MEADOWLAND

TY SPENCER VOSSLER

World Castle Publishing, LLC
Pensacola, Florida
Copyright © Ty Spencer Vossler 2020
Paperback ISBN: 9781953271341
eBook ISBN: 9781953271358
First Edition World Castle Publishing, LLC, November 30, 2020
http://www.worldcastlepublishing.com

Licensing Notes

Cover: Karen Fuller
Editor: Maxine Bringenberg

DEDICATION

In loving memory of my son, Brett Edward Vossler, who lived his life like a candle in the wind.

"The golden moments in the stream of life rush past us, and we see nothing but sand; the angels come to visit us, and we only know them when they are gone." — George Eliot

In small towns, desperate dreams are engineered, seldom built. According to Google, Meadowland is hardly anywhere — a blip midway along a gash known as the San Joaquin Valley. Closer inspection reveals green alfalfa fields of sprouting ambitions. Meadowland's a small California town like most others, populated with dreamers. Some reach for the stars — most are content to gaze up at them from the safety of frayed lawn chairs.

When July the 4th rolls around, children beg parents to take them to the Meadowland fairgrounds. At nine o'clock there's a fireworks show there.

"You can see them from the front yard," they're told by parents.

Kids argue, "Not the same as being there."

With each successive generation, children grow less likely to argue about fireworks. As the world expands, humanity contracts, until one day, we'll all disappear deep inside the social networks.

Weather can be factored into how people act upon dreams. Here's how Meadowland seasons circulate: Winter ushers in dry, brittle cold, yet it rarely snows. In springtime, windows are left wide open to breathe in the voices of youngsters playing outside. The tangy air fosters separate hopes. Like faith, hope can't be explained, only believed in.

Springtime's too short. Wild mountain flowers make a brief appearance, and just as you reach to touch, they curl back like the slippers worn by the Wicked Witch of the East.

Meadowland summers are hot and dry. Hope is born in the early morning and withers by midday around two. Any dreams you may have are baked out of your head.

Fall's an attitude. Leaves hang glide to earth, children are scolded for not raking them, and adults look inward. Their reflective nature this time of year may originate with the spicy smell of autumn, nature preparing to hide her secrets for a winter siesta.

Citizens of Meadowland embrace fall. New rains rinse away old dreams to be replaced by new ones. Meadowland dreams are as refreshing as the breeze they blow in on, so soothing that most sit to admire them as they stray lazily away, not thinking to follow until the final wisp has faded. By then, the trash needs emptying, cars need washing, Facebook needs checking, and a favorite TV show will be on in half an hour.

The end of fall is a bad time to stop at a Meadowland gas station for directions. Most of the town is deep in mourning for dreams that have drifted just out of reach.

CHAPTER 1
Bottom of the Ninth

"Little League baseball is a very good thing because it keeps the parents off the streets." — Yogi Berra —

Main Street in Meadowland has wide sidewalks dotted with large steel pots filled with bright annual flowers and small ornamental trees. Several historical buildings are still standing, and each has a story to tell. Yet no one wants to hear them anymore.

Mom and Pop stores still exist on Main. You'll also find JC Penney's, Sears, Kmart, and one of the last surviving Woolworth stores. Fewer people shop downtown these days. It's easier to visit the mall, where you can find anything you don't need. Meadowland is suffering from the winds of change. It's as though it doesn't yet know what it wishes to become.

Meadowland's a baseball city. Big Ed's Downtown Sporting Goods is doing okay. Big Ed Maple was a minor league first baseman in the late 1970s. A large picture of Ed, kneeling with a bat on his shoulder, is the first thing you notice when you enter his business. He'll greet you with an honest smile, and Big Ed will educate, inform, and entertain you while you shop. Get him started on his playing days, and you'll be there a while, but please don't mention the rival sports store at the mall.

"Bastards wouldn't know a Louisville Slugger from a Fungo bat!" He's been known to say.

With a purchase of anything over twenty dollars, Big Ed'll give you a baseball cap with Make America Great Again embroidered on it.

Meadowland is chock-full of folks like Big Ed, pining for the days when you could get a snow cone for ten cents at the ballgame, when Main Street was a two-lane, and teenage drivers would stop traffic to shoot the shit with friends. You had to drop coins in a slot to make a phone call or to park a car, wrote letters on paper, and checked the TV Guide for your favorite show. For folks like Big Ed Maple, social networking is a weekend barbecue with friends or family, ice-cold beer, potato salad, and homemade vanilla ice cream. Children break into teams to play Wiffle ball, and parents join once the beer's gone.

Big Ed aches for a return to days when black was black, white was white, brown was brown, and never the twain shall meet. He enthusiastically supports the prospect of building a higher wall at the Mexican border and requiring Muslims to carry special ID cards at all times. Two Mexican girls work for Ed part time, and his accountant, Ted Johnson, keeps his books in order.

Grant Wilson is assistant manager at Kmart, located at the edge of beautiful downtown Meadowland, and he's a certifiable baseball fanatic, on a first-name basis with Big Ed. They share lunch once or twice a year at Chipotle, Pizza Hut, or McDonald's and spend the hour arguing about baseball. The only thing they agree about is their reverence for the San Francisco Giants.

***

On typical summer Thursday mornings, Meadowlanders wheeled tall, blue plastic trashcans to the curb for pickup. Grant Wilson's work schedule varied, yet on this particular Thursday, he had switched with Mandy Martinez because it was his son, Robert's, birthday. As Grant parked trashcans on the front curb, he noticed a thick layer of dried sediment blocking the storm drain.

"No wonder it's such a mess after a rain," he grumbled. He saw brush mark evidence, where the street-sweeper had swerved to miss the drain. *Must have been a car parked there,* thought Grant. He went into the garage and returned with a flat shovel, scooping cement-like deposits away from the drainage grate to toss into the trash container. He found the artifacts he exhumed during the process interesting—a beheaded green plastic army man, a faded arithmetic worksheet scarred by red slash-marks, six pennies and a nickel, two Popsicle sticks, fast-food wrappers, three bottle caps, and a condom foil.

"Trojan—your inbound pass to pleasure," he read. *Glad I don't need these anymore.*

Teetering on the edge of the storm grate was a paperback. Grant rubbed the cover with his thumbs and blew it off. Surprisingly, it was still in readable condition. To his eyes, the cover resembled a baseball player facing off with a sun-sized baseball. On the back was a description of the book: *The Journal of Desperate Living* paints a distinctive portrait of America and chronicles one man's search for truth among the....

Grant reread the front cover. "Owen Zzz—whatever," he shrugged. "Must be Polack." After a final dusting, he slid the novel into his back pocket.

Sam, the garbage man, arrived, and Grant stepped onto the

sidewalk. He lifted a hand in greeting and noticed that he'd stepped in dog shit. Lifting his leg, he cursed under his breath and rubbed it off on the front grass. The garbage man's name was embroidered in bright red letters on his orange coveralls.

"Thanks, Sam," Grant yelled over the noise of the diesel engine.

"Welcome," Sam smiled distractedly.

Today was Robert's twelfth birthday, and Grant needed a shower before he started the churner on the homemade vanilla ice cream. Leaving his shoes at the front door, he entered the modest home he and his wife had lived in for twenty years. The house design was known as ranch style. Now it was surrounded by the popular Mediterranean styles.

Grant sat on the toilet and thumbed through *The Journal of Desperate Living,* by Owen Zelenski. The first nine pages came loose. He crumpled them and tossed them into a plastic yellow trash bucket by the sink.

"Two points," he murmured, and randomly selected chapter six, entitled, "Somewhere in Korea." The diuretic effect of morning coffee took effect as he read.

For Larry, it was easy to define his abhorrence for raw fish. The very idea of uncooked fish wrapped in seaweed, and served with a questionable dipping sauce, rubbed against his grain. He tried a bite with horseradish and made a brave face for his companion. Her name was Inki Kim, and he called her Inky, which described her long, black hair to a T.

Inky explained, "Eating sashimi is a spiritual experience."

Chewing slowly, Larry narrowed his eyes, coming to the conclusion that he hadn't gotten to that bite yet. Perhaps he —

Grant tried to turn the page, but it was stuck to the next, so he fanned forward to page 126.

Larry had never absorbed so much heat. The desert inferno, coupled with the fusion of their bodies, made him dizzy. Beneath a makeshift awning, Amunet, which meant Goddess of Mystery, dug her heels into his back and arched to meet Larry's powerful thrusts. The Great Pyramid of Giza stood guard, and a camel bellowed in the distance.

More like it, thought Grant. A rapping of knuckles on the door startled him.

"Fall in? You need to start the ice cream," his wife, Kate, said.

Grant closed the book and stared at his erection. "Yeah, yeah, yeah," adding under his breath, "getting so a guy can't even shit in peace." After dog-earing the page, he dropped the rescued book into a wicker basket next to the toilet and stepped into the shower. *The Journal of Desperate Living* was sandwiched between *National Geographic, Woman's Day*, a Sears Wishbook, and a three-month-old *Sporting News*.

Twenty-one years before, Grant and Kate had met at Meadowland Junior College. Six months later, they married, and after years of trying, Robert arrived. The labor room had a television. When the big day came, Grant's favorite pitcher, Bob Gibson, was a guest commentator for the Saint Louis Cardinals. They'd already agreed on the baby's name — Robert.

"It's a sign," Grant teased Kate as she practiced Lamaze breathing during the labor.

"Hee-hee-hoooo, hee-hee-hoooo!" she answered. In between contractions, she asked Grant if he had a catcher's mitt ready. Grant held his wife's hand, grinned sheepishly, and returned his attention to the ballgame.

After Robert, Kate had wanted a brother or sister for him. For eight years, she and Grant had tried unsuccessfully. Grant used his obsession for baseball to explain why.

"Bottom of the ninth, one out, bases empty."

"Like your head," Kate had shot back.

***

Robert (Bob) Gibson's nickname was Hoot, after a Hollywood movie cowboy, Hoot Gibson. Grant sometimes called their son by the nickname, causing Kate to shudder. She feared the boy would grow into it and turn out looking like a freaking owl. Yet she knew it could've been worse, recalling other big-league monikers—Cookie, Oil Can, Big Unit, Mad-Bum. *Hmm, Big Unit,* she thought—*that sounds promising.*

When Robert was born, Grant used his fifteen percent Kmart manager discount to purchase San Francisco Giants jerseys, autographed balls encapsulated in plastic bubbles, and baseball fundamentals videos. Then he visited Big Ed Maple's Sporting Goods to purchase a child-size baseball glove. Big Ed talked him into the Mizuno GPP1154 model.

"Best goddamn glove on the market," Ed said. "He'll be scoopin' grounders before he learns to walk." And of course, he threw in a free hat for the baby.

Kate loved Grant, yet there were days when she tired of him. Grant was a genuine Little League father and had coached all of Robert's baseball teams. Much to his dismay, their son was a terrible player. Every day after dinner, Grant dragged Robert out to the back yard for a game of catch. He built a regulation mound for him to pitch from, but Robert's fastball wouldn't break a pane of glass.

Their son's greatest asset was his uncanny ability to get plunked by opposing pitchers. Robert leaned so far over the plate he was beaned nearly every game. Kate knew it was only a matter of time before a pitch sent him to the hospital. Baseball left her with a dull, empty ache, and she knew Robert felt the same. But arguing with Grant about it was like complaining to an umpire—she usually got tossed from the game. Kate called

Grant the General when he was too pushy.

Kate tested the frosting on Robert's birthday cake with a finger and made a face. Then she joined her son in the dining room. He was analyzing the presents stacked on the table, trying to guess what was inside. The doorbell chimed, Kate opened the door, and a home invasion ensued.

Twelve-year-old boys could commandeer houses quickly and completely. They were loud, rude, and thoughtless. Kate compared them with the damnable flying monkeys on *The Wizard of Oz*, swooping, swarming, spilling. Most of Robert's friends were on the baseball team. By the time they all arrived, she was ready to climb the walls or drown herself in a bathtub filled with cheap Chardonnay.

The living room sofa was designed to seat four, but Grant was stretched out over its length as he watched a baseball game. The ice cream machine was churning in the kitchen, and when it slowed, he'd take out the dasher to lick it clean. But for now, an over-the-hill Albert Pujols had two men aboard and was long overdue for a blast.

"Checked the ice cream?" Kate interrupted. Grant was a zombie. The announcer was explaining that Pujols had recently visited a children's hospital. "Earth to General!"

"Mmm?"

Kate checked the ice cream herself. On the way, she stopped again to gaze at the birthday cake, diamond-shaped with plastic ballplayers positioned on a brown infield, and a green outfield, and thin, chocolate wafers comprising the outfield fence—all Grant's idea. The first baseman had fallen on his face. She stood him up again.

The ice cream was ready. She unplugged the churner and added salt to the ice bucket. The doorbell chimed, and she knew the pizzas had arrived.

"Pizza," screamed a partygoer, starting a stampede.

No sooner had the pizza landed on the dining room table than kids pounced, ignoring paper plates and napkins, bombing the beige carpet with pepperoni, bell peppers, olive slices, and breadcrumbs. She watched Robert trying to stuff an entire slice in his mouth. A boy named Wesley Hardin laughed and sprayed Robert's shirt.

"Watch it, dickweed!"

"Language," Kate warned her son.

"Let *me* show you how it's done, Wilson," Wesley said—and he did.

Kate listened to the gossip about girls. One, in particular, highlighted their fantasies—Candice Burns.

"Love to see *her* on a beach," said Ramon, "Wearing one of those string—"

"A nude beach," Ethan interrupted.

"Yeah, I'd rub lotion—"

"On her tits!" Robert blurted.

Kate pretended not to hear, quickly walking into the kitchen for a surreptitious giggle. When the pizza was annihilated, the boys went into the back yard to play Wiffle ball. Kate checked on them periodically, yet the game had a calming effect. She watched when Robert was at bat. He hit a towering drive over the wooden fence and into the street.

"Why the hell can't you do that in a real game?" yelled the right fielder, Ramon.

The sounds of live baseball brought Grant to his senses. He shut off the TV to make an appearance, stopping by the empty pizza boxes. "Shit," he grumbled. He watched the Wiffle game for fifteen minutes and then asked, "Hey! You guys ready to cut the cake?"

"I'm ready to cut the cheese," replied Joey Reece, the best

player on the team. He lived west of Meadowland, in a tiny labor camp community named Woodland.

"Not on my watch," said Grant.

The boys boiled back into the house. Grant ambled over to officiate the cutting ceremony. Kate lit the candles. When all twelve were burning, Grant exclaimed, "Candlelight Park!"

After a sloppy rendition of "Happy Birthday," Robert took a deep breath and blew out the candles. The first baseman fell on his face. After the cake was sliced and delivered into cardboard bowls, Grant dropped a scoop of ice cream on top. Then it was time to open presents.

Second baseman Ethan punched Robert's shoulder. "Glad your parents didn't hire a clown...I hate fuckin clowns."

"You read that Stephen King book, *It*?"

"Saw the movie."

Wesley Harden, the team's catcher, shoved the largest gift over. "Open it. Maybe Candice Burns'll pop out!"

The boys erupted into laughter. Robert added, "Naked," and they laughed again.

Robert could easily tell the difference between gifts from his mother and those from his father, even though they said *From Mom and Dad*. Dad—batting gloves, autographed balls, caps, team logo jackets, and trading cards. At first, the cards were interesting. He'd slipped them into albums and assessed their value, yet soon lost interest. Mom—a gumball bank, BMX Bike Magazine subscription, some clothes, and a leather-bound writing journal with a fancy pen.

Grant had added plops of ice cream to the cake slices and considered his part finished. He returned to the game, muttering advice to players and second-guessing coaches.

Amid the chaos of dripping ice cream and the dismantling of the stadium cake, Wesley Harden nudged Robert and pointed to a dad gift—a long, clear plastic container filled with baseball cards. "Coach added to his collection, eh?"

Robert nudged him back with an elbow. Wesley was big for his age and sported a Ruthian profile. He was the only other kid besides Joey Reece to hit a home run that year. Joey hit three.

"Must've been a blue-light special," Wesley taunted, referring to the turnstile light placed to lure Kmart shoppers toward sale items. Robert's eyes were focused narrowly on other presents from his father—a card album, tickets to a Giants doubleheader, and an autographed poster of Barry Bonds.

"Bonds—what a cheat," Wesley snapped. "Who the hell wants a poster of a juiced-up has-been?"

Robert's thumb snapped the plastic fork he was holding. "Know what, Wes? Your brain's so tiny, if you stuffed it up an ant's ass, it'd rattle around like a bee-bee in a tin can." The others howled with laughter.

Kate rushed in from the kitchen. "Who wants more ice cream?"

"Bluelight," muttered Wesley. The room got quiet.

"Wesley, that's enough," Kate interjected

"Bluelight." He silently mouthed the word.

Robert toppled Wesley with a short right jab to the face. The boys gawked at the blood trickling from Wesley's nose. He scrambled back to his feet and staggered to the front doorway.

"Bluelight, bluelight, bluelight!" he screamed and ran out, leaving the door wide open.

"Awesome!" blurted third baseman, Ricky Shepherd.

Kate turned to Robert. "Go to your room!"

Grant arrived, looking confused as the red-faced Robert hurried away.

"What's goin' on?"

"Your son punched Wesley."

"Clocked him good!" added Joey Reece, hitting his open fist for emphasis. The doorbell rang, and parents began arriving to pick up their boys.

"I'll get it." Grant went to the door.

Side-by-side parents stood at the door, smiling in at the mess, not offering to help restore order. Wesley and his parents got a forced apology from Robert. They stood at the door, and Wesley had toilet paper stuffed in each nostril.

"Boys will be boys."

Mrs. Harden smiled. Wesley's father didn't smile. Robert was told to return to his room.

When they left, Kate explained what had happened, and Grant sighed, "Shit, haven't used the bluelight for years." He wandered to the dining room table and scooped a finger full of green outfield icing. "Tastes like Astroturf."

Kate began the tedious task of putting the house back together. She'd been a housewife since the birth of her son and had lately given considerable thought to finishing her associate degree at the junior college and working at a bank or something.

Grant was hovering. Whenever he was upset, he hovered, hoping she'd ask what was wrong. When she didn't, he pointed to the front doorway. "Harden—that little bastard's gonna be trouble when he grows up."

"He's trouble now," Kate amended.

"Yeah, but I mean…one of those guys that beats his wife."

"And votes for women-haters like Trump," she said.

Grant didn't comment. Much to his wife's chagrin, he'd voted for Trump. "Think I'll peek in on the ol' Hooter."

Kate shivered. "Good idea." She was reminded that hooter was slang for a marijuana cigarette and a nickname for tits. There was even a restaurant chain by the name.

Robert was sitting on his bed, thumbing through a BMX

magazine.

"You did okay." Grant surveyed presents spread out on the bed.

"Yeah," Robert said.

Grant thumbed through the new baseball cards, "You know, these rookie cards—some of these guys'll make it into the Hall and—"

"Be worth a fortune," Bob finished. "I know…thanks, Dad."

"Welcome." Grant ruffled Robert's hair. "Maybe later we can have a catch."

"Yeah."

"Figure about another hour ought to do. What you did was wrong, son."

"Yeah." He pursed his lips. *But it felt so good!* he thought.

Grant patted him on the back and returned to the living room to watch the second game of a doubleheader. Secretly, he was proud of Robert—more than he ever remembered.

From the attic window, Robert had a remarkable view of Meadowland life—his father in the front yard, wearing a baseball glove, calling for a game of catch; Mom pulling weeds in the flowerbed; the postman wearing blue shorts and a ridiculous safari hat. Robert marveled at the mailman's mustache—a thick push broom. Cats were stretched out beneath trees, taking refuge from the dry heat of the San Joaquin Valley. The bluish-grey Sierra Nevada Mountains poked up in the background. Robert noticed details—a blackbird bullying a sparrow from its perch on a branch, as others gossiped on telephone lines.

From the attic, Robert felt the town's pulse, slow dancing to the beat of hidden drums. Meadowland was a paint-by-number town—few colors to choose from, one cheap brush to work with. The final result looked okay on the outside, but with time, the numbers would show through.

"Hoot!" his father yelled, wind-milling his right arm to loosen up.

Robert moved away from the window and sat on his grandfather's sea chest to write poetry in a green scribble-pad. Writing was an escape. It never called when he didn't want to come and didn't push where he didn't wish to go. He wrote: When a bee stings, it's the worst of all stunts, take pleasure in knowing that he'll sting only once.

Robert smiled. Poetry was short...to the point. He'd once shared them with his folks. His mother enjoyed reading them, but his father couldn't muster much of a reaction.

"This for school or something?" he'd asked.

"No, I just like making them."

"Hmm." His father handed them back and returned his attention to the sports section. "Buster Posey's leading the league in batting average. Not bad for a catcher, eh?"

His mother still bought writing journals for him, but these days he kept his writings secreted inside this grandfather's sea chest. Robert gazed between his knees to the tarnished lock and leather buckles of the chest. He hadn't known his grandparents—born too late to appreciate the spicy smell of old skin, warm smothering hugs, and "When I was your age," stories. They'd died two months apart, six years before he was born. He examined the cracked wood and rawhide straps. As far as he knew, Grandfather had never used the chest at sea. He'd owned an automotive parts store, a landlubber occupation if ever there was one.

Robert had searched through the silk-lined chest on numerous occasions. Among its treasures were the comfortable odors—the musk of cedar mixed with the fragrance of faded paper documents. There was a letterman sweater with a P sewn to one breast, a love-worn teddy bear with a missing eye, and a tasseled Shriners hat. He'd tried to play the harmonica found there, but the reeds were gummed up. His senses carved an alternate universe from building blocks of pure fantasy, planets and suns void of guilt or expectation—worlds without baseball.

A confused sparrow flapped crazily, trying to scratch its way into the attic through the dirty, cracked window. Robert tried to let it in, but it darted away. He opened the chest to put back his journal and decided to look through the old photo album. Almost everyone in it looked serious as if they hadn't taken a dump in weeks. He opened to a creased black-and-white image taped to a black page—a smiling, handsome, curly haired lad hunched over a giant auto-parts catalog. There were racecar posters in the background and a calendar featuring stacked blondes peddling motor oil. His father said that Grandfather had loved baseball too and had volunteered as a weekend plate umpire.

Robert noticed a tiny corner sticking up behind the photo—another photo perhaps. He pinched it with thumb and forefinger to pull it out and found a baseball card, placed there and forgotten. In place of the usual statistics on back, it carried an advertisement for Piedmont Cigarettes. The card was mint. On the front was a stone-faced, sleepy-eyed image of Honus Wagner. Robert chuckled at the thought of naming a kid Honus.

Robert slipped the card into his shirt pocket to show his father later, then closed the chest and buckled the latches. Again the sparrow was trying its luck against the window. Robert brushed his pants, ran his fingers through his hair, and crept downstairs to the kitchen to see if there was any cake left. All that remained was a single slice of outfield grass.

***

Grant sat on the toilet with, *The Journal of Desperate Living*, by Owen Zelenski, opening to Chapter 9: A Small Town in

California.

All his life, Larry had been what other people wanted him to be. When he was small, he played Little League for his father, took piano lessons for his mother, and chaperoned his little sister to her first dance. After he married, he was the perfect husband, worked hard, spent quality time with the kids, made love to his wife once a week, and kept the lawn mowed.

Everyone has a shadow side, which becomes insistent when continually ignored. His neighbor, Cathy, had borrowed sugar before. But this time, she wasn't there for sugar.

"Larry, are you alone?"

"Yeah."

"Will you fuck me?"

Grant tried to turn the page. "Shit," he hissed. The pages were bonded. He continued the story in his head, substituting Audrey, the pretty next-door neighbor. He couldn't remember the last time he'd jerked off. *Why should I? That's what wives're for.* He flushed the toilet.

Grant conducted a house-search for Kate and found her sorting clothes in the laundry room. He locked the door, raised an eyebrow, and unzipped his fly. Kate half-smiled and continued sorting.

"Bad timing, General," she said.

Grant knew what that meant. He returned to the bathroom, but Robert was there now. He flipped through channels — ice-skating, hunting, and sport-fishing. He watched Big Time Wrestling for a few minutes — Hawkeye Shane Kody had Honky Tonk Man on his back, waiting for the referee to slap the canvas. "Damn." He turned the TV off and got up for a beer. Robert was in the kitchen, pouring soda, and Grant pulled him into an affectionate headlock.

"How 'bout a catch?"

"Sure, maybe later. I'm gonna ride bikes with the guys."

"Barry Larkin's rookie card's gone up fifty bucks since he made the Hall." Grant cranked an invisible one-armed bandit. "Kaching!"

"Great. Later, Dad."

"Yeah, all right."

***

A warm lazy breeze greeted Robert. A jet trail in the sky reminded him of the beads he was taught to make in welding shop. A yellow-jacket wasp buzzed his ear, legs dangling loosely beneath, and he swatted at it. Straddling his BMX bike, he stood on the pedals to accelerate toward his buddies. Ramon, Ethan, and a boy named Mike were there.

His friends used clothespins and playing cards to create motor sounds from the spokes—a cheap thrill. Placed correctly, you could almost get a Harley effect.

"Any more cards?" he asked Ethan.

"Nah, this's what's left of my dad's poker deck. Shit bricks when he finds out. Cool how you fucked up Wesley," he added.

"Got an extra clothespin," offered Ramon, "Wesley, *hijo de la chingada*, that fucker had it coming. Bet he won't play for us anymore."

As Robert leaned on the handlebars, he felt the rigid square of the card in his shirt pocket. In the blue sky above, a gathering of crows patiently rode hot thermals, waiting for the boys to leave. Something was stuck to the pavement below that might be lunch.

"Haw-haw!" they laughed.

"Let's race," said Mike.

***

Grant found a ballgame, but after the second inning, the Blue Jays were down by six, and a third reliever was riding a golf cart to the playing field. He clicked it off, grabbed another beer, and sat on the front cement steps. The bright sunlight made him squint. He took a long swallow and belched through his nose. After another gulp, he scanned the label. "Finest ingredients," he read.

A yellow cat sauntered over to rub against his leg, and then it checked for Crunchy Stars in a green plastic bowl at the bottom step. Grant saw that the dish was full of ants, so he flipped it over to bang them out. The yellow cat purred. In the distance, he heard a clapping sound, as if a bleacher full of Little League parents cheered a final out. He watched as four boys stood on their pedals and raced toward a chalk line scrawled in front of his driveway. Robert was in the back of the pack. Grant's fist tightened around the half empty aluminum can.

"Come on, Hoot, pump those legs." To his delight, Robert swerved left, got even with Mike, passed him, and challenged Ethan for second. With the finish line just ahead, he bumped Ramon's rear tire, overcompensated, and spilled onto the asphalt. Grant sprang to his feet, spilling beer on his shirt. He jogged over to his son.

"You all right?" He helped Robert up and gave him the once-over, as he did when Robert was beaned by a baseball.

Robert's elbow was scraped, and a knee bled through a hole in his jeans. "Think so."

The rear wheel of Robert's bike finished spinning as the others gathered around. "Cool!" Ramon beamed. A stern look from Grant made him roll back a few feet.

Robert brushed off his pants and inspected the bike. His father squinted at the baseball card clipped to the frame and recognized the abused visage.

"Honus Wagner, I'll be darned." Grant had seen that homely face often enough in trade magazines. "An old-timer re-issue," he guessed. Card companies periodically published replicas of old-timers. Originals in mint condition were worth a fortune. He freed the card from the jaws of the clothespin to take a closer look. Wagner's veiled eyes seemed to stare deep into Grant's soul before he turned it over. "Piedmont cigarettes," he muttered, surprised that a replica would carry a cigarette ad. "Hold on there." He put a hand on Robert's shoulder as he remounted his bike. "Where'd you get this, son?"

Robert winced as he picked out a pebble embedded in his elbow. "Grandpa's sea chest."

Grant felt a pressure building behind his eyes, and facial tremors foreshadowed an eruption. He gaped at the faded fortune in his trembling hand. "Know what this is?" His voice was deep and menacing.

Robert shook his head and backed away with his bike.

"This," Grant swallowed hard, "was Honus fucking Wagner!" he rasped. "Know what he's worth?"

"No, sir." Robert stared at the ground.

"Tell you what he's worth now…shit! Not a goddamn red cent!"

"Uh oh," said Mike.

Robert's friends deserted, not wanting to be caught in the tsunami. He was alone…could smell the pungent odor of fear and shame. He quickly turned away to hide tears.

"Jesus fucking Christ!" Molten lava sprayed from his father's mouth. He stood, legs braced, a balled fist on his hip, the other gripping the ruined card.

Kate had been weeding in the front garden and dropped the hoe when she heard the commotion. Now she stood with Robert.

Grant showed her the card. "Your son just pissed away a goddamn fortune!"

Kate put protective arms around her son, who still had his eyes glued to the road.

Haw! Mocked a crow spying from a streetlamp, *Haw-haw!*

"Looks like a piece of cardboard to me," Kate uttered. She let loose of Robert to close in on her husband. Snatching the card from his hand, rage flashed in her eyes like an old dress suddenly remembering how to be worn. "What does your son have to do to make you happy, win a batting title?"

Grant pursed his lips and stabbed at the card with a finger. "This was our dream card!"

Robert looked up fiercely, "Your dream, not mine!" He hopped off the bike, let it drop, and ran into the house.

"Bob!" Grant shouted.

Kate couldn't bear to look at her husband. In the ensuing moment of silence, she heard the hungry squeals of baby birds begging for lunch. She shoved the card into Grant's chest as she walked past.

"Kate?" Anguished sweat rained down on Wagner's beat-up face. "You're right, I know it…."

She whirled to face him. "You know it? You don't know anything!"

"Yeah." Grant lifted the bike, and they returned to the house. Grant went directly to Robert's room. He wasn't there, but a poem lay on his pillow. *I am a hollow tree. There's nothing left of me. An ax will set me free.*

"Robert!" he called out as he handed the poem to Kate.

"Oh, oh my God! I swear, if anything happens to him…." She burst out crying, and Grant held her. She tore out of his grasp and began calling for Robert.

As Kate checked the house, Grant hunted in the yards. Then he saw that the bike was gone.

"He'll be all right. We'll find him. He'll be okay," Grant

nodded vigorously.

They phoned neighbors and friends. No one had seen him.

"The police," Kate said. "Call them."

"They won't do anything—has to be twenty-four hours or some shit."

"Call them," she demanded.

Meadowland police gave assurances that they'd keep an eye peeled. Cruising the neighborhood in his Toyota Corolla, Grant showed a wallet photo to anyone he happened upon— Robert in his baseball uniform, unsmiling, kneeling with a bat on his shoulder.

Grant and Kate sat at the dining room table in the twilight. A baseball broadcast floated in from the neighbor's house. *Audrey likes baseball*, Grant thought. He reached into his shirt to examine Honus Wagner's remains, then tore it into thin strips and watched them flutter to the carpet. Without looking up, Kate slid a hand across the table, and he grasped it.

"I'm goin' out again."

Grant dug into his pocket for the car keys and snagged the Giants ball cap off the coat hook out of habit. He turned it over in his hands for a moment before returning it to the hook. The phone rang, and he rushed for it. It was Audrey, wanting to know if Robert was home yet.

***

Robert knew a place no one would think to look. Summer league baseball season was a few weeks away, and the field was badly in need of a haircut. Grass had begun creeping into the narrows between the base paths. It was too dark for fathers to torment sons with pop-ups and grounders—to live their failed dreams through their sons.

Robert sat in the covered home-team dugout. Visitors sat on an exposed bench, and he guessed that's what was meant by home field advantage. He lifted a paperback from the pocket of his jacket. He'd found it knifed between magazines in the bathroom and had used it to further his education. Within its dog-eared pages, Robert found answers to questions boys his age puzzled about. Using a mini-mag, he turned to the first page.

Chapter One: The Leaving.
Forty years after being coaxed from his mother's womb, Larry walked out of his driveway and into the street, leaving everything he knew behind.

"Boring," Robert scoffed and fanned to page 143:

...she sat yoga-style on the bed, playing the flute. Her eyes danced, and his member began to rise and sway with the music. When it stood rigid, she lowered the instrument and reached for him, using her mouth in such a way that within seconds Larry was spitting....

Robert made frustrated attempts to free the sticking pages, even as his flashlight began to fade and die. The night was warm, and he enjoyed seeing the emergence of stars and the smell of the evening sky. He was glad it wasn't winter. Cold weather ushered evil smells from the Meadowland sewer treatment plant. Sometimes conditions were such that the whole town smelled like shit. He took out his Swiss army knife, selected the short blade, and gouged, BASEBALL SUCKS, deep into the wooden bench.

Hours later, despite a gurgling stomach, a sore elbow, and a banged-up knee, Robert stretched out on the bench and eventually fell asleep. He dreamed of Candice Burns, the girl everyone yearned for at school. She played flute in the school band. His dream evolved as she played. He tried to hold onto the dream even as it morphed into something much less pleasant. Dreams were hard to keep a firm grip on. Now he was in the bleachers behind home plate.

His father stepped into the batter's box and whacked red clay from his cleats with the barrel of his bat. Robert fought desperately to get back to Candice — at least to put her in the stands next to him. A thick fog moved in, smothering everything but the home plate area. The catcher, Wesley, raised his mask to spit, and the umpire hunkered down behind him.

"Bluelight, you ain't no damn good," Wesley taunted.

His father glared back with a mixture of anger and embarrassment. He dug in to face the fog-shrouded hurler. A white blur sizzled out of the mist and popped into the catcher's mitt.

"Stee-rike one!" The umpire took a step back, lifted a knife hand into the air, and chopped down as if signaling a left turn. Grant rolled his head, tugged at his crotch, and readied himself. Another comet blazed, smacking into the round leather pocket.

"Stee-rike two!"

"Keep it on your shoulder, Bluelight." The catcher lifted his mask and spat on Grant's cleats. The umpire called time and removed his mask. It was the mailman. He dropped into a push-up position to sweep the plate off with his mustache. Fog began to lift, and Robert could see now who was pitching…his clone, clawing at the dirt in front of the rubber with a cleat to get it just the way he liked it.

"Shit," Robert gulped as he watched his twin squaring to face his father again. Grant stepped out of the box to face Robert in the bleachers. Sadness was stitched on his face like the seams of a scuffed up baseball.

"Gimmee somethin' I can lay lumber on, son," he begged. "Need to beef up my average."

Wesley stood up menacingly. "Back in the box, Bluelight!"

The pitcher faced his father, waiting for a sign from his battery mate. Wesley squatted and flashed signs. Robert nodded, rocked back, and delivered. His father shrieked as a sizzling fastball greeted his ribcage.

"Take your base," the postman ordered.

Wesley taunted, "Only way you'll ever make it to first, Meatloaf."

The scene disappeared within a swirling fog. Robert shivered, heard his stomach growl, and climbed the bleachers to the concession stand.

"What can I get you, young man?" It was Robert's grandfather. Racing posters from the forties dotted the walls, as well as calendars with ladies in bathing suits hawking air filters and shock absorbers.

"I'd like a large Coke and a bag of peanut M&M's."

"Sorry, kid, all I got's that old gumball machine." The old man jerked his thumb toward a dusty corner. "Oil filters on sale." He nodded toward a stand-up display featuring a buxom beauty covering her bare chest with two of them. Keep it Clean, *read the caption.*

"No thanks. I'm hungry."

"Radiator fluid?" Grandfather smiled. "Fifteen percent off."

"Never mind." Robert turned to leave.

"Hold on a second, son…got just the thing."

Robert's grandfather opened a thick automotive parts catalog to a page bookmarked with a baseball card.

"Here we go." He lifted the card carefully and set it on the counter. "Can't eat it, but it might come in handy." It was a mint Lou Gehrig rookie card.

Robert's eyes lit up. "Thanks!"

"More than welcome," he said. "Was always partial to Lou — such a humble, nice man. Used to have a Honus Wagner…." He pursed his mouth and narrowed his eyes at Robert.

"Yeah," Robert said.

Reaching over the counter, he gently gripped Robert's shoulders.

"Kid?"

　　"Yes, sir?"

　　"Tell that stubborn daddy of yours that the most important thing is what a man carries in here." *He pointed to his heart.* *"Tell him, will yuh?"*

　　"Okay."

Robert's grandfather winked and the dream dissolved. On the way out, Robert followed the sound of a flute, yet Candice was nowhere to be found.

***

Grant cruised the neighborhoods until dawn. A final effort took him past the ballpark. Sun filtered through the trees adjacent to the right field line, casting a strange surrealistic light on the diamond. He read sponsor's names painted on the plywood outfield fence—Kmart was there.

Grant turned his attention toward the infield and saw someone lying in the dugout. *Probably the transient I saw rummaging through the dumpster the other day.* Then he saw a gleam reflecting off the chrome of a bicycle.

Robert opened his eyes. He hadn't slept much, and he was covered with mosquito bites. Someone was walking across the infield toward him. He sat up quickly and stared at the cement floor of the dugout.

　　"You all right, son?"

　　"Yeah."

Grant sat down next to him, nodding and wringing his hands. "Look, Robert...I'm real sorry, I don't know what came over me."

　　"It's okay," Robert mumbled.

　　"No, no, it's not." Grant shook his head. "Baseball's just a game. Guess I wanted you to love it as much as me." He paused to put a hand on Robert's shoulder. "What I'm trying to say is—"

"The most important thing is what a man carries in here." Robert pointed to his heart and looked up at his father.

Grant's eyes widened. "Daddy used to tell me that." He took Robert in his arms.

Robert liked the way it felt to hug his father—couldn't remember the last time it had happened. Then he recalled the dream.

"The card!" He pulled away from his father and emptied his pockets—a burned-out flashlight, a pack of gum with one stick left, and the paperback.

"Where'd you get this?" Grant reached for the book.

Robert blushed.

His father smiled and ruffled his son's hair. "Time for a man-to-man...after we take another peek at Dad's chest."

***

The next morning the paperboy delivered a fastball from his bicycle to Grant's doorstep, hitting the front door with an obtrusive thwack. The rubber band snapped—news splashed on the doorstep and flipped the cat's dish over. Standing on his pedals, the young fire-baller sped toward his next delivery.

A sparrow landed, hopping and pecking at the spilled cat-food. It crapped on the sports page of the *Meadowland Chronicle*, which headlined the recent sale of a baseball card.

Wagner Card Goes for $940,000

Union Oil executive Daniel Foster paid $940,000 Friday for a Honus Wagner baseball card from a series issued in 1909 and 1910. After the auction at Sotheby's in New York, Foster, who lives in Santa Barbara, said, "Well, it's just kind of fun knowing you own the best in the world."

Only forty Wagner cards are known to exist....

The bird cocked its head and flew away, not wanting to press Lady Luck.

CHAPTER 2
Fly in the Ointment

"The golden moments in the stream of life rush past us, and we see nothing but sand; the angels come to visit us, and we only know them when they are gone." — George Eliot

A gopher emerged from its tunnel just as sunrise formed a pink halo over the Sierra Nevada mountains. A patient cat pounced. She carried her struggling breakfast across the street, narrowly avoiding a garbage truck.

"*Pinche gato!*" Sam scolded as he slammed on the brakes.

Sam wore an orange hardhat, long-sleeved orange coveralls, and a pair of leather gloves — an outfit that left him feeling like an overripe persimmon. He cruised to Meadowland's newest gated community, where houses were the color of mashed potatoes and gravy, yet sold for more than he'd earn in ten years. Meadowland was a Y-town — white folks living in the main body, separated by railroad tracks from Latinos and blacks, who resided in the opposing arms. The sleeves of his coveralls secreted jailhouse tattoos — a reminder of the past.

Sam sipped from a water bottle.

"*Salud y pesetas,*" Sam toasted sarcastically, knowing that the wealthy held all the cards and always would.

Sam was uncomfortable collecting there. Yet everywhere he went, he enjoyed watching children, who were fascinated with the crushing drama of the trash compactor, the shhh of hydraulics, and the ping of the diesel.

Sam Villarreal, thirty-six, lived a simple life when measured by the keys in his pocket — one for the '82 Firebird, the other for a modest fixer-upper he shared with his wife and two young boys. Trash pick-up wasn't prestigious, but it kept food on the table. He deferred personal dreams to a secret realm in his heart labeled *Someday*.

On November 8th, he didn't vote because he didn't like either candidate. Miriam, his wife, had voted for Hillary Clinton. "Lesser of two evils," she was fond of saying. She'd been so upset with the results that she tried to call in sick. Ironically, the manager of Rite-Aid (a black man) had also called in, so Miriam had to cover for him.

At noon, Sam parked beneath a stand of pine trees at the city park to eat lunch and read a few pages from a magazine, newspaper, or a book he'd rescued. He made a game of it — finding reading material for his midday repast. As he read, static-filled voices wrestled for understanding on the CB. Antonio was informing dispatch of an oil leak. Dispatch was sending someone to check it out. Mario was taking his lunch break, and Pete was heading to the city dump.

After forty-five minutes, Sam glanced at his watch and closed a rescued book he'd struggled to read for three lunchtimes, *The Labyrinth of Solitude*, by Octavio Paz. The front cover was missing, and it carried a Meadowland Library stamp on the first page. Emily Brisk, Lupe Payán, and Frank Beckworth had previously checked it out. Sam studied signatures and due dates, wondering if either of them had paid a late fee. How it ended up in the trash was anybody's guess. Sam's lack of education caught up on page thirty-six, and he returned it into the hungry jaws of the compactor.

***

Donna loved the smell of the new house. The mixture of Berber carpet, unsullied paint, and unused appliances made her giddy as she scouted a location for the wedding portrait. She held the picture to her face and admired Warren in his black tux, her in the plunging white dress, only three years before.

"Love a well-dressed man." Her southern lilt drifted through the house, adding warmth to the virgin stone fireplace. She calculated space above an antique secretary desk, held up the portrait, shook her head, and sat on a leather sofa. She stretched her arms, reached back to unsnap her bra, and admired her nipples beneath the Nike logo of her T-shirt. "That's better." She tousled her bleach-blonde hair and heaved a sigh.

Donna was tall enough to cut Warren down to size. She raised other men's eyebrows whenever she was out and about. Thirty-four, she was the youngest of three daughters born to Mr. and Mrs. Thornton. Her mother kept house, while her father, born into old money, dabbled in real estate. When she was seventeen, Donna ran away with a black boyfriend she'd secreted from everyone. It'd taken her father a week to find them, holed up in a cheap hotel in downtown Raleigh. The boyfriend disappeared, and after the abortion, Donna studied fine arts at the University of North Carolina. She was never very close to her father after that.

Briefly, she was married to a tax attorney, yet after less than a year, he hired a detective to prove she was fucking a supermarket manager. Donna moved back into the family house for a time. Shame kept her on a sharp lookout for another alternative…and along came Warren.

Warren was forty-nine, fifteen years her senior, partnered in a successful family medical practice, and hailed from a prosperous old-moneyed North Carolina family like hers. His father was retired from his law practice and had once run for Republican governor. Warren's young-adult children still lived with their mother. Donna's only experience with them had come in the form of a scathing RSVP refusal to attend their father's wedding to her.

Warren was well preserved and exercised regularly at the Meadowland Fitness Center, where Donna took aerobics three days a week. Physically, the initial years were satisfying. Donna lifted the portrait and smiled as she reminisced about their first time together.

They met at a cocktail party fundraiser for a future Republican senator. Guests wafted through rooms in the palatial southern mansion like a humid breeze, towing shallow conversations along with them. Donna noticed Warren drifting about and greeting other guests. She initiated the first round by intercepting him as he neared the open bar. She'd arrived at the gathering with a lawyer named Brit, who was busy schmoozing the budding senator. Round one:

"Rather warm, don't you think?" She fanned herself.

"Especially in this monkey suit," Warren joked, smoothing the front of his Armani.

"Oh, but you look so very handsome," she said.

"Mmm, so do you, I might add." He noticed her empty glass, "What're you drinking?"

"Vodka tonic."

"Perfect. I'm Warren, Warren Smythe." He held out his hand.

"Donna Thornton." She held his hand longer than necessary.

"Two vodka tonics coming up." He strolled with her to the bar.

She smiled and watched him appraise her as they waited for drinks. There was a bit of a line, so she touched his arm and said she'd wait by the grand stairway.

Round Two: As he joined her, Donna was halfway up the stairs pretending to admire staggered paintings hanging there. As he arrived, she climbed ahead to provide him an excellent view of her backside beneath the pleated filigree skirt. She gazed at a renaissance nude—a woman lying on a bed of steaming autumn leaves, in the arms of a satyr.

Warren smiled and handed her the drink, gesturing with his glass. "Lovely."

"Yes, it is."

"The painting is nice too," he said. Donna smiled and tried her best to blush. "Such passion," he added.

"Dyin' trait." Donna sighed.

Round Three: Donna studied Warren like a foreign language that begged understanding. His cologne planted a field of cotton in her brain.

"Passion and spontaneity—doesn't this painting make you want to seize the moment?" Warren wrinkled his forehead and sipped.

Donna remembered that as being the deepest thing, Warren ever said. Primal emotions absconded with lingering doubts, and she lured him deeper south.

"Certainly does." She set the hook.

Round Four: Warren swallowed hook, line, and sinker, kicking toward her boat to be gaffed and netted.

"Hmm, wonder what's up here?" She ascended the stairs without waiting for an answer, and he followed. Donna opened the first door on the left and was pleased to find an empty office.

"This's where our host plots conquests," Warren said.

Donna veiled her eyes and set her drink on a chessboard table. Carved onyx pieces were lined up, ready to do battle.

"Play?" he asked.

"Afraid I don't know a king from a pawn."

Round Five: Warren abandoned his glass next to hers and put his arms around her waist. After the first kiss, Warren locked the door. Subsequent kisses were followed by his pants being drained to the ankles, her skirt lifted up around her waist. Donna kicked her panties aside and sat on the edge of the large, mahogany desk.

"God, you're beautiful," he said, lifting her knees and shuffling forward.

As he slipped inside, she buried her head into his shoulder to keep from rousing the entire household. "Ohhh, yes, darlin', ohhh yes."

Final Bell: Lasted less than five minutes.

"Oops." Donna regarded a pool of semen on the desk as Warren helped her to her feet.

"Leave it," he suggested.

"Why, Mister Smythe, you naughty boy."

"Inspired by you." He took her into his arms.

"Need a lady's room."

She found one in the next room, and Warren waited at the top of the stairs. When she rejoined him, she straightened his collar. As they turned to descend, there was Brit, leaning against the banister at the bottom of the stairs, staring up with narrowed eyes.

***

Squealing brakes interrupted Donna's remembrance. Warren had reminded her that morning to put out empty moving cartons that were stacked in the garage.

"Shit," she muttered, hurrying into the garage. The bright sun hurt her eyes as the garage door lifted. The garbage truck stopped at the curb.

Sam saw Donna dragging boxes and met her halfway. "Let me give you a hand."

"Thanks."

More boxes were stacked next to Donna's BMW, and he brought them to the curb. After three more trips, the task was done.

"Thanks so much," Donna said as Sam fed them into the compactor.

"*De nada.*"

Donna shielded her eyes and squinted. One of her favorite pastimes was sizing up men, creating a mental checklist. *Good-looking. A little chunky, and yet, look at those big, beautiful, brown eyes.*

"You always come on Thursdays?"

"Just Thursdays," he replied.

"Thank you, Mister…." She leaned closer to read his name, embroidered to his coveralls.

"Sam Villarreal, but please, call me Sam."

"I'm Donna." She offered her hand. "Donna Smythe."

He smiled and removed a glove. "Pleasure."

"Pleasure's mine, Sam. Thanks again."

"Next Thursday."

"Try to stay cool."

He squinted up at the blazing sun and smiled. "Pretty tall order."

Donna added, *Dazzling smile*, to the checklist.

***

Sam climbed into the truck and watched Donna disappear

into the garage. Absently he touched his stomach and felt a flabby roll. The garage closed, swallowing any other thoughts he may've had.

Late that afternoon, Sam parked the sanitation truck in the service lot and drove home, where he parked his '82 Firebird in front of the garage next to a worn minivan. There was no room inside for cars. The garage was a storeroom for the collected detritus of life—junk too precious for Miriam to part with.

"*Buenos tardes*," Miriam greeted him from the kitchen.

"Hi, baby-doll." He pecked her lips, and she returned to cooking.

Ten-year-old Ramon and eight-year-old Joseph sat on beanbags watching cartoons. Television was neutral ground, a Christmas truce from ongoing sibling rivalry. Green plastic soldiers and Star Wars figures littered the burgundy shag carpet around them.

"Hey, guys." Sam waved. A Japanese cartoon had lobotomized them. "How was school?" he tried. No response. Abstract humanoids were blasting three-headed snakes. "Robbed a bank today." One of the snakes was hissing, *You cannot hope to defeat us!*

Sam turned to Miriam with hands in the air. She smiled up from a steaming pot of rice.

"Ice cream!" he screamed.

The boys' heads jerked up. "What flavor?" they chimed.

Sam shook his head and sank to his knees to roughhouse with them. They jumped on him and twisted his arms until he submitted with a cry of, "Uncle!" Then he sniffed his armpits. "Think I need a shower; what do you think?" He chased the boys around the living room with arms raised high over his head.

"Phew! Get a bath," Joseph said.

"Smell like a buffalo!" added Ramon.

"Yeah, guess I'd better."

"Don't be long. Dinner's ready," Miriam's voice followed him down the hallway toward the bedroom.

Sam stripped and threw his orange coveralls into a wicker laundry basket, then stepped into the shower and let cool water run over him. This was his personal form of Zen. Meditations sometimes returned him to the barrio of his youth, scratching out a living in the fields, waiting tables, cutting lawns for rich people...gangbanging.

Sam was taught when he was young, not to expect much out of life. Sandwiched between six brothers and sisters, he'd nearly disappeared. He founded a gang, painted walls, got into fights, and used drugs. Sam didn't ask for this life—hadn't wanted to come to Gringolandia, leaving grandparents and sisters behind. His father, Pedro, had sent money to hire a coyote to smuggle Sam across the border with his mother and two older brothers. Sisters were less useful, so they stayed in Mexico. Before coming to North America, Sam had seen his father only twice. Each time, before returning to el Norte he made sure Mother was pregnant.

His father had crossed many times and loved bragging about his journeys to friends and family. Sam's mother hated hearing about it. She recounted her first and last experience with loathing and disgust—climbing into the back of a cargo van, packed like sardines with twenty-five others, including Sam and his two brothers. They'd nearly suffocated on the seven-hour journey before the van stopped in the middle of nowhere.

Their clothes were soaked and smelled of piss and vomit. They gasped for air as the back door opened. Several were passed out on the filthy floor. His father was there and barely said a word as he drove seven more hours to a one-bedroom shack in the labor camp community of Woodville, in California, twenty-five minutes west of Meadowland.

What Sam remembered most was standing under the showerhead with his brothers, eyes closed, letting the cold water run over them—one of the best feelings he ever had.

At Woodville Elementary, he began losing his Mexican identity. Friends preferred burgers and pizza to beans, rice, and tortillas. Soon he was spending more time in the assistant principal's office than the classroom. After a certain age, his father decided it was better for Sam and his brothers to work in the fields rather than waste time in school. Sam's mother lamented the decision and tried to persuade Pedro to reconsider.

"Education will provide them with a better future," she argued.

"Gringos don't want us to have a future," he snapped.

They migrated to wherever crops needed harvesting, returning to Woodville at the end of the season. Truant officers never found them. For the children working in the fields, there was never time for make believe, and they were too tired for games when the day was done.

"*Ay, perder la infancia,*" Sam sighed. "No time to be a child."

"Dinner's ready." Miriam interrupted his thoughts. Her blurred image showed through the shower door.

"Yeah, okay."

That evening Sam announced his intention to lose weight. Miriam eyed him from across the dinner table, and Sam could hear what she was thinking. Miriam was shy by nature, yet her thoughts weren't bashful at all. She was pretty, with a long, black waterfall of straight shining hair reaching almost to her waist.

She was thinking, *Same old story. He'll last until dessert.*

"Sure?" She gestured to a steaming bowl of spiced rice.

Ramon tipped his milk over.

"*Ay, cabrón*," Sam blurted.

"Daddy said *cabrón*," Ramon complained.

"I heard." Miriam reached for a kitchen towel.

Surprisingly, Sam held firm, eating small portions and doubling up on green salad. After dinner, he found a pair of old gym shorts and his beat up running shoes. Summer evenings in Meadowland were sultry, and Sam took it slow. Asphalt and baked earth sponged in the afternoon heat and released it at sundown. He felt queasy at first before settling into a rhythm.

In bed that night, Sam replayed Donna's tickling southern lilt in his head. He turned on his side and pressed himself against Miriam. Her eyes opened in the darkness. She slipped down her pajama bottom, moved to her back, and lifted her knees. No words were needed as Sam climbed between.

Afterward, Miriam used her panties as a diaper and hurried into the bathroom, where she let Sam's seed drip into the toilet. When she returned, Sam was fast asleep. The swamp-cooler kicked on, and its steady hum helped her to drift off.

***

Donna finished slicing a fresh tomato into wedges as Warren arrived from work. Exhausted, he gave her a peck. "How was your day, sweetheart?"

"Same ol' same ol'." He went into the living room and settled into his favorite recliner to watch the evening news.

Donna began tearing lettuce. "Was thinking we should go to the condo this weekend." She raised her voice a notch to be heard over the TV. "We could invite that couple we met at the fundraiser."

"The Kmart manager?" Warren returned.

"They were nice, don't you think?"

"Mmm." He watched numbers roll by as a laconic market analyst Dow'd this and NASDAQ'd that. The economy had begun to tank since the election of the new president, and it worried him.

Donna chopped radishes to toss into the salad, shoving scraps into the disposal. She ran cold water and flipped the switch. The gargling irritated Warren, and he pumped up the volume. She could hear his thoughts—loud, echoing, empty. She tightened her grip on the knife and shoved a perfectly fine stalk of celery into the black hole.

After dinner, she sulkily thumbed through a few magazines as he watched television and then finally turned it off.

"Is there anything you wanted to watch?" he asked after it was already off.

"No." She tossed a magazine onto the coffee table.

Warren took her by the hand and pulled her off of the couch. He kissed her and then led her into the bedroom.

They fucked. Foreplay was condensed into a few pecking kisses, followed by penetration.

Dow's up, mused Donna, as Warren worked back and forth predictably. She made a mental list of to-dos for the following day: Red wine, cauliflower, and feta cheese.

Finally, he growled and shuddered. "Mmm, you felt great," Warren sighed. Immediately he padded into the bathroom. As he brushed his teeth, Donna sat on the bidet.

"So, what do you think of going to the condo?"

"Mmm. Can't this weekend, maybe next," he said with a mouthful of toothpaste.

Donna wiped and went to bed.

The next morning Donna cooked breakfast and kissed a crumb from Warren's mouth as he made for the garage.

"Mercedes's low on gas. Mind if I take the Beemer?"

"Sure, honey, have a nice day."

Donna wore a tiger-striped outer piece for the aerobics class at the club. Recently, she'd tried spicing things up with William, an elementary teacher enjoying summer vacation. He lifted weights, and her scouting report had been promising — nice looking, early thirties, well built.

She'd decided to play with William after Warren snapped at her for not picking up the dry cleaning. "What do you do with your time?" His words crashed into her brain like a Walmart sales stampede. He phoned later to apologize, and flowers followed. But the damage was done.

"Alrighty then," she'd murmured as she slipped into her leotard. "I'll use my time...you bet."

Donna paced the weight room as William used various machines. One particular machine's instruction plaque said PecDeck. Donna asked him innocently what muscles it worked, and William happily explained. Then he invited her to work out with him. After simple introductions, they took turns doing sets.

"I'll be sore for a month." She touched the tops of her breasts when they were done.

"Not if you stick with it," he said. "I'm here at the same time, Monday, Wednesday, and Friday."

"Won't I slow you down?"

"Nah, you'll push me harder."

Afterward, he treated her to a mineral water at the juice bar and asked her to call him Bill. She sipped and narrowed her eyes to extract vital information with lilting queries. He provided a resume: *Married, two youngsters, just bought a Lexus SUV, wants to run a marathon.*

"See you on Wednesday, if I'm able to crawl out of bed," she joked.

"You'll be fine, Donna. Soreness will leave after the first week."

That Wednesday, after their workout, Donna showered and changed into a thin cotton skirt with a peach blouse. Bill walked out with her to show off his new toy. He keyed open the passenger door of the Lexus for her, fired it up, and clicked on the air conditioning. He demonstrated how the rear seats eased down into a bed with the touch of a button and explained how smoky privacy glass made occupants invisible to outsiders.

"Why, it's a regular motel on wheels." Her words flowed like Karo syrup.

"No need to register under a false name." His eyes roamed over her.

"Air conditioner feels good." She leaned back into the leather seat and touched his thigh.

"Wanna check out the back?" He leaned in for a kiss, and she offered the tip of her tongue.

"An indecent proposal?" Her hand rubbed up and down his thigh.

"Don't have a million dollars," he said.

"Put me on layaway," she smiled.

"Okay." He crawled over the armrest and into the back, holding out his hand to help her through.

Kneeling, they faced each other and kissed. Wasting little time, he lifted her skirt and tugged down his pants. Donna slid off her panties and lay on her back. Bill lifted her knees and scooted forward. As he pushed inside, his cock lost stiffness. He pulled back on the skin, yet it continued to soften. He tugged at himself as they kissed — still nothing.

Donna took him into her mouth, and he hardened again. Quickly he placed himself at her entrance and pushed inside. A few seconds later, he grunted, pulled out, and spurted heavily over her cotton blouse.

"Jesus. Oh shit, sorry, Here let me get you a—"

"It's all right." She cleaned herself with a hand towel from her gym bag.

"This never happens to me," he insisted. "Just couldn't hold off."

They redressed, and Donna started to leave.

"Friday?" Bill queried.

She gave him a hurried kiss and slipped out of the new Lexus without answering.

***

William never returned to the club. Donna saw him at a grocery store one afternoon with his wife and children in tow. He shrank beneath her gaze. She reached into her shopping basket and playfully waved a polska kielbasa at him. He sped away with the shopping cart.

"Slow down, we need pasta sauce!" scolded his wife.

Following the van shenanigans, Donna was unfulfilled. When Warren came home, she attacked with every inch of her body, guiding him like a Sherpa to the highest peak. Afterward, he stood on quivering legs and wobbled into the living room to watch *60 Minutes*. Donna reached down to finish what Warren hadn't even started.

"Commodities are down one-point-three," droned a market analyst.

Donna pushed angrily through the next aerobics class, and if men were eyeing her, she didn't notice. "Just bought a Volvo," the aerobics instructor told Donna at the sports bar afterward.

"Volvo...sounds like a Swedish erogenous zone," Donna said. The instructor gave off a shrill, forced giggle.

***

Sam's alarm chirped like a tortured sparrow, which was

less irritating than using the radio option. Moving across the FM dial in his head—Mexican, country-western, conservative talk, hip-hop, Mexican, pop, and more pop—he found not a decent rock station in the mix. Sam thought of a TV program he'd watched when he was a kid, *The Andy Griffith Show.*

Meadowland is Mayberry, he reflected. *Floyd's the barber, Barney's the law, and Miss Crump still won't put out for Andy.*

Sam's shoulders relaxed as he jogged. The old feeling returned—a picnic with body and spirit. He was out of shape, heart drumming between his ears, throbbing painfully in his throat, yet it reminded him he was still alive.

No pain, no gain. The tired cliché sneaked through cracks in his subconscious. Earlier, he'd seen a plastic tampon dispenser on the ground. Feel fresh all day had popped its corn into his brain. He realized that most thoughts were manufactured products, put there to sell something. His originality was sold long ago, and now the shelves were nearly empty.

Sweat stung his eyes. He passed beneath a giant oak, and the lower branches knocked off his Giants baseball cap. As he stopped to pick it up, he heard a child squawking for something it didn't have, and crows in the upper branches spread rumors about where breakfast could be found.

A short distance away, Sam saw an obscene radio tower topped by a blinking red light. It pointed a skeletal middle finger toward a fading half-moon. KJUG was a country station. They towed around a giant moonshine jug stuffed with speakers and blasted away at every public function. It sat in front of the station now and fouled the air with tunes that reflected trailer-trash mentality.

As he resumed running, a voice twanged on about oceanfront property in Arizona. He knew the playlist by heart. The next song would be about cocker-spaniels having puppies, or worse, an idiotic post 9-11 song, where God blesses America by blowing the shit out of the Middle East. *Yeah*, he thought, *I should've voted.*

Sam smelled fresh-cut lawns and stagnant water from the irrigation canal. Sprayed blue or red on the back wall of a warehouse was the angular placa of gang-bangers — dogs pissing on clumps of grass. He'd been one too. As he jogged, he looked down at his knuckles and could clearly see the permanent dots there. He'd often thought of having the tattoos removed by laser, but his insurance wouldn't cover it.

The word soldier was scrawled across a bicep, while a long knife with a pair of handcuffs ran down one forearm. The name Cassandra forever reminded his wife, Miriam, of the woman who preceded her. It had been engraved in jail with homemade black ink and a Macgyvered cassette player.

One of the hieroglyphic writings caught Sam's eye: You're born so you can die — the rest is just a lie. Below that, Little Puppet had signed his autograph in blue.

The smell of sweat reminded Sam of swathing grapes and the summers of his childhood. He remembered finding a clear blue marble beneath a vine and keeping it in his pocket for years because what were the chances of finding something like that in the middle of a vineyard? He'd given it to Miriam on their second date.

Sam didn't need a watch to know when it was noon. The Wilson house was right around lunchtime, and then he was off to the gated gabacho community, where Donna lived. He braked at the Wilson's curb. Kate Wilson was carrying a book to add to the trash, followed closely by her husband, Grant.

"Haven't finished it," Grant argued in a voice that wasn't soldierly enough to live up to his name.

"I found it hidden in your son's underwear drawer, and the

sex scenes are dog-eared."

"Boys will be boys," Grant argued.

Kate answered by lifting the garbage lid and letting the book drop from her fingers as if it were a soiled diaper.

Grant shrugged at Sam and followed his wife back into the house. Sam had seen Grant rushing, approving checks, straightening displays, and greeting K-Mart customers. When the temperature soared, he envied Grant, working inside a bubble with air conditioning.

It was over a hundred degrees, and trash was beginning to cook. The reek of human accomplishment—sweet, sour, bitter, salty, and spicy—assaulted his nose. Sam tilted the Wilson's blue plastic container into the waiting jaws of the compactor. After ten years, he'd whiffed it all—dead pets, rotting food, wilted flowers, putrid lawn clippings, and everything in between.

Sam jerked the lever to initiate the trash-hugging mechanism. *Hugging comes in handy*, Sam thought. *Junk cars get a final squeeze. Adam's snake slithered into Eve's garden after one.* He thought of Miriam. *I'll need a hug tonight.*

As the diesel engine revved and the compacter squeezed, Sam wondered when Meadowland Sanitation would modernize. New trucks sported hydraulic arms with pincers. But his arms and shoulders flaunted the results of the heavy lifting he'd done over the years. Miriam enjoyed trailing her fingers over his muscles as they made love.

Sam finished emptying the Wilson trash and spotted the paperback resting against a milk carton. First, he read the back of the carton—a photo of a missing child with attendant information. Then he rescued the book and tossed it onto the passenger seat. His mother had died illiterate, yet insisted, *Un libro cerrado no saca letrado*—a closed book never made a scholar. Sam believed it. He couldn't remember ever seeing his father read, not even in Spanish.

As he drove to a nearby park to eat lunch, he drummed on the steering wheel as a song from The Fabulous Thunderbirds filled the cab. He hadn't lifted his guitar in years.

"Would've been pretty damned good by now," he muttered.

***

Donna paced her new home. The historical romance she'd been trudging through was boring and predictable. With any one of them, she could thumb three-quarters into the book to find the hot spot. She phoned a few friends for lunch, but they had other plans. After emailing her older sister in North Carolina, there was laundry to do, and then the car needed washing. It felt good giving a two-dollar tip to the Mexican who waved his towel when it was done. After puttering around in the garden, it felt good to skinny-dip in the kidney-shaped backyard pool. She wondered if neighbors ever spied on her as the lukewarm water caressed her naked body. Donna didn't know her neighbors—had only seen them come and go. They smiled and waved from their driveways.

Her house was a four-bedroom/three-car garage Mediterranean-style, and when Warren had opened his practice in Meadowland, she welcomed the newness. Yet Californians were an odd bunch, and her southern charms had yet to defrost their reserve. She paced like a caged lioness. The fresh smell of the house was beginning to fade. She thought of shopping, but for what? She didn't really need anything.

In the distance, she heard the ping of a diesel, reminding her that she hadn't set the trash out. A blast of hot air smacked her face as she wheeled a container to the curb. She thought of how tired and thirsty the garbage man must be, exposed to such a furnace. She rushed back into the kitchen to fetch a tall glass of iced tea and returned as the truck squealed to a stop at the front curb. She handed Sam the tea with her best southern smile.

"*Muchas gracias*, Donna."

She was impressed that he remembered her name. "*De nada*," she replied.

Sam raised an eyebrow to show appreciation for her use of Spanish.

Donna made a mental checklist as Sam gulped down the tea: *Not as chunky as I recall, soft, deep voice, and sexy brown eyes.*

As Sam finished, the ice that had stuck to the bottom of the glass suddenly rushed to the top to splash his face. He laughed.

"Let me get you another," offered Donna.

"Don't trouble yourself."

"No problemo," she called back.

When she returned, Sam asked, "*Habla en Español*?"

Donna laughed and shook her head. "I've exhausted my high school Spanish."

"Least you tried," he said, taking an ice cube into his mouth and then returning it to the glass.

"More?" she offered.

"No, thanks." He handed her the glass.

"Thursday," she smiled. "*Hasta luego.*" She turned to walk away.

"Hey, Donna, I was wondering…?" Sam stopped her.

"Yes?"

"Any fish in that lake?" He nodded to the artificial pond across the street.

"Honestly, I have no idea," she smiled.

"Just wondering."

"I'll ask," she promised. Donna walked into the garage, and she knew that Sam followed with his eyes until the aluminum door finished closing. "Nice man," Donna smiled. The air conditioning was too cold, so she switched it off. She searched her memory for other remnants of high school Spanish. Maybe later she'd study a few phrases on the Internet.

Donna slipped down a strap on her tank top. "*Me gusta caliente,*" she crooned, circling the remaining ice cube from Sam's glass over a nipple.

She didn't remember to switch on the air until Warren returned.

"Christ, it's boiling in here—air conditioner busted?"

Donna shrugged, "*Me gusta caliente.*"

"Burrito supremo to you too," he answered.

"Means, I like it hot." She lifted a corner of her mouth.

Warren's switched the air back on, "Hot, eh?" He tugged her into his arms, and after a short kiss, he towed her toward the bedroom.

"No," she said, "right here." She pulled him down to the living room carpet.

The change of scenery didn't inspire Warren. A few kisses, a flick of tongue where he'd previously camped out before they were married, and then it was off to the races. Nowadays, he rarely took her to the finish line. Donna closed her eyes and fantasized about the garbage man as Warren worked back and forth. Sam's rugged, swarthy face surfaced—orange shirt unbuttoned, hair in disarray, coveralls drained to the ankles. The smell of work was on him, and his brown eyes blazed as he thrust.

She felt a familiar ache, and a guttural moan escaped her lips. "Ohhh god." She lifted her hips and dug her heels into Warren's ass. "Yeah, baby!"

Warren bombarded her from above with thick drops of perspiration. He suddenly stiffened, and she was afraid he'd finish early again.

"Jesus Christ!" He pulled out and flipped onto his back.

"What's wrong?" Donna bolted upright. Warren was rolling from side-to-side in agony. "Honey!" Donna jumped to her feet.

"Back, shit, goddamn, fuck!"

"You scared me to death! I thought you were dyin'!"

Warren gritted his teeth and glared at her. Donna helped him into her car and drove him to the chiropractor. Doctors were terrible patients. He ranted and raved like Edgar Allan Poe on a drinking binge. A steady river of molten gutter-language flowed from his mouth. Donna sped along wordlessly, self-indulgently recreating the image of Sam, who'd nearly gotten her off.

"God*damn* it, you missed the fucking turn!" Warren's lava boiled over the side of the mountain and headed for the village. Donna hooked an illegal U-turn.

***

The alarm chirped at five on Tuesday morning. Sam merged with the hot, dry air. He ran faster now, focused on losing his spare tire, ignoring the writing on the walls and the shrill catcalls of crows. When he returned, Miriam had clean orange coveralls spread out on the bed for him, along with light clothing to wear underneath.

"Tired of looking like a fucking fish-stick," he murmured.

"Clothes don't make the man," she reminded and gave him a peck on the lips.

"Mmm." Sam's pants were loose now. He rummaged through the closet and found a pair of faded button-fly blue jeans he hadn't worn for five years. They fit perfectly. After showering, he studied his nakedness in the mirror. His cheeks were thinner, and it gave his eyes more intensity. Sam started liking himself again. He turned sideways. His large cock looked even bigger now. *Damn*, he thought, *a weapon of mass destruction.*

He drove to work with the windows down and felt a sudden urge to dig out his guitar. "Wasn't bad," he remembered, taking his hands off the wheel to strum his shirt. "Could've been a player."

They'd called themselves The Smokin' Lizards. Ten years earlier, they'd played rock'n'roll oldies in bars, county fairs, and high school dances. Chupa, short for chupacabra, played bass. His teeth were crooked, eyeteeth sticking out like a pair of fangs and hooking over his lower lip when his mouth was closed. Chupa had a garage, and they practiced there after work. Pancho played drums that were held together with duct tape and baling wire. Sam was the voice and reminded some of Stevie Ray Vaughn. Music kept him straight for a while. Sam worked a variety of jobs during this period of his life — construction, house painting, landscaping, anything that required muscle. His gang tattoos made it impossible to find any other work.

By then, his sisters had been brought over from Mexico, and the whole family applied for green cards. Sam didn't enjoy the few times they'd visited Mexico. *Had to use a bucket of water to flush the toilet. Fuckin' cops pulled us over for bribes. Mexico is so broken. Terrible roads, crumbling houses, corrupted government.* The only thing he liked besides the delicious food were Mexican girls. They played hard-to-get, but he'd caught a few anyway. In fact, one of his Mexican cousins told him that Sam had knocked one up, which was yet another reason never to return.

Sam's brothers and sisters were scattered all around the country like candy from a piñata. The sisters followed North American expectations by getting pregnant and becoming single moms. The brothers, in turn, became dead-beat fathers with dead-end jobs. Sam would've followed them if it hadn't been for Miriam. Just out of high school, she worked at the Rite-Aid. They met when the Smokin' Lizards played at a Cinco de Mayo festival in Meadowland.

Love blinded Miriam from Sam's dark side. She liked hearing him play. Soon after they met, Sam backslid and was arrested for cocaine possession. Miriam stuck with him through six months in county lockup and a long period of subsequent unemployment.

They shared an apartment, and she paid the bills. It was the first time in his life that Sam felt loved. Eventually, his luck changed, and he landed work with the Meadowland Department of Sanitation. Miriam got pregnant, and they married at a drive-through in Las Vegas. Sam hustled trash, ate three squares a day, and snuggled into bed with an affectionate wife.

Miriam had worked at Rite-Aid long enough to avoid working the customer courtesy ice cream counter unless it was an emergency. Now, she was an assistant manager-in-training. She attended occasional weekend workshops to learn the ins and outs of Rite-Aid corporation philosophy.

Sam smiled as he ran. Life was better now. He was living the American dream — wife, two kids, two cars, a mortgage, and credit card debt.

During lunch, he retrieved the novel he'd salvaged from the Wilson trash. Earlier, it'd fallen to the floorboard when he slammed the brakes to avoid a filthy mutt, covered in a tangle of mangy dreadlocks. It sat in the middle of the road licking its butt. Sam bumped the horn, but the dog didn't budge.

A homeless man appeared, carrying a gunnysack over his shoulder. He paused to lock eyes with Sam before scooping up the dog and disappearing down an embankment on the other side of the street. Sam recalled, *Man's eyes were greener than fresh grass clippings*. They'd reflected a painful history that Sam could only guess about.

He inspected the cover of the paperback, crusted with thick, green cake frosting. The odor had abandoned ship, and many of the pages were stuck together. Some of the best adhesives known to man were in the back of the truck. Sam theorized that leftover oatmeal was stronger than Krazy Glue when it dried. On the cover was a man that seemed to be facing a large trashcan lid centered between mounds of rubbish. The book's title was scratched, yet Sam puzzled it out — *The Journal of Desperate Living*. The author was Owen Zelenski. The first nine pages were missing. He turned to ten.

I'm a simple man. Doesn't take much to make me happy. All I seek is an answer to the question…why?

"Fuck this," Larry murmured to himself, "I'm finished waiting for enlightenment to bite me on the ass."

Larry left before the kids returned from school, before his wife came back from the grocery store, and before a neighbor popped over to borrow sugar.

Sam furrowed his brow. He preferred mystery and horror. Flipping to the middle of the book, he read:

The road split, and Larry had to make a decision. One path was paved, the other overrun with bullhead stickers and razor grass. Larry returned to a campground he'd walked through earlier that day. He'd decide which path to take after a night's rest.

"Should've left this book where I found it." Sam shook his head and tossed it onto the passenger seat.

It was time to pick up in Donna's neighborhood. More than once in that neck of the woods, he'd sifted through unwanted items set out for Goodwill. Many things looked new to his eyes. Arriving at the gated community, he punched in a code at the security island, and the metal gates swung open. In many of the driveways sat cars that cost more than he and Miriam made together in a year.

Sam wondered how Donna kept busy — *fundraisers, Macy's, little get-togethers, kids in private school, pool in the backyard*? People living behind the gate were from a different planet as far as he was concerned.

***

Donna moistened her lips when she heard the truck. She peeked through the mini-blinds and did a short-range reconnaissance as Sam stopped at the neighbor's house. *Nice ass, taller than most of his kind.*

Sam drew up next to Donna's curb. He emptied a container, and when he turned to lift another, she was there, standing in the blazing heat, wearing an Indian skirt and a cream-colored blouse. He smiled and shut down the engine when she offered a glass of iced tea.

"You're going to spoil me."

"Hardly think so, Mr. Villarreal — maybe if it was a Long Island ice tea."

"Please, call me Sam."

"Okay, Sam. Why don't you come in out of this nasty ol' heat for a spell?"

Sam did as he was asked. He took off his gloves and slipped out of the orange coveralls, setting them on the driver seat. Donna led him into the house, where the air conditioning quietly and efficiently cooled them down.

"Nice place." He nodded as he swiveled his head.

"You must be dyin' of thirst."

Sam followed her into the kitchen, where an iced pitcher of tea sat on a cooking island.

"House still smells new," Sam grinned as he accepted a glass and took a long drink.

"New is excitin', don't you think?"

Sam arched an eyebrow as she topped off his glass.

"Thanks," he smiled. "Yeah, I've always thought so."

"Sometimes, I get to feelin' a little crazy."

"Yeah?"

She put a hand on his arm, "Don't you sometimes?" Donna's voice dragged lazily across the vowels.

"Got me into trouble more than once."

"Don't mean that kind, silly. I mean, the sort that makes you feel alive."

The tone in her voice was unmistakable. Sam's heartbeat pounded in his throat. Her eyes softened.

The front door swung open, and Warren rushed in out of the heat, resting his briefcase on the dining room table before noticing them. Donna straightened and slipped into her best mask.

"Sweetheart, you're early. I didn't hear you drive up."

Warren gave a half-smile and nodded. "Had a cancellation. Thought we'd try out that new Japanese place."

"Honey, this is Sam."

"Pleasure," Warren nodded. "Saw your truck. Thought you'd broken down."

"Your wife invited me for iced tea." His voice struggled past the knot.

"Southern hospitality...nice to meet you, Sam." He excused himself into the living room.

"Like some tea?" Donna called after him.

"No thanks." He winced and pushed on his lower back before sitting in the recliner. "Martini is more like it."

"Thanks for the tea," said Sam.

"Thursday?"

"Yeah."

"I'll have something waiting."

"Don't trouble yourself."

"No trouble." She frowned toward Warren, sitting in his pew. "No trouble at all."

After Sam left, she started dinner until Warren reminded her that they were going out.

"Honey, I don't really feel like it."

"You all right?" He got up and came into the kitchen.

"Just a little headache." Her legs were still quivering.

"Hope you're not coming down with...." Warren put a hand to her forehead. "I'll get you an aspirin."

Donna knew aspirin wouldn't put a dent in what ailed her.

***

Days fronting Thursday were dipped in molasses and rolled in chicken feathers. The crystal on Sam's watch captured the sun's rays and deflected seconds into his eyes. Each moment brought him closer to Donna. No mistaking the vibes. He shed three more pounds and stepped up his running mileage.

That weekend he purchased some new clothes at JC Penney. He carried a small bottle of cologne in his lunch box and tried out a newfangled vibrating razor with four blades. Vibrations were damned expensive.

Thursday, he pinched his stomach and smiled. Orange coveralls protected a new white shirt, tucked into a crisp new pair of button-fly Levis.

***

Thursday morning, Donna made sure Warren had a full schedule at work.

"I'll be late," he said. "Gotta give Ralph Parker some bad news."

She knew what that meant. Family physicians were prepared for birth and death, hello and goodbye. As he drove away, she marched into the walk-in closet and flipped on the light to appraise rows of hanging possibilities.

"Accessible," she decided. A familiar tingle raised goosebumps on her arms and motivated her nipples to sit up straight in their rosy seats.

***

Sam's stomach grumbled when he parked for lunch. He took out the large salad Miriam had prepared for him. She was impressed by her husband's willpower and had decided to support him. His efforts inspired her to take aerobics at the Meadowland Sports Center. As a Rite-Aid employee, she didn't pay an initiation fee and qualified for a membership discount.

At lunchtime, Sam read from the shoddy novel he'd rescued from the Wilson family garbage. It helped distract him from his anxiety.

Chapter 16: The African Sahara
Larry's cheeks knotted. She'd been the one, he was sure — it felt right. They'd fused together, simmering like ingredients in a zesty soup. He'd poured his essence into her like the bubbling waters of an eternal spring. Afterward, he whispered three words to her — the same ones that could destroy or give eternal life.

"Nyama Namungu" she purred.

Larry didn't know what it meant, and she only smiled when he asked. Then she went out for cigarettes and never came back.

Tears rained from Larry's face. He beat his fists against the soft side of his backpack, then stepped out from the motel room and into the scorching sun. Yet even the sun felt cold...so fucking cold.

Sam laughed and checked his watch. He reached out of the window to test the weather. "Hot...fucking hot."

He started the engine, hating the sound. It reminded him that he was a garbage collector, not a corporate executive, a doctor, or a trust-fund baby. He sometimes joked about being an environmental engineer to camouflage indignity. Bottom line, he picked up other people's trash. Suddenly, reality slapped him hard across the back of the head.

"Who do you think you are?" he said aloud. He shook his head and spit out the window. *What the hell was I thinking? What could this woman possibly want from me? She's just a tease,* he thought. The more he reflected, the angrier he got.

Snapping out of his daze, he sped past a city cop doing twenty over the limit. The officer was busy arresting a sub-sandwich and reading Miranda rights from the back of a 42-ounce Big-Gulp.

***

Donna touched cologne to the inside of her thighs. She admired her reflection in the floor-length mirror and reviewed the personal checklist: *Flower-print silk skirt, check; white blouse unbuttoned three notches, check; tousled hair, like the mane of a lioness, check.* She smiled and quaffed from her cup of sensuality—a tangy blend of spontaneity and passion, topped with whipped need. She touched her forehead and wondered if it was time for another Botox treatment. She hung gold loop earrings and walked out of the bathroom with a sidelong glance.

"Showtime," she whispered, pausing at the front door to listen. She heard the steady hum of the pool filter, the thundering closure of a neighbor's aluminum garage door, and a tomcat yowling as it stalked a prospective mate. She crossed her arms and rubbed her nipples until they stood out like the tips of baby carrots.

***

Donna's garbage cans crouched like escaped felons, dark and round-shouldered against the hot sun. Sam hoped there were no grass clippings, which smelled like the breath of a vegetarian alcoholic. Barrel after barrel, he moved closer until he was finally there.

As Sam lifted the first container, Donna emerged from the front door. She flowed like a frothy wave poised to break, defying gravity and holding her curve. She carried a glass of iced tea, and Sam knew his thirst was about to be quenched.

"Come on in out of that nasty ol' heat, Sam."

Sam slipped out of his coveralls and followed her like a puppy. When they were in the kitchen, she turned to him. "So tell me, Sam, what happens if you're a little late getting' back?"

"Nothing."

"Good."

Donna smiled and stepped toward him. Sam met her halfway, turning into putty as her soft tongue caressed his lips and slid into his mouth. Moments later, the living room carpet was strewn with the bottom halves of their clothing.

***

Sam hadn't written poetry for years. Responsibilities had dulled his artistic senses. Now, like a Saturn rocket wheeled out of storage and dusted off, his pen streaked across a worn Scribe notebook.

> You're easy to love
> Passion stirred with honesty,
> poured upon my soul —
> bathed in your ocean eyes

Creativity returned, a trusted bartender blending the perfect foo-foo drink. The sky reflected in the watery moons of Donna's eyes. The curve of the Sierra Nevada's signified her peaks and valleys. She combined with nature. Together they lived inside him now. It had been three months since the fateful afternoon when he'd discovered he was more than just a garbage man.

Donna called it an affair.

"Affairs begin and end," Sam argued. "My feelings for you are endless."

Donna's heart melted when he said that, yet she warned against using the *L* word. "People love pecans, cell phone plans, Rocky Road ice cream, and shoes. But what does it mean when they say it to a person?"

Sam searched for alternatives. *Adore, worship, revere, idolize, need. She is afraid of being needed too…that won't do.* Sometimes Donna hinted about ending their relationship, and Sam grew desperate.

"There's a lot at stake, Sam. We can't get caught."

Donna made safe, well-planned, and intricate meeting arrangements. Sometimes she let his landline phone ring just once, signaling that she was thinking of him. Two rings meant it was safe to call her cell phone. Yet he wasn't allowed to signal her. She was careful never to leave messages on his cell and warned that he shouldn't either.

"What if you forget it at home, and your wife reads them?"

Occasionally, after a few glasses of wine, she'd break her own rules and call Sam's home phone from a bathroom, while Warren tranced out on television. Sam cleverly camouflaged their conversations, especially if Miriam was near.

"Hi Ed, how're you doing?"

"I want your big cock inside," Donna would moan.

"Sure…."

"Deep inside, right now." Her drawl was more pronounced with wine.

"Yeah, been a while. When?"

"Can't. Warren's home. Tonight I'll have to perform my wifely duty."

"Don't think the Giants can pull it off. Their hitting's weak."

"Tomorrow afternoon?"

"Sounds good."

"Bring the mini-van."

"Shouldn't be a problem, Ed, see yuh then."

Sometimes Miriam studied him after Donna called. He avoided eye contact and focused on healthy baseball thoughts.

***

They met in black holes. Sam gained an erotic appreciation for seedy motels, underground parking lots, and weedy pull-offs. When he was out with family, he drove past sacred grounds — Edgewood Park, an orange orchard, the Ponderosa Motel.

Donna wouldn't risk fucking at home again. The longer she lived there, the more likely it was that a friend would drop by unannounced. "Never shit in your own backyard," she remembered her father advising her in the wake of the famous Clinton/Lewinsky sex scandal.

Sam pulled strings to be with her. They constructed a freeway divider, separating realities. Sam wrote a poem about returning home after being with Donna.

> Swallowed by dim light,
> black and white,
> as the garage door
> closes tight

Donna grew impatient with Warren. She had trouble partitioning the two worlds and often caught herself daydreaming, staring at a corner of the ceiling. She phoned Sam more often, and then one Saturday she steeled herself to end it, once and for all.

"Kissing Warren's like licking the sofa. I'm obsessed with you, and it's fucking up my home life. I have to keep him happy."

Sam trembled, gnashed his teeth, and turned toward the Disney character wall-calendar tacked up next to the phone. He felt Miriam's eyes on him.

"Okay, Jack. Listen, we'll talk later about this." His voice caught.

"No, Sam, it's really over." She hung up.

Sam escaped into the bedroom, and Miriam's eyes stabbed him between the shoulder blades as his sons battled for supremacy over the television remote.

"Dad, Ramon's hitting!"

"You're dumb!"

"Stop it!" demanded Miriam.

Sam felt like the empty hourglass in *The Wizard of Oz*. He found his notebook, and wrote:

Silent, swift-legged spider sticks my soul to the center of her web
Races to cover me with silk — drains me
A warm breeze tugs, lifts my hollow shell
She watches me drift away
Waits for another vibration

"Vibrations are goddamn expensive," Sam murmured, feeling bankrupted.

Early Sunday morning, Donna phoned from aerobics. Sam heard the irritating thump of techno music in the background. The boys were watching an old *He-Man* cartoon, and Miriam was showering after a night shift.

"Can't do it, Sam—I want to see you." Her words caressed,

and his heart healed as if touched by ET. "But there has to be ground rules, my friend. *No* sex." She paused, and Sam was silent. "It's too intense. After being with you, I've got nothing left for Warren. Those're the rules."

By the power of Grayskull, I have the power, He-Man proclaimed, transforming from a wimp into a hunk.

"Yeah, okay," Sam answered numbly. When he thought of losing the pleasure of their lovemaking, a lump formed in his throat. "Just want you to be happy."

"Doesn't mean forever, just for now, until things smooth out."

"Okay. I wrote a new poem."

"Okay?"

"Yeah."

"Sure?"

"Yeah."

"Read it to me."

"All right."

He-Man turned back into a wimp.

Three days later, Donna invited him to her home. Warren had flown to a conference in Miami, and she was feeling bold. Sam showered her with poetry, Donna engulfed him with flames that licked and scorched into the wee hours. Miriam thought Sam was watching Sunday football with buddies at a sports bar. When he turned on his cell phone at 3:45 AM, there were five messages.

"Lost track of time," he told her.

Miriam's eyes were slits, and when he slipped into bed, she turned away from him. He thought to reach for her, yet felt it would add insult to injury. He secretly dreaded a confrontation. He wasn't sure what he'd say if her thoughts formed into words.

The following day, Sam left a poem taped to the inside lid

of one of Donna's trashcans. She read it back to him when they met again.

"Wish I could write you a poem," she lamented.

"You *are* poetry," he said.

Donna's husband spared no expense to keep his high maintenance wife happy. One Sunday morning, a gleaming new Mercedes, license plate DONNASM, was parked in the driveway when she went out for the newspaper. That evening, Sam received another *we have to talk* call.

"Can't anymore…it's tearing me apart," they usually began.

For Sam, the following days were vacant and punctuated by fatalistic poetry.

> My paintings deteriorate,
> brush lines fading,
> one color blending into another

Inevitably Donna called — a stay of execution, followed by upbeat poems.

> Hanging in the silence,
> dancing on the breeze,
> a proud, golden lioness,
> brought me to my knees

Sam accepted the mood swings, comparing them to a rollercoaster at Magic Mountain.

"Don't know how you put up with me," she said during an orange-grove reunion in the minivan. "I'm so neurotic."

"You're not neurotic."

"Yes, I am, but I'm glad you still like me." She lifted her ass to tug down a pair of snug-fitting jeans and straddled him.

She gripped his shoulders as she impaled him. "Ahhh, damn you...." Her fingers closed playfully around his throat. "You're a fly in the ointment." Then she began moving her hips, and any further thoughts were drowned by immediate needs.

***

Sam and Miriam decided to take the boys to Disneyland. The two young warriors negotiated a temporary ceasefire so their parents wouldn't cancel.

The day before the phone had rung, and Sam sensed it was Donna. The boys were in the back yard, throwing a football, and Miriam was trimming roses.

"Hi, Dave," he said.

"Yesterday I was Ernie."

"Yes, I remember."

"Keeping it light?"

"Practically weightless," he replied.

Recently Donna had separated the two worlds by bringing more levity into their relationship. She reasoned that connections withered as a result of over-seriousness. Earlier that week, Sam had gifted her with the book he salvaged from the jaws of the compactor — *The Journal of Desperate Living*, by Owen Zelenski. She gained a measure of revenge by reading excerpts to him over the phone.

"Why would anyone trash this book? Listen to this, page seventy-six, somewhere in Denmark." And she read:

"Larry wished he were a giant squid. At least then, he could unleash a cloud of ink to escape enemies (Donna giggled). *But he was defenseless. He thought to return home — yet to what? The window of his crumbling rental looked out on an isolated gift store where hardly anyone shopped. The storekeeper emerged to stroll every ten minutes up and down the street.* (Donna cleared her throat). *Fuck this! Fuck everything! Larry opened the window. 'Knep!' He cried in Danish."*

Sam chuckled, "Ever been caught knepping?"

"Don't laugh. This book is changing my life." She lowered her voice. "I think I'm ready to accept Christ as my personal savior."

Sam burst out laughing at the same moment Miriam came in from the backyard with a basket of cut roses. Her mouth tightened at the corners.

"Is that right? Well, Dave, that changes the whole ballgame."

"Certainly does. Well, I'll let you get back to the battlefield, sweetheart. Have fun at Disneyland. Think about me when you're on the Pirates of the Caribbean."

Miriam was in the garage now, sorting laundry. Sam whispered, "I'll be thinking of your booty." Sam started to hang up.

"Oh, just one more thing...." She paused for effect. "I think I love—"

***

Warren was suddenly there. "I'd love to," she amended as Warren slowly set down his briefcase and lifted a questioning eyebrow. "Okay, Barb." Donna's throat tightened. "Uh-huh, see you Tuesday. Okay, bye-bye." She gave a beaming smile to Warren and shuffled submissively into his arms, "Didn't hear you come in. How was your day?"

Warren wearily slid off his jacket and hooked it over a dining room chair. "Same'o," he droned, yet she saw a storm brewing on his forehead, suspicion scrawled with thin black marker at the corners of his mouth. She quickly brushed past him into the laundry room to gather her wits, along with warm clothes from the dryer. She threw them on the master bed and began folding.

"God*damn* it," she muttered, massaging her temples. In the bathroom, she found Valium. She put two in her mouth, took a handful of water from the sink, and tossed her head back. The pills slid dryly down her throat.

***

Sam sneaked quietly into the shower after his morning run. He hadn't finished rinsing shampoo when the toilet flushed in the boy's bathroom, followed by a sudden jolt of cold water.

"*Puta madre!*" He backed away from the nozzle and waited for warmth to return.

Sam was on top of the world. Donna had been close to saying the magic words, and he couldn't wait to hear them flowing out like melted caramel. He was ready for the whole nine yards — divorce, genesis, and a life he hadn't known was missing until Donna emerged from the garage that day.

He finished his shower, got dressed, and broke up the first fight between the boys. Then he took the initiative to fix breakfast while Miriam showered...and broke up another fight. Finally, he delivered an ultimatum. "Next peep I hear...." He shook a finger.

"Yeah, stupid," Joseph muttered to Ramon.

Sitting in the front driveway next to the Firebird was the battered mini-van, resembling a loaf of wheat bread.

"Mom's car," he said when Ramon asked which car they'd be taking to the Magic Kingdom.

"*My* car?" Miriam snipped, her hair still damp from the shower.

"You know, I've been thinking that we ought'a get an SUV."

"Yeah?" Miriam countered. "Who's going to pay for it?"

"Found somebody interested in the Firebird. Remember the tax guy, Johnson? His stepson likes it."

They sat down for breakfast, and the boys wolfed down eggs and toast, anxious to begin the journey. Sam tried to bring up the SUV subject again, but Miriam quickly put an end to it.

"Forget it, Sam. Boys, get in Mommy's car."

"We'll talk later," he said, slipping into the driver's side.

The boys each had portable DVD players and were quickly immersed in an alternative universe when he started the engine.

Sam snapped his fingers. "*Ay, cabrón*, forgot my sunglasses."

"Dad said cabrón," the boys chorused without looking up from their screens.

"I heard," Miriam acknowledged.

As Sam entered the house, the phone was chirping. "*Bueno*?" he answered cheerfully.

"It's over, Sam. Warren knows." Donna's voice was distant, as though she were speaking into a coffee mug.

Sam felt dizzy and sat on the carpet next to the phone. "What?"

"Remember last night?"

"Sure."

"Get another call after that?"

"A hang-up." Chills ran down his back and into his arms.

"He knows. When I was in the bathroom, he checked my cellphone."

"You tell him?" His heart felt like pounded cube steak.

"I'm no good at this." Her voice cracked with emotion.

In the background, Sam heard an aerobics instructor shouting instructions over a monotonous techno — boom, boom, boom — screech — boom, boom, boom — screech!

"Said it was a guy I met in aerobics — that we were only flirting. Think he bought it, but I never want to feel like that again."

"Listen, we'll work it out — "

"It's finished."

"We can set new ground rules — I love you." The last three words leaked out. There was a long pause.

"Had to make a choice, Sam."

"Listen, let's—"

"Don't make it harder. We're both married, you have kids, and besides, we're from different worlds." Her words trailed off.

"So, that's what it boils down to," he choked.

"Gotta go," she answered. "Bye, Sam."

The phone clicked and then buzzed like a squadron of killer bees. Sam drew his knees into his body. Ramon stormed in and didn't see him.

"Dad?" Joseph yelled.

"Probably taking a dump," said Ramon, and they returned to the car.

A moment later, Miriam came in. She saw the phone cord dripping down the wall and knelt in front of him. She'd seen the look before, years back when Sam was sentenced to county jail.

"What happened?"

She'll be back, Sam reasoned. *She always comes back.*

He got to his feet and hugged his wife, who looked very pretty just then. Lately, she'd been taking better care of herself— wore new clothes.

"Hank was fired."

"Oh, that's terrible."

"Cutbacks, or some shit."

Miriam didn't know that Hank had been terminated the previous month.

"Any chance you'll—"

"Nah, been there too long. Hank only had three years in."

"Yeah. You okay?"

"Let's go."

For Sam, the Magic Kingdom was another prison,

surrounded by concrete walls, roaming security forces, and employees wearing character costumes. Only Tinker Bell caused him a doubletake. He went on the scarier rides with Joseph and Ramon because Miriam suffered from motion sickness. They stayed for the fireworks and then headed for home. The boys fell asleep, and Miriam stared out her side window.

The following morning he tried Donna's cell phone, but the number was no longer in service. He'd no way of knowing that Warren had flown with her to Paris for a week, to glue the broken fragments of their marriage.

That Thursday, he stood in front of her house, distractedly emptying trash barrels, absently spilling grass clippings onto the street. Summer was over, and a cruel October wind tossed his hair around. A child was walking her brown dachshund and stopped to watch the machine do its job.

"Want to pull the lever?" he asked.

She nodded, and Sam lifted her. She grabbed the rubberized tip, and Sam put a gloved hand over hers to help. Her mother arrived and smiled at the kindness. The dog bridled as the compacter went into action. The mother took the leash from Sam and backed away. When the job was finished, he returned the child to earth.

"What do you say?" the mother said in a fawning voice.

"Thank you," said the little girl.

"You're welcome. You did a great job."

"Thank you," repeated the child.

"My pleasure." As they walked away, a lump formed in Sam's throat.

Sam left work early the next day, complaining of a stomachache. Indeed, his guts were tied in knots. The kids were at school, and Miriam, on her day off, was probably shopping. They'd recently switched cars, and he noticed small repairs the van needed — torn upholstery, a broken cup holder, and a lengthening crack in the front windshield. He sat on the edge of the bed staring into the open closet at his black guitar case.

***

Hours later, Miriam returned and was greeted by sounds she hadn't heard in years. She straightened her dress, ran a hand through her hair, and walked quietly into the bedroom. She'd never heard Sam sing more soulfully.

"Green man grows, poor man breaks his back, that's just the way it is when you're born on the wrong side of the railroad track...."

Miriam sat quietly next to him on the edge of the bed until the song was finished. "You write that?"

Sam looked up like a child who'd just fallen off a bike. He nodded, burst into tears, and buried his head in Miriam's chest. She rocked him, stroked his face, and focused on the bare white wall next to the vanity. A moment later, the phone rang, and she felt Sam stiffen.

Miriam's heart raced, and then she began to relax. *I'll call him back later*, she thought. *Sam needs me. Gotta keep the troops happy.*

CHAPTER 3
Double Cross

"Religion is regarded by the common people as true, by the wise as false, and by the rulers as useful." — Edward Gibbon

Jim remembered, *She hardly ever wore dresses. Nothing more attractive than a pretty woman in a nice dress.* These days, casual style was the in thing. Teenagers came to church wearing ripped up Wranglers, black T-shirts fronted with band logos, or a corporate moniker—Hello Kitty, Van Heusen, Quicksilver, Eddie Bauer—the list went on—advertising for a bunch of rich bastards. *Good rule-of-thumb for bachelors—avoid designer-jeans girls.*

"Ginny sure looked fine in a dress," Jim muttered.

The attic smelled stale, full of memories that hadn't aged well. The refurbished Victorian was over a century old. Sitting on a frayed lawn chair, Jim furrowed his eyebrows and read Ginny's letter beneath a naked bulb that dangled from the ceiling. He searched for hidden messages, a hint that she was still waiting, but the letter was thirty years old, and the distance between them was complicated by more than just time. He'd kept it hidden in a wooden Roi-Tan cigar box, camouflaged by forgotten Christmas decorations and a hoe with a broken handle. Jim lifted the letter to his nose, and the stationery whispered through his fingers. Ginny's flourishing handwriting caressed his heart. The paper had long since lost the fragrance she'd sprinkled it with.

"Here, kitty-kitty-kitty!" Mildred's voice blared, dissolving his reflections like a foghorn on a stygian night. The reverb trudged up the stairs and into the attic, pounding his brain like a meat tenderizer. Jim's fingers tightened around the letter, and he slumped forward.

Mildred's voice emerged from a cold, frothy sea and echoed within the bone-chilling mist that she carried everywhere with her. Jim compared her voice with the beautiful black saleslady who recently sold them a coffee table. Her voice had warmed his ears like the crinkle of onion paper in his Bible. "Can I interest you in anything else?" she'd asked.

Lord, Jim thought, *if she could'a read my mind, she would've slapped me...or maybe invited me for coffee.*

"What do you have in end tables?" Mildred replied from a throat begging to be cleared.

Physically, Mildred was pleasing enough—tall, slender, ramrod straight. But, it was clear to Jim that attitude was sculpted with a mallet and chisel, thus shaping our faces. Mildred had crow's feet around the eyes. Negativity had dragged the corners of her mouth downward. *Person's view of life reflects on their face. See the world through a negative lens, and a corresponding mask forms.*

Jim and Mildred were childless. "Jim's seed isn't viable, but the good Lord has blessed us with many young lives to care for in the church," she tirelessly reminded the congregation.

Mildred lacked passion, the zest for life that separated menial existence from thriving fellowship. As far as he knew, Mildred had never experienced an orgasm. She considered sex a wifely duty, like cooking eggs in the morning, doing laundry, or pulling weeds in the garden.

Jim focused on the letter again, and his hand made the words tremble. With his free hand, he explored his face. Despite Mildred, it had resisted the chipping and fading that occurs when attitude is left out in the weather. A salty tear splashed the date on one corner of the letter:

January 14, 1974
Dear Jimmy,
I love you, and I always will. You've a gift for writing feelings. The poems and letters you've given me are reminders of how much we've shared. I still have the first one: You shed light on my sleeping hopes, and on this day, loneliness set sail.

You said you needed time to think about our relationship, and it's been over a month. I know you're busy with the church, but what's that got to do with you and me? Isn't there room in your heart for both?

All of this waiting is tearing me apart, Jimmy. I need to know what's going on in your head. I'm jealous of God — angry that He makes you feel guilty for what happened. I love you, Jimmy, but I won't wait forever.

Love always,
Ginny
PS: This isn't very good, but it's the best I can do: What's the sense in loving if freedom turns to stone, pouring two glasses, just to drink alone?

Jim touched the final word with his finger and squeezed his

eyes shut. The attic surrounded him with lost things. *Alone*, he thought.

"Jim! Dinner's almost ready," Mildred trumpeted. Her words circled the musty attic like bothered hornets.

"In a second," he called down.

"Don't let it get cold," she warned.

Jim clenched his teeth and cracked his neck from side-to-side. Ginny's lipstick signature was still there. He lifted the letter to his mouth and closed his eyes.

"Jim, did you hear?"

"Yes!"

His river had meandered for thirty years, following a predictable path. The storm began with a few pattering drops on Ginny's letter. Within seconds the banks overflowed, drowning theological fruit trees carefully pruned and protected for thirty winters. Jim felt like a child, sent to the back of the class simply for not knowing the answer.

"Thy rod, and Thy staff...," he whispered, desperately filling sandbags with scripture. His nose dripped, and *Love always* was magnified for a moment.

"Jim!" Mildred clomped up the stairs like a Nazi soldier searching for hideaways. Boards creaked beneath the pressure of her coming. Jim was reminded with every step — thirty years shot to hell in the blink of an eye.

"Lies," Jim muttered. "Thy rod and staff are no comfort at all." Jim ran fingers through his graying hair and flicked tears from his eyes. Mildred was a silhouette in the doorway.

"You've been crying."

"Mmm," he grunted.

"Never known a man to cry as much as you." Then, in a gentler voice, "Coming down?"

Jim tried to smile. "In a bit, dear."

Mildred blinked and shook her head. "It's getting cold." She turned on her heel and left.

Dinner cooled with each moment, threatening to lose flavor if he waited longer. The odor of dinner stalked the stairs and assaulted his nose. Pot roast. He hated pot roast. It could wait.

The attic was closer to Heaven than the living room or office. From the attic, Jim prayed that God would inspire The Big One — the elusive Holy Grail of sermons that every preacher dreamed of. The Big One would have them standing in the pews, stumbling toward the altar like zombies. He'd anoint them, ask for the world, and they'd give it to him on silver collection plates. Then he'd march the lemmings over a cliff and watch them splash their souls on jagged rocks. God would name a drink in their honor, served in a dive-bar at the corner of the universe.

"Martyrita," Jim smiled. "On the rocks."

Jim would write the Big One in the attic, where heat rises, carrying with it the smell of faith and pot-roast. He set the letter down and gripped his notebook and pencil. His Bible lay heavy in his lap, and he opened it.

The letter — aged paper and faded ink. Could just as easily tear it up, let it swirl down a toilet.

Mark, 2:27: *But the Sabbath was made to benefit man, and not the man to benefit the Sabbath. And I, the Messiah, have authority even to decide what men can do on Sabbath days.*

Jim smiled as he read the verse. He knew that youngsters in the flock would rather scoop dog poop off the back lawn than waste Sundays with him. They whispered while he sermonized, passed notes, giggled, tapped toes against pews, and doodled on programs. They were plugged in and tuned out, gaming, texting, Tweeting, What's Upping. Social networks were more important than whatever he prattled on about.

"Technology creates sociopaths," he nodded, picturing youths with ear-buds clogging up their perceptions. *Perhaps I should address the issue in a sermon.* He studied what he'd scribbled so far — JESUS, in block letters, and beneath it, GINNY. Jim lifted the letter. *Not just paper and ink*, he thought. "Love always," he read the words aloud.

A sharp pain shot down Jim's left shoulder, and he swung his arm in circles. He fondly remembered the lustful ache Ginny had caused when they kissed. Jim remembered another Bible passage: Matthew 24, verse 12: *Sin will be rampant everywhere and will cool the love of many. But those enduring to the end shall be saved.*

Jim had counted on it. His parents had steadfastly maintained their faith throughout his life. Everything was connected to the Eye in the Sky. As a result, Jim had been a joy for them — never any trouble, good grades, and even when he was bullied for his faith, he endured. Jim was an island surrounded by holy water. Faith bubble-wrapped his world with truth, interpreted by doe-eyed Sunday school teachers.

Back then, Jim had looked forward to the end times. He prepared for Christ's second act like a spiritual packrat, memorizing gothic passages from Revelation and watching the skies. As years passed, the memory of Ginny, his high school sweetheart, faded. He met Mildred in 1975 at the Fresno Bible College. They shared quiet dinners, G-rated movies, and the few times his hands explored beyond her moral boundaries, she reminded him of how special it would be if they waited. He'd waited, and it hadn't been.

Like a rock crab, Mildred dutifully wedged between her dual role as minister's wife and caretaker of the faith. She considered herself the First Lady and kept her foghorn well-oiled to keep Jim on the straight and narrow.

The attic crackled and popped like a bowl of Rice Krispy's. Old houses settle, and wood flexes with heat and cold. Jim concluded that life is never settled. After thirty years, it was increasingly difficult to extract sermons from the Good Book. When he strayed too far from the usual drivel, the flock furrowed brows and slipped into masks of indifference. Indifference yanked his chain. It was a wrinkle practically impossible to iron out. Indifference fostered passivity, which in turn engendered stasis.

Jim stared at the letter. "Isn't there room in your heart for both?" Ginny had asked. *Sweet Jesus, I was a high school senior, barely eighteen,* Jim recalled. Ginny was sixteen. They attended a church where his father was an elder, and his mother supervised bake-sales. Ginny was his first real girlfriend, and they dated three months before temptation rang the doorbell.

***

His parents were celebrating their twentieth wedding anniversary, Meadowland style—dinner and a movie. He and Ginny were alone in the house, listening to records in his bedroom. Jim being alone in the house with Ginny wasn't a problem for his parents. They liked her and believed God would keep watch. Jim and Ginny talked, danced a bit, and ate pizza. He put on her favorite '50s tune, "Only You," and she wilted against him. "Oh-oh-only you," the song claimed, "can make my dreams come true."

They kissed longer than God would've liked. Jim shuffled Ginny over to the bed, and she smiled nervously as the singer crooned, "Oh-oh-only you." They lay side-by-side, tongues dancing. He unzipped Ginny's dress and slipped a hand inside, fumbling for the latch to her bra.

Jim thought she'd stop him, but she reached back to help. His hand cupped a small breast, and a nipple tickled his palm.

When he rolled on top, Ginny's hips writhed, and her breathing was erratic. The odor she gave off was different than fear or exertion. He pulled the bottom of her dress up. Ginny lifted her hips as Jim hooked thumbs beneath the elastic of her underwear. He nearly fainted when he saw the wondrous triangle and fell off the bed struggling out of his pants. He quickly climbed back on. She pulled away from a kiss as he probed with his hardness.

"Shouldn't you be wearing a thingy?" she asked.

His wallet was in his pants, with a condom neatly tucked in a credit card sleeve. He'd found it bookmarking a library paperback at the high school. Jim kissed her, and her query wasn't repeated. He lifted her knees, and after several awkward pecks, found what he was searching for.

Ginny felt a discomforted pleasure as Jim pushed inside. "Huh, ouch...slow Jimmy...uhhhn...slow."

Jim fought the urge to erupt. He closed his eyes and gritted his teeth.

"Ohhh, Jimmy, I love you," she said. "Huh...ohhh!"

A few strokes later, Jim surrendered and felt lifted toward Heaven.

Jim wanted to pull back a dusty sheet in the attic, to reveal a time machine. He'd climb in, pull a lever to travel back to those moments when he was neither alive nor dead, but somewhere in between as he spurted inside Ginny. Immediately afterward, he felt guiltless. God waited patiently for the second cumming, when he lasted longer, and Ginny tolerated it more easily.

Jim had wanted her again soon after, but the garage door opened. Ginny pushed him off, scrambled for her clothes, and ducked into a bathroom. Jim fell over again, trying to step into his pants. He tucked in his shirt, smoothed out the bedspread, started a record, and took a bite of leftover pizza.

Without knocking, his mother stuck her head through the

door. "Hi hon, did you take Gin home?"

"She's in the bathroom," he answered. "How was your evening?"

Jim's mother narrowed her eyes on the quilt covering his bed. There was a large wet spot in the middle.

"We went to that...new steak house on...Main," she answered distractedly. "What's this?" She entered the room and bent over the stain.

"Sorry, I spilled some Coke. Gin says it'll wash out," he managed.

She sniffed the stain and crinkled her forehead. "Well, I certainly hope so." She waved a warning finger. "No crumbs on the carpet."

Jim owned a Chevy Nova, and the good Lord rode shotgun as he drove Ginny home. He kissed her at the front door and began stiffening.

"I still feel you inside." She smiled and touched her belly. Then she kissed him slowly so that he felt pre-cum soaking into his underwear.

"Night, Gin," he said. At that moment, he wanted the whole nine yards. But, God had other plans. Jim went home and stepped into the shower. God waited patiently as Jim replayed each magical moment beneath the water as he masturbated.

***

Jim was pulled back into the present. Beneath the Bible in his lap, his hardness throbbed. He lifted the book and let it drop. He couldn't remember the last time Mildred had performed her wifely duty.

Could do a people search on the Internet and find Ginny, but what good would it do? Wood fibers that still held her words together caused pain and regret. Thirty years shot to hell, but her memory still gave him a hard-on. He remembered Ginny's breathy voice on the phone after his shower. She called as he forced his way through a nightly Bible study.

He'd opened to Corinthians 10:13: *And no temptation is irresistible. You can trust God to keep the temptation from becoming so strong that you can't stand up against it, for He has promised this and will do what He says.*

"Hi, Gin," Jimmy greeted as he highlighted the passage with a yellow overliner.

"I love you!" she gushed. "Can't stop thinking about us. I called earlier—"

"Was in the shower."

"Wish we could've showered together. You made me tender down there."

"Sorry," Jim said, guilt beginning to fuel his resolve.

"Let's go to Rite Aid after school tomorrow."

"Why?" His cock refused to follow his resolution, and he thumped it with the Bible.

"Why do you think, silly?" Ginny teased. "We need to be more careful, don't you think?"

"Oh, yeah." Lying on the bedstead was his wallet, where the condom slept. The Bible felt like a brick in his hand as God launched weapons of mass destruction.

"Still there?" Ginny broke the silence.

"Yeah, well, I don't know, Gin. Don't you think we should slow it down?" The pressure in his pants was unbearable, and he squeezed it through his pajamas.

"Yeah, okay, sure. I guess, if you think it's best."

"Meadowland's a small town, and we know half the people at Rite Aid."

"Someplace else then," she argued. "Or...I read that if you pull out before—"

"What if something's already happened?" he interrupted.

God zeroed in. Jim's question sped toward the primary target.

"Pretty sure it all leaked out."

"Listen, I gotta go. See you at school tomorrow, okay?"

"Okay…do you love me?" She'd wanted to hear the words.

"Yeah, of course. See you tomorrow."

"Night, Jim."

"Night."

In the following weeks, he avoided Ginny, explaining that he needed time to sort things out. Ginny was patient, calling him only to say that she'd started her period.

Jim smiled, looked heavenward with uplifted hands, and cried out, "Thank you, Jesus!"

He hung an iron cross around his neck to serve as a reminder. It bumped against his chest when Ginny was near. Slowly, God gave him strength to endure temptation. Then, one afternoon Ginny cornered him at his locker and pulled a small box from her purse.

"Where'd you get…?" He looked around furtively.

"Rite Aid. Don't worry, there wasn't anybody we know at the checkout." She fingered the top button of his shirt. "Wanna go for a drive after school?"

"Listen, Gin, I need a little more time to…."

Ginny stepped back, her mouth quivering. She threw the box at his feet. "Fine, take all the time you need!" She hugged herself and walked away from his life.

Jim swooped up the box, stuffed it in his jacket, and walked toward a bubble-headed trashcan. *Punch it through,* he commanded himself. His fingers tightened around the iron cross. "Lord, give me strength," he said, yet his other hand was already returning the box to his pocket. He was ready to run, catch up with Ginny, and apologize. He knew of an abandoned barn where they could —

A voice startled him from behind. "Hi, Jimmy." It was Ms. Dunlop, his English teacher.

Jim nearly broke his hand, punching the box through the spring-loaded trap of the trash barrel. "Hi, Ms. Dunlop," he winced.

"Ready for graduation?"

"You bet," Jim replied. As far as God was concerned, he'd graduated with distinction.

Through faith, Jim acquired immunity from Ginny's soulful stares at school. She was waiting for the words he longed to say that he felt deep in his heart, deeper than his love for God. Yet he never said them.

Ginny abandoned the church. He thought of persuading her to return but knew it was a bad idea. The crucifix served as a spiritual condom, and his Bible was a leather-bound umbrella to keep Satan from pissing on him.

The next day, Ginny gave him the letter he'd kept safe for thirty years. At first, Jim safeguarded it as a reminder of his commitment to the Almighty. Now, it represented so much more, a haunting voice that beckoned; a beautiful, whispering melody, barely audible, yet deafening to his ears.

***

"Dinner's cold. I'm going to bed." *Mildred's voice is steel wool on a greasy frying pan,* thought Jim. He started a poem beneath the scratched-out beginnings of his sermon. He hadn't written poetry for thirty years. After Ginny, his attempts amounted to no more than shallow foolishness. An idea formed, and without thinking, he wrote:

Guilt is a quilt
Squares of immaterial stitched together,
patterns to follow, threads to clip,

needles to poke reminders,
half-moon glasses in a dull light

"Never wrote back," Jim whispered hoarsely. He reread the poem as Mildred slammed dresser drawers, flushed the toilet, and marched. March, march, march, always marching, like a good little Christian soldier.

Before graduation, Ginny hooked up with Richard Ivonkovich, a popular jock at Meadowland High. In the locker room, Richard had earned the nicknamed Big D, an abbreviation for Big Dick. Jim suppressed jealous rage when he spied them walking hand-in-hand or smooching in the parking lot. At times like these, the cross was heavy around his neck.

A few days before graduation, Ginny confronted him at his locker. "Hi, Jimmy."

"Hey, Gin."

Nervously, she glanced around. "I was wondering," she whispered conspiratorially. "Do you still have that box?"

Jim could barely shake his head. A knee to his nut sack would've proved less effective than her inquiry.

"Thanks anyway." She turned on her heel and hurried away.

Good Lord Almighty. Jim winced at the memory, "Sure as hell had it coming." Richard Ivonkovich, lucky bastard. Jim had waited thirty years for the Big One. Big D carried his with him everywhere he went.

Still hurts. Why does it still hurt? Jim's hands trembled. "Goddamned fool." Painfully, he realized that, even if Ginny walked through the attic door, straight-arming Mildred like a fullback at the goal line, it would never be the same. But her words endured, reached so deeply.

"Thirty years." Jim sadly realized he'd never written

anything to last that long, except the poem reprised in the letter. He wondered if Ginny still kept his poems—if she ever thought about him. "Maybe she still feels...something." *I love you, Jimmy, but I won't wait forever,* she'd warned.

"I'm going to bed." Mildred's voice snuffed the moment. He hadn't heard her come up. She stood at the attic door in a flannel nightgown. Light from the stairway highlighted the outline of her body and the triumph of gravity.

Jim blurted, "Sorry, be down in a minute."

"Said that an hour ago." She turned, and the wooden steps of the stairway creaked as she made her way down.

"Night, Gin," he whispered, folding the lawn chair and leaning it against a web-tangled coat rack. The same cross he'd worn for thirty years still bumped his chest. He slipped the letter into his back pocket, flipped off the light, and closed the attic door behind him.

Jim sneaked downstairs, trying to avoid the squeaks and groans that come standard with ancient Victorian houses. Centered on the dinner table was a large, brown lump of meat. Surrounding it were overcooked potatoes, steamed carrots, a bowl of gravy, and slices of bread. He carefully slid the pot roast into the refrigerator and crept into his study.

When they'd purchased the house thirteen years ago, Mildred intended for the office space to be a sewing room. Jim had taken a rare stand. Consequently, she refused to clean there. Surveying the dusty bookcase, Jim saw the spines of books he'd been warned to avoid—the *Upanishads, Tibetan Book of the Dead,* the *Apocrypha,* the *Quran*—all leather-bound with ribbed spines.

"Bible's the word of God," his theology professors had claimed aggressively. "All that other stuff'll just confuse you."

Jim chuckled as he slid a particularly contentious book

from its slot, *The Bible as Fiction*. He held it gingerly, like a boy who'd absconded with his father's December issue of *Playboy*. He collected religious writings yet only skimmed the surface of them. He found his copy of *The Origin of Species* considered a threat to Christianity. The Christian philosophy taught that you should never allow facts to interfere with faith.

Dolefully Jim shook his head as he pondered the ignorant attempts by Christians to replace science with Creationism, gift-wrapped as Intelligent Design. Another work caught his eye, trapped between *Theology Today* and a battered hymnal: *The Journal of Desperate Living*, by Owen Zelenski.

The book had been stuck in a hymnal rack on the back of a pew. He'd brought it home and skimmed a few dog-eared pages before stowing it in the bookcase. The book was water damaged, and the first nine pages were missing. On the cover was the silhouette of a man facing a condom that rested between a pair of breasts. Jim settled into his leather office chair and opened it to a random page.

"A little death" is how Shakespeare described orgasm. Larry agreed. There was a moment during orgasm when time stood still... separated from everything but the moment. Larry's moment was at hand. Isabel's brown legs were clamped around his back, and she was dying beneath him.

Jim sighed. "Can't recall the last time I experienced a little death. Doubt Mildred ever has. A little death," he considered. "Hmm."

Hidden in the file cabinet of his desk, Jim found an unopened bottle of cheap red wine. He fished in the top drawer for his Swiss army knife, which had a corkscrew. After a satisfying pop, he lifted the bottle to his lips for a long swig. Mildred didn't approve of alcohol — as good a reason as any to get stinking drunk.

"The Big One," he said morosely, followed by another long swig.

***

Sunlight sifted through the mini-blinds and filled the empty wine bottle with a greenish light. The cackle of crows outside the office window startled Jim awake. He'd suffered a terrible nightmare, filled with blood and pot roast. Now he suffered a sulfite headache.

"Shit, I need to ask the wizard about a brain." He rubbed his temples. *Haw-haw*, laughed the crows. "Haw-haw, right back at you," Jim answered.

Jim shuffled to the refrigerator with his Swiss knife and corkscrewed it into the pot roast. Then he lifted the cross from around his neck and hung it from the hilt. Yawning, he peeked in at Mildred, still in bed, mouth ajar, dreaming of end tables, no doubt. The cat was snuggled next to her. It was gray-striped and had wandered into their yard one day. Jim didn't care much for cats, although it paid more attention to his lap than Mildred.

Jim washed his face and hands, remained in the wrinkled clothes he was wearing, and drove to church. Mildred was a late riser and would join later to take her rightful place in the front pew. Even before he arrived, he saw the cross, raised on a steel beam from the center of the roof. He guessed that it defended the church from the wrath of God during thunderstorms.

The parking lot was empty. In a few hours, it would be filled with a variety of mostly white conservatives. When he arrived, he wheeled in a large dry-board from a Sunday-school classroom and placed it on the stage to face the congregation. With a red dry marker, Jim constructed a poem.

Prayer's nothing more than fear and ignorance,
woven into words

And when it's all said and done,
you're not kneeling next to anyone

Jim knew the flock wouldn't understand. He just wanted to see confusion carved all over their foreheads. Unshaven, he greeted the congregation at the entrance of the sanctuary an hour later, with the odor of sour wine still on his breath. His clothes were rumpled, and there was a red stain on his shirt. He shook hands and offered his patented fatherly smile.

"Feeling all right, Pastor?" inquired Mrs. Abernathy.

"Never better," Jim answered, squeezing the Bible in his hand. Ginny's letter was in there, and he could almost feel her reassuring hand in his. The congregation marched past, each shaking his hand, except for the teens, busy staring into the rectangular faces of their plastic gods.

"Wake up on the wrong side of the bed this morning," she joked.

"Could say that," Jim answered.

The organist accompanied the arrival of the flock with reflective mood music, and then the doors were closed. At a preordained moment, she played melancholic music intended to prepare the hearts of believers. Instead, it provoked thoughts of death, taxes, Sunday football, and cases of Budweiser. The morose vibrations from the organ pipes sent shivers down the spine of Jim's Bible. He wondered, *What inspires lyricists to pen such depressing swill? Perhaps they have wives like Mildred.*

The organist was a heavy, dyed blonde woman in her mid-fifties. She rocked and smiled, banging out the kind of tunes you might hear in a documentary about the Holocaust. Then, music-minister Burt led the flock in song. They droned hymns that sounded like funeral dirges. Teenagers cast eyes heavenward, praying for new material, something from Taylor

Swift, Bruno Mars, or Justin Bieber. Jim listened patiently as Burt tortured followers by asking them to stand, sit, and stand again, as though one dismal song deserved more reverence than another.

The choir's robes were bright burgundy, the color of usher jackets at the Meadowland Cinema. They clutched black velvet folders, and Burt waved his arms as if he were swatting locusts. Combined voices tried to breathe life into "Onward Christian Soldiers," but it was dead on arrival.

Burt was replaced by the youth-minister, Kenny, a timid, jittery young man. Occasionally Jim allowed him to deliver a Sunday sermon, yet today his job was making important announcements and inviting everyone to evening Bible study.

"Won't you please stand while we pray?" Kenny smiled and bowed his head. This was Kenny's spot in the sun. He prayed on and on, making up stuff as he went. His prayers ran the gamut—asking God to heal a tumor, helping Kate Wilson find her reading glasses, guiding the government's newest preemptive war effort. Anything was fair game.

Then, after reviewing important bullet-points on the program sheet, Kenny sat down between the organist and music-minister, Burt, whose hands were piously folded over the Bible on his lap.

Jim stood before the congregation without the podium, gazing out at the sea of familiar faces. Bob Cranfield and his wife sat in front. A few weeks earlier, Jim had been shopping at Walmart and spotted Mrs. Cranfield in the cereal aisle. He rolled his squeaking cart toward her as she reached for a box of Wheaties. Accidentally, she nudged several boxes off the shelf, and they tumbled to the floor.

"Jesus Christ!" she hissed.

Jim turned away and pretended to check the grocery list

Mildred had written. She saw him.

"Pastor Jim, how are you? How's Mildred?" Mrs. Cranfield's mask was barely held together by the threads of her counterfeit smile. A famous sports figure recently arrested for spousal abuse grinned up from the cereal box in her hand.

Three pews deep was Vernon Klemke, who shouted amen at odd times during Jim's sermons. Recently, mention of Mary Magdalene's occupation as a prostitute brought forth a particularly loud one. "Amen, thank you, Jesus," Vernon lifted his hands in appellation to Heaven.

No doubt, Jesus got it for free, thought Jim. In the back pew sat the new visitors, candidates for future harassment. An usher would ask them to fill out a requisite visitor card. Later in the week, church volunteers would swoop into their homes unannounced, knocking when there were enough crumbs on the carpet to feed Bangladesh, interrupting a lovemaking session or quality time with the children. Christian soldiers would strut past the front door and judge.

Like the inquisitors they were, environs would be inspected, they'd study the faces of the children, and smile fawningly at family portraits hanging on walls. They'd notice every stain on the sofa and leave something behind when they finally left, an unwelcome guest taking up residence who never paid rent — guilt. Guilt sustains churches, overflows offering plates, and gets stuffed into plastic bread loaves. Guilt comes crawling on hands and knees.

Jim scanned the flock, heads cocked, mouths gaping like baby birds waiting for regurgitated worms, hungry for a return on their investment. He thought of thirty years divested. He'd sacrificed Ginny as a down payment on a thirty-year loan. Thirty years speculating on his condo in Heaven, streets paved with gold, the promise of paradise.

The latest president came to mind, a billionaire monster that fit easily into the book of Revelation. *Yet*, he thought, *What choice was there — a woman who never wears dresses, married to a womanizer?*

Jim turned to face the towering wooden cross behind him, bolted high on the wall. His hand tightened on the Bible, Ginny's letter tucked between the imitation leather cover. He heard throats clearing, a sneeze, followed by "God bless you," and a baby in stage two of a tantrum. The high ceiling of the church trapped the tiniest sounds and rained them down.

"Where's my return?" Jim said to himself, yet the tiny wireless microphone clipped to his lapel captured the words, hurling them into the audience from wall-mounted speakers. Jim could almost feel the breath of the flock on his back.

"Amen!" Vernon Klemke screamed.

"You promised." Jim's voice was husky with emotion. "Said you'd care for me." He swiveled to face the congregation. Where was Mildred? Jim shuddered, and his arm ached. *Probably overslept*, he thought. *That woman sleeps like the dead.*

He backed up to the dry-board and slapped it with his Bible hand. The dry-board shuddered and pivoted Jim's poem upward so that God, sitting in his La-Z-Boy recliner, was the only one that could read it. Ginny's letter escaped from Jim's Bible and fluttered to his feet. Jim wanted to scream but couldn't find his voice. The flock was in V formation, heading south. His chest had the weight of God's thumb pressed on it. A series of broken sobs spilled from his mouth.

"Thirty years. Thirty goddamned years!"

Jim didn't remember falling. Voices climbed in and out of his consciousness. He opened his eyes, and everything was coated in Vaseline. Music-minister Burt noticed that Jim was trying to say something and put an ear close to his mouth.

"Follow the...yellow brick...road," Jim whispered.

Burt looked up and shrugged. A siren was heard in the distance.

A sweet voice filled Jim's head. "Love always." He smiled and closed his eyes. "Ginny," he whispered.

***

The new minister, Ron, kept his sheep well pastured. Basically, he fed them the same diet as before, with a louder, more evangelical squelch.

The coroner reported the cause of Jim's death—a massive coronary attack. He announced that Mildred's death was caused by a single puncture wound to the heart, via corkscrew from a Swiss army knife. The murder weapon was found imbedded in a refrigerated pot-roast.

"Corkscrew...that'll do it every time," Detective Milken murmured to his rookie partner. "Damnedest thing I ever saw," he repeated as he wandered through the house, twirling a crucifix necklace around his finger as he walked. It'd been slung over the murder weapon. Because he was a detective, he also noticed that the Swiss knife didn't have nail clippers.

"Should you be handling evidence?" inquired the rookie.

"Cut 'n dry, bright boy," Milken answered. "Witnesses, suspects, victims, all worm's meat."

Detective Milken didn't give two shits about motive, opportunity, and other sorted details. The ones with the answers weren't talking. He wandered into the study and found a book lying open next to an empty wine bottle, *The Journal of Desperate Living*. He skimmed through it as his stomach gurgled, trying to get a handle on four glazed doughnuts he'd wolfed earlier.

"Pepto-Bismol time." He patted his tummy and read a section.

Chapter 19: Somewhere in Italy

Larry didn't care about tourist trap Italy, depicted in glossy brochures and embellished in travel magazines. He wanted a full dose of the real deal. He strolled with Domenici Ruffino, whom he'd met at the Roman Coliseum a few days earlier. Dom spoke excellent English and translated when Larry ran into stumbling blocks. In return, Larry paid for Dom's meals.

Today Larry let his nose tell him where to go. He detected a foul smell on the breeze and followed. Dom argued about the direction they were taking, but Larry was stubborn. He smelled truth wafting in from the south, along a narrow, cobbled street. Tall tenant buildings stood on each side, connected by laundry lines, with clothes flapping in the steady breeze. The smell emitted from an open sewer, built along a broken side-path. Larry heard people cry warnings from above as they lowered plastic bags full of rubbish out of windows and into the street.

"What're they saying?" he asked Dom.

"Something like, look out below."

Larry laughed and thought of how universal language was.

"Hungry?" Dom asked.

Larry ignored the question. Dom was always hungry, and lately, he'd been asking for startup capital to open a small fruit stand.

A short time later, a group of tourists stopped ahead of them. The guide pointed to a third-story window and said something. Tourists looked up expectantly before continuing on.

"What were they looking for?"

"There," Dom pointed, "lives Roberto Rossi, the poet."

"I've heard of him."

"He hasn't written for thirty years."

"Wonder why?"

"Who knows? Perhaps he suffers, how you say, writer's block, eh? How about we get something to eat? I know a place just around the corner."

Larry glanced up as Dom walked away. Someone was at the window. Larry squinted against the sun. Yes, someone was staring down at him. The window slowly slid open, and a withered hand emerged, holding something. With a flick of the wrist, a paper plane was launched. It circled, bumped against the building, and spiraled gently toward Larry.

"First poem in thirty years," *chortled Larry, as if he'd won the lottery.*

Inches from his outstretched hand, a gust of wind carried the plane out of reach and dashed it to the street. Then it skittered into a foul-smelling gutter and floated away. As he reached for it, the wind caught it, lifting the plane into the sky. Larry sprinted and hopped. Dom watched the crazy American run past him.

"The paper...." *Larry gasped.*

A boy straddling a rusted bicycle snatched the paper out of the air.

"Thanks," *Larry panted.* "Grazie."

"No." *The boy backed away from Larry's open hand.*

"You don't understand, the paper is mine, very important. Molto importante, capisce?"

"No." *The boy placed his foot on a pedal and held the paper plane to his chest.*

"Okay, I get it," *Larry fumbled for his wallet,* "Here!" *He fanned an assortment of lira frantically in the boy's face.*

"No," *the boy repeated, taking the money and keeping the paper.*

Dom caught up and smiled knowingly.

Larry dug into his pants, filling his hand with loose change and giving it over. The boy took it and dropped it into a shirt pocket. Then he shook his head and tapped his wrist.

"Jesus!" *Larry took off his watch and handed it over.*

The boy examined the watch. "Okay." *He handed over the paper and sped away, turning once to yell,* "Baciami il culo!"

"What'd he say?"

"You don't want to know," said Dom.

Larry turned away, unwilling to share the moment. Carefully he unfolded the paper plane.

"Can we eat now?" Dom asked.

Larry turned away from him to read the bold capitals scrawled in permanent black marker. **FUCK YOU!** *He looked back and saw a head poking out of the window. Even from that distance, he could tell that the old man was laughing to beat the band.*

Detective Milken screwed his face up and tossed the book onto the desk. He opened the junk drawer in Jim's desk, adding the cross to an assortment of nuts and bolts that had no place else to go.

CHAPTER 4
Owen Hears Voices

"How starved you must have been that my heart became a meal for your ego." —Amanda Torrani—

Owen liked the word, fuck—an attention getter, rebellious, agitating, connected to reality. He added the word to his laptop dictionary so the spell-checker wouldn't highlight it as a mistake. Owen was nearly finished creating a dream...his vision: *The Journal of Desperate Living*.

He considered how to sign his name. *O. Zelenski sounds scholarly. Better yet, Oz. That sounds more commanding.* A hundred and eighty-nine pages deep, Owen typed:

Chapter 22: Somewhere in Mexico
"In between the small things we are unwilling to do and the large things we think ourselves incapable of comes the risk that we do nothing," Larry explained to his beautiful brown lady-friend as they sat on the sofa.
Maria unzipped his pants to gather his cock in her hand, "This

big t'ing, you put in my little t'ing." Larry followed her to bed.

Owen had written with his high school teaching colleague, Mariana Payán, in mind. Ms. Payán wore beautiful Mexican blouses, flowery skirts, and her voice sounded like the whisper of a breeze through a field of wildflowers. She inspired fantasies and drove him to surf the Net for Latina porn. She had a twin sister, Lupe, who taught at Woodland Elementary School, less than an hour from Meadowland.

Owen's fingers flew, and his eyebrows twitched as he wrote. He kept peanut M&M's in a bowl, popping four at a time, sucking until the candy coating and chocolate were gone before biting the nuts. Occasionally he pushed up his half-moon glasses and cracked his spine on the back of the office chair. It was early summer, and he'd worked on the book for two years—papers ungraded, sick days used up, summers spent in front of a computer screen. Safely tenured at Meadowland High School, he'd soon quit and dedicate himself as a full-time writer, as soon as *The Journal of Desperate Living* was published. Then he'd move out of his downstairs apartment and buy a house.

During the school year, Owen woke up at 4:00 to write for a few hours before dressing for work. Each morning he examined his reflection as he shaved. Lately, he'd noticed subtle changes. His head was topped with curly gray-peppered hair, the mouth curved down slightly—the eyes...yes, the eyes troubled him now. His sparkling green eyes were mocking as if they didn't belong to him. He blinked hard until the feeling faded. He opened the medicine cabinet, took a prescription bottle in his hand, and read the instructions—Take once a day with a meal. *Flush'em down the toilet*, an inner voice advised. Owen returned them to the shelf and closed the cabinet. *The eyes. Yes, they're changing. Idiopathic, that's what doctors call something when they don't know what it is.* Doctors had never been able to put a definitive finger on Owen's mood swings and depressions. It was easier just to give him a prescription with a list of countless side effects.

"Get to work." Still in his pajamas, he made coffee and went into his office.

Three hours later, Owen finished *The Journal of Desperate Living.*

Chapter 23: Somewhere in Germany

The sun made a lonely ascent into the cool gray sky. A gust of wind rattled leaves hanging from the branches of a thick, wrinkled oak. Larry sat with his back against the gnarly trunk. He brushed away black ants that were using his legs as a highway. He'd earned this spot in the universe, had searched for truth, and felt on the verge of discovery. Yet for now, he was enjoying a simple sunrise, ants or no.

"I'm not merely a part of the universe; I helped construct it," he blurted without thinking.

Larry sat up straight, repeating the words in his mind before saying them again. "I'm not merely a part of the universe. I helped construct it!"

The search had finally ended. Larry smiled down at the ants beating a path over him. They followed ancient trails just as he had. He looked at the sun, one of his creations. It warmed his face and felt good, fucking good.

Owen scrunched down in his chair and leaned his head back. He studied a collection of dust spilling over the blades of the ceiling fan and smiled. In the apartment above, he heard a couple making love, a rhythmic tapping of headboard followed by appreciative grunting.

Owen rubbed a hand over his face. It was finished. He'd dedicate the book to his children, Patrick and Tracy, with special thanks to Shirley Bitterman, his high school English teacher. He fondly recalled the afternoon she confiscated a pornographic pastiche he'd written as the English class discussed, *Lord of the Flies*. Owen's version of Golding's classic put girls on the island. Catalina Rodriguez sat in front of him. She turned and snatched the story off his desk. Still in the early stages of feminism, Catalina marched to Mrs. Bitterman's desk to hand it over.

"This's what Zelenski writes in class."

Owen remembered his teacher's eyebrows fluttering up and down as she read.

"Boy're *you* gonna get it," Catalina said.

When Mrs. Bitterman finished, she set the story down and glanced up at Owen. "Mister Owen, I'd like to see you after class."

Owen expected the worst. Instead, she offered reassurances and called his work, "Questionable, but well written." If she were still alive, he'd send her a copy, and one to ex-wife Nancy, and of course, copies to Tracy and Patrick.

Lately, he'd been worried about the children. Patrick avoided him like the plague. Nancy called one evening to say their son was hanging with the wrong crowd. Owen reminded her that the boy was over eighteen and could make his own choices.

Tracy had multiple body piercings and a rose tattooed on her ankle. Nancy had caught her with cigarettes. According to Owen, it was nothing to worry about.

Owen edited the novel with Grammarly. It highlighted mistakes and offered alternatives. For the next few weeks, Owen searched the Net for publishers. He signed up for Duotrope, a search engine that narrowed possibilities. There were a few publishers, mostly Canadian that only accepted snail-mail, and for those, he provided self-addressed stamped envelopes along with a query letter, summary, and an excerpt of the novel.

Dear publisher,
    The Journal of Desperate Living *is a contemporary allegory about one man's search for truth. Larry's globetrotting journey is dramatized by the philosophical lessons he learns along the way, and....*

The letter went on to explain how timely the book was for Americans, who he felt were wrestling with unfulfilled, desperate lives, as if the American spirit was slowly fading, like a pair of Levi's with a ripped out crotch.

He placed snail-mail queries in a community mailbox slot just as the mailman arrived. A white Jeep with a blue postal service insignia pulled up to the mail hop, brakes squealing. The driver wore navy-blue shorts, a light blue shirt, and a beige safari hat. His mustache was thick, perfectly trimmed, almost fake looking. Owen thought, *I know Meadowland's a jungle, yet that doesn't warrant a safari hat.* The mailman greeted Owen with a smile.

"Query letters to publishers," Owen volunteered. "Just finished a novel."

"No kidding?" he answered, handing Owen a stack of junk mail.

"It's called *The Journal of Desperate Living,* and —"

"Desperate what?" A glazed look of indifference dribbled down the postman's face like print from a wet newspaper.

"Living," Owen repeated slowly, "Desperate *Living.* It's

about a—"

"Well," interrupted the mailman. "Wish you luck." He gunned the Jeep toward another community box ten yards away.

"Jesus." Owen shook his head. "Seems like nobody's interested in anything these days." Undaunted, he returned to the house and celebrated alone with a bottle of almond flavored sparkling wine. Picking up the *Meadowland Chronicle*, he pursed his lips and perused the front page: Middle-east conflicts, a Texas man shot his three children, his wife, and then himself, president meets with Putin, and the Meadowland City Council voted to annex farmland for an apartment complex. "Christ."

***

Summer ended, and school began. Autumn came and went, and winter was the coldest in recent memory, covering front lawns with frost and making it harder for ever-present crows to find sustenance.

Owen stirred his Scotch on the rocks with a lazy finger. Almost all of his e-mail queries had been answered with generic rejections: *After careful consideration, we have determined that your work does not suit our publishing needs at this time—best of luck in placing your work elsewhere.*

Spring—Owen idled the hours away. It didn't take long to prepare classes. These days the Department of Education prescribed texts and materials, and all he had to do was follow the teacher's guide. The school provided an overhead document camera, and prefabricated assessments were given at the close of each chapter. At the end of each year, students took a standardized test, which measured how standard they'd become.

"Lab rats could teach," Owen reflected. Once published, he'd enroll in an online MFA program and teach at Meadowland

Junior College. After two years, he'd get a job at Fresno State. Perhaps his efforts would entice Ms. Payán to see her way clear, giving him a shot.

The end of spring arrived, and not even a nibble on his book. He became depressed. Owen went into the bathroom, opened the medicine cabinet, and shook two small white pills into his palm. *Why are you trying to keep us out?* asked the voices. He ran water in the sink. The pink pills were mood elevators covered by school insurance, manufactured by Pfizer—happy pills. He held them in the palm of his hand until they began to get sticky. *Yeah, chug'em right down, be a happy boy, see where it gets yuh.* Owen washed the pills down the sink, turning it pink.

Summer arrived with few mail deliveries. Spiders used the vacant slot as a summer rental, filling the emptiness with silk-wrapped insects. Summer ended, and a new school year began. Two weeks later, he received a letter. *We apologize for having to respond to your query with this form letter, but the sheer volume of queries we receive makes it impossible to answer each one personally.*

"Blah-blah-blah!" Owen huffed.

The next day two more arrived. *Regretfully we have determined that your work is not appropriate for our list. We are currently inundated with manuscripts....*

"Yaduh, yaduh, yaduh," he spat.

A week later, he got five, one taking the cake for malicious simplicity. *NO!*

E-mail rejections were more civilized yet did nothing to dull the ache of rejection. Owen pursed his mouth, frustrated by the overwhelmingly impersonal nature of the publishing industry. It was hard to keep faith when no one gave a rat's ass.

Then, hope arrived.

Trapped between a phone bill and a pre-approved credit card offer, the letter almost went unnoticed. He pursed his lips and prepared to add Vortex Publishing to the stack of rejections on his desk. His knuckles whitened over the hilt of the butter knife he used as a letter opener. "Fucking waste of time," he murmured as he put on his half-moon reading glasses.

Dear Mr. Zelenski,

Although we cannot consider your work at this time, it sounds promising. Have you considered self-publishing? A lot of great writers got their start that way. I would also add that Vortex offers this service at a reasonable price. We offer quality full service — cover design, publishing, distribution, and press releases. In either case, we wish you the best of luck with The Journal of Desperate Living. *Thank you for your interest in Vortex Publishing.*

Respectfully,

William Yates

Owen reread the letter, and a pleasant feeling of warmth replaced his melancholy. True, it was another rejection, but at least Yates offered encouragement. He even signed his name at the bottom. Hmm, self-publishing. Owen considered it; "*A lot of great writers....*"

It was a mild dawn, and the fingernail moon faded like disappearing ink as the sun peeked up over the Sierra Nevadas. Early birds hurried to catch the worm. Two crows hopped and flapped over scraps of dried rabbit glued to the warm asphalt road. Dogs barked just to hear themselves. The barrier of the gated community was open for repairs, and Owen veered off the main road to jog there. Each house was a variation of the other. Lawns were immaculate, driveways were hosed clean, and in the freshness of early morning, Owen heard a couple arguing inside their garage.

"Yeah, run away! You're good at that!" the woman

screamed.

The garage door lifted, and the man peeled out of the driveway in a Mercedes. As he raced down the empty street, birds held their breath before resuming morning gossip. The lady stared coldly at Sam, and he sped up.

Owen sped up again, smelling road oil and earth. He was thankful for a relatively simple life. After years without exercise, he'd taken up jogging again. In the early morning light, demons fled his mind, and his thoughts were clear. A few times, he'd crossed paths with a garbage truck driver, Sam, and they exchanged greetings. Before that, he'd only seen him on the Tuesday pickup day, wearing bright orange coveralls and looking like a member of the county jail road crew.

When he was married, Owen had slipped into the cool mornings to jog at a nearby park. He ran in a variety of weather, including the infamous San Joaquin Valley fog, which appears suddenly, smelling like a cheap damp carpet. Fugitive dogs barked within its frigid mists, traffic looked surreal, and headlights appeared and faded as drivers crept cautiously toward their chosen lives. Owen remembered one particular foggy morning. He got up from bed while his wife breathed softly beside him, and the children dreamed of green dragons or pink Easter bunnies. He quietly tugged on his warm-ups, tied his running shoes, and left the warmth of their tract-home.

Water dripped from trees and bushes. Small birds scurried within the branches, bumping into twigs and chirping obscenities. He jogged, gulping mouthfuls of mist, having it open and close around him without a trace. Like a slice of potato poking up from a steaming cup of clam chowder, an elderly woman materialized, mummified in a scarf, snowcap, boots, heavy jacket, and a pair of mittens. Dangling from her wrist was an empty dog leash. As Owen jogged past, the woman gave a frightened cry, "Oh my word, you startled me!" She patted her chest and glared reproachfully at Owen.

Owen trotted on. Soon he heard a rustling in some bushes, followed by an unwelcome pressure on his lower calf. Instinctively he kicked, dislodging the attacker. A tiny dog rolled, popped up, and darted in again, yipping and snarling.

"Fuck off!" he shouted. It was the kind of dog that brought shame to the species—a tiny, leftover spaghetti-looking mutt. Owen was ready to test its shape with his foot as it crouched to spring.

"Tiger," yelled the old woman, "come!"

Luckily the little bastard had only managed to snare his pant leg. Owen resumed his steady pace. "Use the leash," he scolded the old woman.

Without apologizing, she scooped up the wooly atrocity and trudged on. As Owen circled again, his neck hairs bristled. Up ahead was the woman, carrying an empty leash.

"Tiger!" the woman bellowed.

Owen swiveled, and the dog couldn't stop in time. Owen stepped forward and swung his right leg up. The dog sailed—a shag-carpeted football splitting the upright of the woman's outstretched arms.

"It's good!" he shouted and resumed jogging.

Tiger's shrieks were so delicious that the sun punched a hole in the fog for a moment just to listen. The old woman hurled a steady stream of epithets. Owen turned and pumped his fists like Rocky Balboa.

"Tiger, come, baby. I'm calling the police. Come here, precious. I'll have you arrested. Oh, my poor baby." She hugged the shivering mass of fur and fang.

Eons ago, he reflected, shaking his head to force the past back onto a dusty shelf. Any day now, *The Journal of Desperate*

Living would arrive on his doorstep. The project had cost a pretty penny. He hired a Vortex Publishing artist to render the cover design—a man facing converging mountains with the rising sun slotted between. Owen paid extra for marketing services too.

Any day now, advance copies would arrive. William Yates had his people arranging newspaper interviews and radio appearances. Owen's English classes perked up when he mentioned the book, yet when he elaborated, lethargy returned.

"Will we have to read it in class?" asked one student.

Owen never admitted to self-publishing. Vanity houses carried the stigma of last-ditch alternatives for losers, authors with money enough to feed their egos. He'd ordered a thousand copies.

Owen shook his arms out and moved to the far side of the road when a Honda Civic slammed past, windows down, hip-hop blasting, "Don't want no short-dick man!" Owen caught a glimpse of the driver's angry face, his baseball cap turned backward. Crow's drifted up and landed softly to resume their meal, pausing to add *haw-haw-haw* to the rap.

As he neared the apartment complex, the landscape changed. Fast food packaging dotted the gutters, and landscaping took on a somber, minimalistic tone. Renters didn't have the buy-in to care about their surroundings, and owners sure as hell weren't about to invest toward brightening things up with flowers and trees.

***

One frosty morning, weeks later, a UPS truck arrived. There came two loud knocks on Owen's apartment door. Owen signed a receipt for his box of courtesy copies.

"Hang on, I'll sign a copy for you. You'll be the first," he offered generously.

"Thanks, but I've got a ton of deliveries." The deliveryman's breath fogged like cigar smoke as he clomped away.

Owen sat the box on the snack bar and snatched a kitchen knife. He cut away the postal tape, lifted the cardboard flaps, and pulled the bubble-wrap away. On top of the books lay media-kit freebies — five posters, fifty business cards, twenty postcards, and thirty bookmarks emblazoned with the book cover, along with ordering information. He set them aside and reached in for a copy of *The Journal of Desperate Living*. Owen Zelenski was printed in bold at the bottom. Seeing his name in print was overwhelming. He held the book to his nose, fanned the pages, and stopped at a random page.

Chapter 4: Somewhere in Hollywood
In the corner shadows of the hotel bar, Leslie's face radiated. They entwined fingers and looked deep into each other's eyes. He wanted to say just the right thing at that precise moment. Leslie touched his face as she worked a stick of gum, and suddenly the words spilled.

"Our time together…you've helped me to stay on the trail, to find meaning within the confines of our universe."

Leslie stopped chewing for a moment, smiled, and squeezed his hand. In that moment, they formed a new pair of galaxies.

"You're a heck-of-a-nice guy," she said.

Larry had discovered another piece of the jigsaw. He ordered another round of vodka-tonics, and then they returned to room forty-six.

Owen smiled, remembering his inspiration for the chapter. Her name was Lesley, spelled with a Y. Lesley was a seventeen-year-old Meadowland High School senior. She rarely turned in homework and spent class time gossiping, texting, or asking to use the bathroom, where she rendezvoused with friends. She was pale, slender, pretty, and her hair was the color of adobe bricks. Toward the end of the second semester, she began showing up after school a few minutes each day. She needed Owen's class to graduate, and yet the numbers didn't add up. She always stood close to him when she visited, sometimes leaning over him as he graded so that her breasts pushed against his back.

"Mr. Z, could you, like, give me extra credit work or something to, like, bring up my grade?"

He gave her make-up assignments, and when they were due, she didn't deliver.

"Mr. Z, I really liked class today," she often claimed during an afternoon blitzkrieg. Yet subsequently, she flunked a prefab test over the same material.

After the final test, students stampeded out with the bell, except for Lesley. He remembered what she wore that afternoon— *red mini-skirt, white silk blouse, with a gold crucifix swinging from breast-to-breast, and black spiked heels. She was chewing gum – a veritable pin-up girl.* Even now, when he caught the scent of the perfume she'd used, it gave him a boner.

Owen smiled up from his desk, "How do you think you did, Lesley?"

She'd been pretending to read announcements and famous quotes on his bulletin board. Lazily she walked over to his desk and sat on the edge, folding her hands modestly in her lap. "Not so good, and I swear to god I really studied hard. My parents're gonna freak!" She waved her arms frantically.

"Shall we take a look?" he suggested.

"You're sweet, Mr. Z." Lesley stopped chewing, and her mouth curled sensuously. "Has anyone ever told you, you have, like, the most amazing green eyes?" She hopped off the desk and placed her face in front of his. "I've wanted to do this for, like, forever."

His heart stampeded in his ears as she lowered her lips to his and slipped her soft tongue, along with the gum, into his mouth. He remembered her breathless inquiry as she drew back from the lengthy kiss.

"What flavor?"

"Spearmint," he smiled and chewed.

As he stood to take her into his arms, she allowed a much shorter kiss and then gently pulled free. "Gotta go. My boyfriend's waiting. Oh, by the way, did I pass your class?"

"I think you'll squeeze through."

"Thanks, Mr. Z." The door closed, and Owen rested his forehead on the desk.

That afternoon he had called Nancy to say he was stopping at the microbrewery with colleagues to celebrate the end of another school year. He sat alone in a darkened corner and quaffed four pints of Guinness.

"Lesley with a Y," he murmured. He'd desperately wanted to lock the classroom door and take her on his desk. Instead, he'd watched her skip out, holding his job in her delicate, spider-webbed fingers.

Everyone was asleep when he arrived home. Stripping in the bathroom, Owen lifted his shirt to his face to sniff her perfume. He fingered the starchy splotches of dried pre-cum on his underwear. Lesley's image filled his head as he masturbated in the shower. When he emerged, four-year-old Patrick was there, giggling and wearing Larry's shirt, sleeves dangling to the floor. He lifted it to his nose and loudly announced, "Foo-foo!" his word for the fragrance his mother used.

Owen smiled sheepishly, hoisted Patrick into his arms, and marched the evidence into the garage, where the washer and drier were. Then he carried Patrick back to bed. As he tucked him in, his son sang a song he learned at school.

"Skinuhmuhrink-a-dink-a-dink, skinuhmuhrink-a-dink-a-do, I love you."

"Goodnight, buddy," Owen said.

On the way to his bedroom, he paused to peek at Tracy. She looked so small. Her tiny face reflected in the glow of a seashell night-light, and her toes rubbed against the clean white sheets. She was two, and he wondered what two-year-old's dreamed.

Slipping into bed next to Nancy, Owen felt like a stranger. In thirteen years of marriage, he'd never experienced as much passion for her as he had during the fifteen seconds with Lesley. He couldn't remember when he stopped loving Nancy. Perhaps he never had. He remembered the rush of dopamine the first time they'd had sex, mistaken for love. Then, after they'd been married a few years, Patrick came along, and they both switched to autopilot. Owen didn't bathe every day, and Nancy wore sweatpants when she was home. Owen wondered if it was the same for other couples—the honeymoon ends, and the digging begins. He and Nancy dug out the worst in each other. She was a hoarder. The cars were parked in the driveway because of all the crap in the garage. Her mantra was, "You never know when you'll need it."

She, in turn, hated when Owen forgot to erase the history on the web browser, and she discovered porn sites he'd visited. She hated that Owen was an atheist and had wanted her to visit an adult store with him to buy toys. He wanted to spice things up, and she wanted to tone it down. They dug into each other until the hole was deep enough to bury each other.

That summer, Owen didn't know how to feel better. He thought of buying a new car or taking the family on vacation—San Diego, or even Mexico. But he couldn't muster the energy to look for package deals. He considered using the pills in the medicine cabinet—happy, happy, happy pills. He wanted real happiness and didn't know where to look.

Nancy asked him one night in bed, "Owen, what's wrong with us?"

"Nothing. We just...I don't know."

"Are you seeing someone else?"

"Don't be silly. It's nothing like that. We just...I can't explain it. We've changed."

"How?" She reached over and took his hand.

"I don't know. Tomorrow let's go to that new Italian place on Main."

"Maybe we should get counseling. Have you been taking your pills?"

Owen lifted her hand to his lips. In the darkness, he imagined Lesley with a Y lying next to him. He pulled Nancy closer and kissed her.

"You'll need jelly. I'm really dry," she whispered.

"Okay."

Six months later, he asked Nancy for a divorce. There wasn't much discussion about it. Neither of them fought to salvage the marriage. Nancy got custody of the children, the house, and hefty child support payments. Owen kept his late model Toyota Corolla and moved into a studio apartment with green shag carpeting. A year and a half later, she married an accountant she met at church.

"An accountant, for Christ's sake," Owen hissed. He rubbed a newly minted copy of *The Journal of Desperate Living* against his cheek and fanned the pages again, enjoying the smell of the paper.

Owen was a celebrated local author for two days. He met smiling colleagues in twilight hallways, who insisted that they looked forward to reading the book. He donated five copies to the Meadowland Public Library. William Yates sent advance copies to newspapers, radio stations, and the local cable television studio. Owen created a Twitter account, revamped his Facebook, and signed up for LinkedIn. Then he created a blog on Wix, where he offered writing advice.

Owen steeled himself for celebrity. He'd invite Ms. Payán to lunch and see where it took them, knowing well and good where he wanted it to go.

Days turned into weeks. *The Meadowland Chronicle* wrote a short, kind review and gave him a three-inch space tucked deep inside, just before the obituaries. A local radio station invited him and then canceled. It was as if his novel had been born, only to suffer crib death. He phoned Vortex Publishing to inquire about alternative marketing strategies.

"Doing all we can on this end, Mr. Zelenski." Yates was annoyed. "Success depends on John Q. Public, and you know how fickle they can be. We guarantee our services, but we can't guarantee your success."

Resting on his bed one afternoon, Owen sipped Scotch and vaguely considered calling the kids. Tracy was unemployed, living with Nancy and her husband. Owen didn't know if Patrick worked, only that he rented an apartment on Evergreen Street, not the best area to live. He shook his head sadly. He hadn't phoned for six months. Last Christmas, after sending them Kmart gift cards, he hadn't even received thank-you cards. Occasionally he bumped into them at Target, Ross, or Pizza Heaven. Chance meetings were stiff and uncomfortable.

Two months earlier, he'd spied Tracy with a boyfriend at Rite Aid. He ambled over with a shopping handbasket.

"Hey, honey, how's it going?" He gave Tracy a stiff hug.

"Hi, Dad." Tracy's face turned crimson as she introduced

the boyfriend.

As they shook, Owen saw a spider web tattoo on the webbing between his thumb and forefinger. The boy's ears were rimmed with metallic studs. He had a silver loop in his lower lip and two through his left eyebrow. When Tracy spoke, Owen saw a BB gleaming on her tongue. *What possesses youngsters to maim themselves?* he wondered. They were standing in front of a condom display, and the boyfriend had a box in his hand. "Miriam, check please," was repeated twice over the loudspeaker, and then the hits from the seventies resumed.

Another time Owen wanted a used acoustic guitar and surprised Patrick at the pawnshop in downtown Meadowland. Patrick was selling items.

"Hey."

"Hey." Patrick barely glanced up as the owner counted bills out in his hand.

"Need cash?"

"Why else would I be here?" his son said in a monotone.

"Can I help?"

Patrick looked up and didn't hesitate. "Sure, if you want to. I'm sort of short this month."

The owner of the pawnshop stared at the two. He'd been in business long enough to know the kid's story as well as the father's. He'd watched it play out time and time again. His business thrived on desperation—on those who lived hand-to-mouth—people like this kid with the hollowed out face and the bad teeth.

"Let's go get a coffee." They crossed the street to a Starbucks.

Patrick was thin and jittery. His eyes were sunken, hair straggly long and unwashed looking. He wore a T-shirt and a pair of shredded Levi's. His eyes were as green as his father's, yet something was lost from them. Owen bought coffee and sat in a booth across from his son.

"So, how're you doing?"

"Okay." Patrick's legs jiggled nervously.

"Where're you working now?"

"Odd jobs here and there, you know?"

"Still at Evergreen?"

"Yeah."

"How much do you need?"

Patrick stared at the top of the table, "Five hundred would see me through, I guess."

Owen nodded. "Thought of going back to school?"

"Yeah, I've given it some thought."

"I remember how you used to love dinosaurs," Owen smiled. "You knew all their names."

"Yeah. Hey, Dad, I gotta go pretty soon."

"Okay. There's an ATM on the corner."

"Mmm," he nodded.

"Anything else I can do?"

Patrick shook his head. "I'll pay you back."

"Don't worry about it."

For a moment, Patrick looked up, and seeing into his eyes was like looking at his own reflection in a mirror. Patrick stood to signal the end of the reunion. They walked to the ATM. Patrick pocketed the money, thanked his father again, and walked quickly away. Owen had a sick feeling in the pit of his stomach as he watched his son disappear around a corner. Then he stared vacantly across the street at Big Ed's Sporting Goods. The manager of the Kmart emerged with Big Ed. An Out to Lunch sign was flipped over, and they began strolling down the sidewalk. Big Ed wore a cap with Make America Great Again, fronting it. Owen felt his stomach growl.

***

Owen phoned Nancy the weekend after he sent her a copy. "I've only skimmed through so far, but I'll make time to read it," she promised. In the background, he heard the husband, "Honey, you seen my calculator lying around?"

He found Mrs. Bitterman's address in the phonebook and sent her a complimentary copy. He phoned a week later. She was eighty-four and couldn't remember him. "From what I've seen so far, there're quite a few grammar errors," her voice quavered.

"Next time, I'll ask you to proofread," he joked.

"What did you say your name was again?" she answered.

A deep melancholy swept through Owen like the unshakable smell of three-day roadkill. He thought of Henry David Thoreau, who'd said that we're strangers to everyone but ourselves. He tried shaking himself free, giving pep-talks to himself.

"Pats on the back are for kids playing team sports," he philosophized. Yet the prospect of marching through life alone was troublesome. He tasted bile in his mouth and closed his eyes to the sound of his heartbeat, pounding harshly between his ears. A voice in his head returned. *Fuckup*, it said.

"Leave me alone," Owen begged.

You are alone.

"Patrick, Tracy." Owen filled his head with pleasant memories of his children when they were young — when he still felt like a father. He pictured Patrick climbing the tall pine at the park and playing catch, and Tracy playing with Barbies, him whirling her around in circles by her arms. "Faster, faster, Daddy," she said.

They're not here, the voice taunted.

For years Owen had the kids every other weekend. But they'd stopped wanting to come. "Stopped wanting to," he sighed.

Total fuck-up, the voice insisted.

The phone bleated, and Owen jumped as if a creature living in the closet of his mind tapped him on the shoulder. The landline sounded like a cricket cheerleader or Mickey Mouse giggling at Goofy's dirty joke. *Certainly isn't a woman*, he surmised. Internet sites he visited attested that he hadn't been fortunate in that department for some time. Owen answered on the fifth ring.

"Mr. Zelenski, this is Bill Yates."

"Oh, hi, Bill."

"Good news. Your book found its mark. We just sold all but fifty-six copies."

"Say again?" Owen's depression evaporated.

"You'll be getting a nice check in a few days."

"Amazing! What…how…?

"That's the nature of the beast—feast or famine."

"Wow, I don't know what to say."

"A second run?"

"Sure. What do you think, another thousand?"

"Why not two?" Yates had perfect timing. "Your profits'll cover the cost."

"Sounds fine."

Owen kissed the phone. From now on, he'd welcome its eunuch screech. Acceptance was just a call away.

Two days later, a certified letter arrived.

Dear Mr. Zelenski,

My name's Jack Skag, and I'm the mayor of Weeville, Texas. Came across The Journal of Desperate Living *by accident. Recently had business in Bakersfield and found a copy in the bathroom stall of a Denny's. Started reading and couldn't put it down. I ordered a passel of copies off Amazon and gave one to darn near everybody I know.*

Every year the Weeville Literacy Council selects an author to help celebrate the Fourth of July with a public reading, a writing workshop, and whatnot. Last week the council announced that you've been selected Weeville's author of the year, all expenses paid. We hope you'll accept our invitation. Let us know as soon as possible, and we will arrange your flight.

Look forward to hearing from you.
Sincerely,
Jack Skag.

Owen immediately responded over the Internet and received an email from the mayor's secretary a few hours later, including flight information. She wrote that the mayor would personally meet him at the airport. Owen reread her response a dozen times, words filling him until he could hardly breathe. He Google'd Weeville—a flake of dandruff in the middle of Texas, twenty-five miles east of Dinosaur Valley National Park. The closest airport was in Grandbury. The flight from Los Angeles would only take a little over two hours.

"Author of the year," he repeated. "Kids loved dinosaurs when they were little." He remembered Patrick creating a dinosaur land in the back yard, replete with a shallow lake for the brontosaurs to muck around in.

Owen emailed a thank you and went for a jog. Later that day, he bought a shiny red 150 cc Moped. When he twisted the throttle, it sounded like a leaf blower. In his youth, he'd ridden a Honda Shadow when weather permitted.

What the hell, he thought. *Time enough for a Harley later.*

***

Owen soaked in the soft Texas drawl of the stewardess. The sensuous texture filled his head with helium. It was the first time he'd flown first class. *Could get used to this*, he thought.

"Get you anythang?"

He'd heard rumors about the Mile High Club yet thought better of asking. He'd show her a thang or two in the airplane john. The woman sitting in the window seat next to Owen was pretty too. Her short black hair brushed her collar as she swiveled her head to see out the window. Her face was interesting—sleepy blue eyes, expressive lips. After a few drinks, he tried thinking of a way to make her acquaintance.

She was pleasant but seemed wary. He set a copy of *The Journal of Desperate Living* on his food tray and looked away.

She tucked away the free in-flight magazine she'd been thumbing through and glanced at the book. "Is it any good?" Her voice tickled his ears better than the flight attendant's.

Owen folded his wings and plummeted like a hawk through an opening in the clouds. "Pretty darned good." He handed it to her.

She studied the cover and turned it over. When she saw his picture on the back cover, she raised an eyebrow. "That's you."

"At your service."

She took his proffered hand. "I'm Glenda." She was visibly impressed and turned to the first chapter. "Zelenski. Unusual name. Polish?"

"Schizophrenish."

Glenda's laughter was more of a giggle. Subsequent chat began at the beach, tiptoed into the water, and then waded deeper. She leafed through the book as they talked.

"Hot spots?" Her eyes narrowed mischievously.

He smiled and pulled the book from her fingers, fanning to page one sixty-three and handing it back. "You be the judge." He noticed that she wasn't wearing a wedding ring.

Chapter 7: Somewhere in North Dakota

Jenna's breath issued in short jerky spurts as Larry unbuttoned her pants and swiftly tugged them down to the ankles. She stepped on the tangle and lifted her legs free. Larry slowly removed her top. They lay on the bed, embracing, enjoying the pulse of their bodies together.

"Jenna," he whispered hoarsely, kissing her inner thighs. "You believe in synchronicity?"

"Ahhh," she returned. "Huh, sure, yeah, ohhh…yeah…right there."

"God?" He flicked his tongue.

"Ayyy, God, yeah…get inside."

Jenna dug her heals into his lower back as Larry entered, and a short time later, he clenched his teeth and spurted. Still breathing heavily, he slipped out of bed to reach for his pants.

Jenna looked up, dreamily. "Where you runnin' off to, baby?"

"Out," he replied.

"Hurry back. We'll take it slow and easy."

"I won't be back."

Jenna sat up on her elbows. "Huh?"

"Sorry, Jenna, it's not happening for me."

"What the — what's not happening?"

"I'm searching for something."

"What?" Her voice was louder.

"You wouldn't understand. Thanks, Jenna."

"Fuck you, Jack!"

"Larry," he said, "Name's Larry." A dirty ashtray thunked against the door as it closed behind him.

Glenda closed the book and stared out the window, wanting desperately to laugh, fearing it would hurt Owen's feelings. Instead, she focused on the cloud layer outside her window.

"Well," Owen broke the silence, "hot enough?"

She set her jaw and turned toward him, "It...." A giggle started high in her nose as if a soda bubble had lodged there. "It was...," she tried, but the giggle wedged deeper, morphing into a rich, honest laugh. Owen's face grew stormy. She lifted the book to hide her face. After a moment, she composed herself. "You misspelled heels — it's ee, not ea." She wiped tears from her eyes. "You use Grammarly?"

Owen turned away. The man across the aisle thought Owen's look was meant for him, and he glared back.

"Oops," Glenda whispered.

The word *bitch* pinged around in Owen's head, and he tipped his plastic cocktail glass to gnaw on a chunk of ice.

The lilting voice of the stewardess filled the jet with much-needed distraction. "Please fas'in yer seat belts," she advised. "We're expectin' some turbulence."

Later the co-pilot talked about dinosaurs and put in a plug for Dinosaur National Park. "Paleontologists generally agree that many dinosaurs were warm-blooded, intelligent, and much more active than was previously thought. It's now believed that present-day birds are the living descendants of dinosaurs."

Owen glanced at his seatmate, still clutching the book and gazing through the window. "Eh-hem," he cleared his throat and gestured to the book.

She pursed her lips and handed it over. "What're you writing now?" She tried to make amends.

"Doubt you'd be interested," he said.

Glenda looked out the window again. The clouds were breaking up, so she celebrated by ordering a double-shot of tequila before dozing off. Owen watched a few minutes of the in-flight movie — a Chinese martial arts film with warriors fighting from swaying treetops, snatching flying daggers out of the air and vowing vengeance every few minutes. A short time later, the copilot announced they'd be landing shortly. Owen had just nodded off and wiped drool from the corner of his face with a drink napkin.

As the jet taxied to a stop, Owen narrowed his eyes and tried small-talking with Glenda. "Where are you headed?"

"Weeville. My father's picking me up."

He drew in a breath. "Weeville? Your father, is his name Jack?" Her answering expression was more reprimanding than incredulous. "Synchronicity," he whispered as passengers stood, opened overhead bins, and crowded into the aisles.

"What?"

"I don't believe in fate, must be synchronicity. Your father's picking me up too."

Glenda stared a few seconds before commenting. "How well do you know my father?"

"Why?"

"Hope things've changed."

"Meaning?"

Her mouth tightened, and she refused to elaborate. They were the only passengers left on the plane.

"Lose somethin'?" the stewardess drawled.

"No, we're fine," Owen answered.

As they were stepping off the plane, he touched Glenda's shoulder. "Your last name—Stoakes."

"Divorced. Haven't been back in six years. What does Daddy want with you?"

"I was voted author of the year."

She smiled and nodded.

The dry Texas summer morning smacked them in the face like the fetid breath of a velociraptor. The area around the airport was hemmed in by barren hills as if a brown serape had been tossed over a series of half-inflated beach balls. After collecting luggage, they were greeted in the arrival area by the smiling mayor. Jack Skag was short, built like a rough-hewn block of granite. His ruddy complexion contrasted starkly with the biggest, whitest teeth Owen had ever seen.

"Glenda darlin'!" he took her into his arms. "Saw you two were on the same flight—saved me from havin' to make two trips."

"Hi, Daddy." She patted his back and smiled wanly.

Pushing her to arm's length, he said, "Lemme get a good look at you. Great to have you back. We got some catchin' up to do. What's it been, three years?"

"Six."

Jack gave a sidelong glance to Owen. "You must be Mr. Zelenski." He stuck out a meaty hand. "An honor. I take it, you two've met."

Owen fought the urge to roll his eyes. "We sat together, actually."

"Well, I'll be, what a coincidence."

"Synchronicity, Daddy. Mister Zelenski doesn't believe in coincidence."

A snarling, life-size allosaurus replica guarded the airport exit. Next to it was a large billboard plastered with the goofy face of George W. Bush welcoming everyone to the great state of Texas. Jack led them to an older model Mercedes sedan. Glenda sat in the back, and Owen was next to the mayor.

Jack attacked the hills in the dusty Mercedes with the sunroof open. Wind scooped Jack's carefully coiffed hair, revealing a shining desert beneath. "Sorry." He wiped his sweating forehead. "Air conditioner's broke. Think it's the compressor."

During the drive, Glenda offered short, terse responses

to her father's superficial inquiries. "Darlin', you read Mr. Zelenski's book?" He glanced in the rearview mirror.

"A few pages," she blushed.

"By the way, your room's just the way you left it."

"Hmm," she nodded.

"What's your ex up to?" he finally asked.

"I've no idea."

"Least there was no kids."

Glenda glared at her father, then stared at the floor mat. Owen felt intrusive. He looked out the side window and observed a small bird badgering a hawk high in the sky over the hills.

"Hey, read about the preacher that murdered his wife up your way. " Jack swiveled his head toward Owen.

"Yeah, that was terrible."

"What would make a God-fearin' man do such a thing?"

Owen shrugged and shook his head.

"Had a little somethin' on the side, I'll bet."

"Maybe. They're still investigating."

"Sheesh." The mayor shook his head.

To change the subject, Owen asked about the weather in Texas.

"Same as California, dry as hell. Don't get some rain soon we'll all end up like the dinosaurs."

"Global warming," Owen commented.

"Global warming...bunch of hogwash if you ask me," Jack said a bit too loudly. "Naw, this's just Mother Nature doin' her thang."

Owen resisted the temptation to argue, knowing that non-believers couldn't be persuaded, just as church members are undeterred by the truth behind the myths they live by.

It got quiet, and Owen nervously opened his book to page

thirty-two. Larry was somewhere in Sri Lanka.

The moonlight reflected off the water, and a line of waves pursued the shoreline, depositing shells, seaweed, and plastics. Larry sat in the sand.

"Pointless," he breathed. "Nothing here."

He listened to the whisper of the ocean. Shhh, it warned. He punished the silence by heaving rocks into the surf and whipping the lapping water with a rubbery length of kelp. Clouds covered the moon, and a light drizzle drifted down. Then the drops got heavier until they pelted him. Larry stood to raise a middle finger at the sky. Immediately, a thundershower poured down on him.

"Fuck you!" Larry shouted at the top of his lungs.

A jagged white ribbon lit the sky in response, accompanied by a low, castigating rumble.

Larry tilted his face into the rain and smiled. He'd found another piece of truth for the puzzle of his life.

Owen noted that he should've checked to ensure that kelp grew in the seas around Sri Lanka. His discomfort evaporated as they coasted down the final beach ball into town. A huge banner spanned the entrance to Main Street: *Welcome to Weeville, Mr. Z!* Beneath it, a small elementary school band sweltered in full uniform, and a plump, fretting maestro waved a thin wand. The band squeaked out a frenzied, fissured, Souza march. Glenda rubbed her forehead and looked at Owen with half-a-smile and a raised eyebrow. He glanced back and returned the smile.

Owen surveyed the town. There were few trees, yet daisies, pansies, snapdragons, begonias, geraniums, nasturtiums, poppies and other assorted flowers spilled from window boxes and sidewalk planters. They frothed out of anything that would hold dirt, offering breathtaking contrast to an otherwise plain-looking town. Children chased each other, and mothers scolded them. Men adjusted straw cowboy hats and knifed their hands into back pockets. There were about two hundred people milling around. Curious faces appeared in shadowy doorways as baton twirlers performed in front of the band, occasionally pulling up the thin straps of their tops.

Carnival booths selling pink and blue cotton candy, sodas, and half-price Weeville High School Raptors T-shirts dotted the main street, blocked to traffic by two police cruisers. A table hawked copies of *The Journal of Desperate Living*. Taped around the edge were children's renditions of the book cover. Cheerleaders chanted, "O-W-E-N, Owen yes he can, he's our desperate livin' man!" They finished with an enthusiastic, "Yay!"

Batons were flung into the air, most bouncing crazily off the pavement. Owen noticed signs posted reminding folks to reelect Mayor Skag, and several people wore baseball caps fronted with Let's Make America Great Again! The mayor parked his crippled Mercedes, and Owen stepped into a smattering of applause.

"Daddy, see you back at the house," Glenda said and pecked him on the cheek.

"All right, darlin', in a bit, then. Front door is unlocked."

A fragile autograph seeker greeted Owen. "I'm ninety-two years old," she announced stoically. Her face was covered with deep wrinkles, moles, and warts. One of her eyes was nearly closed by a drooping lid, yet the other gleamed at him.

He took both her hands in his. "You don't look a day over seventy," he smiled. The old woman's face was implacable. He scratched out his first autograph for her. Then the mayor ushered him to a comfortable chair at the book table.

"Got a speech ready?"

"Yeah, I put something together."

"Okay, then. I'll announce you in a little while. Got a little business to attend first." Jack walked away to shake hands with his constituents.

Glenda had quietly slipped out of the crowd and walked across the street to a liquor store. She emerged a few minutes later with a brown paper sack twisted at the neck, and then scurried down the street, turned the corner, and was gone.

After an hour, Owen shook out his cramped fingers. Friendly townsfolk pressed him for the chaotic mass of swirls that constituted his signature. Compliments showered, erasing earlier uncertainties. Within the bubble of celebrity, he wondered about the process for having a book considered for the Pulitzer.

"Wunerful writin' — real interestin' — never read nothin' lak it — where you git such idears?" were some of the comments he heard.

"What you thank 'bout gun control?" asked a middle-aged man wearing a Dallas Cowboys cap. Then, he unleashed a dark stream of tobacco juice into an empty soda can. "I thank it's bullshit, you ask me."

Weeville, thought Owen, *a land once ruled by dinosaurs*. "I had a bee-bee gun when I was a kid," he answered.

The mayor stood on a temporary stage in front of a wooden lectern and gestured for silence. "Testing, testing," he tried the microphone. The accompanying squelch made everyone plug their ears. Dozens of faces turned toward the platform — children smeared with chocolate faces, squinting into the sun faces, choking on popcorn kernel faces, juicy gossip faces, and blank text-messaging faces.

"Testes, testes," a young jokester called out.

"Friends." The mayor held up his hands to begin the welcoming ceremony. "Weeville has a proud tradition of honoring outstanding contributors to literature...." He paused, trying to control a gas bubble that had reached the end of its journey. "And it's my great pleasure to introduce a man whose writin' has nourished our minds with food for thought. Friends and neighbors, please give a warm Weeville welcome to Owen Zelaski!"

The band stumbled into a short introductory tune over a generous applause, providing cover as Jack let out a long ragged fart. Owen winced at having his last name butchered. When he reached the podium, a malodorous fragrance assailed his nose. He adjusted the microphone.

Pausing for effect, he began with, "I'd like to thank Mayor Skag and the wonderful people of Weeville for this great honor. I can't begin to tell you what a joy it is for me to see such an interest in literature. In an age when computers, cell phones, and social media are separating us further and further from each other, it's heartening to see that books are still revered in Weeville. This gives me hope that future generations will choose paper over plastic.

"*The Journal of Desperate Living* was born of my need to find out about myself, my purpose in life. Not long ago, I believed no one would be interested in reading anything I had to say. You've proven me wrong." People clapped, and a firecracker went off close to the stage. Owen's audience began shifting on their feet, and Owen knew he was beginning to lose them. Quickly he jumped to the end of his speech. "As I look upon the fine people of this lovely town, I'm reminded of Lou Gehrig, the great Yankee first baseman—" A long feedback squeal allowed Jack the luxury of another blast.

"Shit," a father cried out when the toddler he was holding

sneezed a mouthful of nachos onto his neck. The horn section of the band blew into spit valves.

"Lou Gehrig," Owen began again. "The Yankee great ended his farewell speech at Yankee Stadium by saying, 'Today, I am the luckiest man on the face of the earth.' That's just how I feel. Thank you."

Townsfolk clapped and whistled enthusiastically. Owen gazed over their heads and saw Glenda leaned up against a dinosaur-shaped trashcan with a book in her hand. She was shaking her head and smiling.

***

Jack wouldn't hear of Owen staying at the Motel Dinosnores.

"Nope," he shook his head. "Got three empty bedrooms. Wife passed away, and my little punkin went off. Shoot, there's been nobody around to soak up my opinions. They just sit around and get moldy."

"Sorry to hear about your wife."

"Yeah, well, she was really somethin', my Maggie."

Jack drove Owen to his restored two-story Victorian. Its bluish-gray skin was trimmed white. A seven-foot brick wall surrounded the property, and a pair of horse-shaped bonsai's reared on each side of the main entrance. The massive front lawn was dotted with mature magnolias. The border gardens were profuse with pink lilies, magenta hollyhocks, multicolor peonies, roses, and other flowers separated by boxwood hedges. Jack noticed the admiration in Owen's green eyes.

"Cow shit," Jack explained.

"Pardon?"

"The flowers. My Mexican gardener uses cow manure. That's the secret."

"Oh." They strolled up the brick walkway. "Reminds me of an English tea garden."

"Been to England?" Jack inquired.

Owen shook his head. "Only in magazines."

"Well, that Mexican really knows his shit, pardon my French."

"You've a beautiful home."

"Keeps me off the streets," the mayor beamed. Then he noticed a fresh hump of fine earth on the lawn. "Sum'bitchin gophers."

"Is being mayor a full-time job?" Owen asked as they entered the house through the heavy French door.

"Naw, I dabble around, little this, little that," he answered.

The house was impeccably furnished with antiques, Native American rugs and pottery, western paintings of cowboys riding lonely trails or herding cattle, a portrait of Sitting Bull, and one of Wild Bill Hickok.

"Got something to show you." The mayor ushered Owen into a large den. One entire wall was lined with tall bookcases, and there was a rolling wooden ladder to reach the uppermost shelves.

"Impressive." Owen walked over and pulled out a crackling new hardback copy of *Gulliver's Travels*. He opened to an illustration of tiny Lilliputians holding Gulliver in bondage.

"Classic example of S and M," he joked, holding the book for the mayor to see.

"Yeah, well, I collect all kinds of stuff." The mayor gestured to an elegant display case centering the room. "Especially rare children's books."

A pretty Mexican woman brought in a silver tray with two tumblers, an ice bucket, and a bottle of single-malt Scotch. Jack smiled. "Gracias, Josefina," staring after her as she left. "Sorry," he focused again. "Didn't ask if you were a drinkin' man."

"Been known to." Owen replaced Gulliver.

Jack used tongs for the ice and poured two fingers worth in each glass.

Owen stood before the display case and saw that the books were indeed very old. An original *Tarzan and the Golden Lion*, assorted Zane Grey hardbacks, as well as a threadbare copy of *Maidenhead Stories*.

"*Little Bear's Adventures*," Owen pointed. "Read that as a child."

"Yeah, that's a favorite of mine. Still have your copy?"

"Afraid not. My childhood headed out the door along with my father. He used to read to me." Owen took a long sip, and ice tumbled against his teeth.

"That's the trouble, kids don't get read to. Mother and father divorced?"

"When I was five. They're both gone now." He took another swallow.

"Sorry to hear that. Brothers or sisters?"

"Nope."

"You want some whiskey with that ice?" Jack smiled and gestured to the empty glass.

"Thanks."

Jack refilled Owen's glass, and he let the amber liquid glide down his throat, thankful for the numbing effect.

"Married?"

"Was."

Glenda's heels tapped rhythmically on the tile as she entered the library with a knowing smile. "Thought I'd find you here."

"Just showin' off the collection, sweet-tart. Remember *Little Bear's Adventures*?"

Glenda put a finger to her temple. "About the cub that ran away from home and found out that his parents hadn't prepared him for the real world, so he failed miserably?" Her eyes tapered. "Is that the one?" She turned toward the serving tray, but there were no more glasses.

"Guess it all depends on how you look at it." Jack's voice was stern, and he could smell that she'd been drinking.

Owen wandered over to a window and looked out. Another sparrow was pestering a hawk. He wondered if they were the same ones. If so, how frustrating for the hawk and tiring for the sparrow.

"I'll start dinner," Glenda said. "This little bear is starving." She whirled and clicked away.

Jack looked down at his feet and stirred his ice with a finger. "Hmph...kids grow up so fast, and before you know it, they're gone." He pursed his mouth. "And then they come back." His eyes were glazed, and frustration creased his brow like a jailhouse tattoo.

"Know what you mean." Owen did the mental math to figure how old Patrick and Tracy were, but he would need a calculator. Their goddamn stepfather would have one.

***

As she waited for the onions to caramelize and the mushrooms to sauté, Glenda read snatches from *The Journal of Desperate Living*. She'd purchased it half-price at the liquor store counter.

Chapter 3: In the Sierra Nevada's

From the top of Moro Rock, Larry could almost see the whole world. Steps leading to the top were well worn. Moro was a popular tourist attraction.

Larry arrived just before dawn. He wanted to be alone with the yawning planet — watch the sun rise from the top of the world. Only in this way could he hope to catch a glimpse of slippery truth. The journey had taken him on countless adventures — his perceptions were keen. He could hear the heartbeat of the universe as he traveled through it.

When he reached the top, he saw a large triangular shape poised at the edge of a cliff, silhouetted against the beginning edges of dawn. It resembled a giant orange butterfly.

"Good morning," Larry greeted.

"Goot mornink," a man replied in a Russian accent, adjusting the straps on his hang glider.

"You really going to jump?"

The man smiled, "Konechno." Then he translated, "Of course."

"What's it like?"

"Vel…." He scrunched his face. "Imagine how vould be to soar like hawk — free as vind. Dat vat is like."

Larry nodded, pondering the image.

"Vel, enjoy your day." The man sniffed, cleared his throat, took ten paces back, and ran, leaping from the edge.

Larry rushed forward and was horrified as he watched the hang glider spin wildly out of control, screaming, "Nye-e-e-t!" He thumped against the mountainside and was spread like margarine against the bread of the earth below.

"Jesus!" Larry rushed down to find a ranger.

Glenda tossed the book on the counter and returned her attention to the onions and mushrooms. She reached for the cognac she was using in the recipe, sloshing some into a heated saucepan and raising the bottle to her lips.

Dinner began quietly. Glenda served a lovely filet mignon, paired with a French Burgundy.

"Didn't have to go to all this trouble, honey-pie — I was set to take y'all out to Busby's for ribs."

"No trouble…I enjoy cooking."

"It's really delicious, Glenda." Owen reached for his wine glass.

"Thank you, Mr. Zelenski."

"Please, just call me Owen."

Jack picked up the bottle. "French," he grumbled.

"Exquisite." Glenda took the bottle from his hand to refill her glass. Her father glared and then went to work on his fillet. "Tell me, Mister Owen...the adventures Larry has in your book—are they connected to your personal experiences?"

Owen recognized a challenging tone in her voice. "Experience—yes, of course, very important, yes. Every writer uses experience in their writing."

"Ever been to Egypt, Italy, India, any of those other places you write about?"

Owen cleared his throat. "Spent a few weeks in Cabo last summer."

"Kabul?" she asked.

"Cabo with a C. Cabo San Lucas, in Baja, Mexico."

Jack wiped his forehead with a napkin and mopped his plate with a hunk of French bread.

"Tell me something," Glenda continued. "Your book is about finding the truth. Isn't truth subjective, like our perceptions of beauty?" She refilled Owen's wine glass and poured the last in hers.

"Good question, Glenda. Don't know where to start." He put his fork down and took a sip of wine.

"It's always best to start at the beginning, and all you have to do is follow the yellow brick road."

Owen sat up straight. "Well, I think we find pieces of truth and spend our lives trying to fit them together."

"See what you mean," Jack fumbled. "Like a road that ends, and then you double back to find out how you got there." He stuck a toothpick in his mouth and sucked on it.

"Something like that," Owen nodded.

"Ol' Larry should've stayed on with Jenna. She might've taken him down a road less traveled." Glenda's voice trailed off luxuriously.

"How do you mean?" Owen dabbled at the corners of his mouth with a cloth napkin.

"Use your imagination. One thing's for sure, ol' Larry doesn't have a clue about what a woman wants or how she wants it."

Jack's eyes bulged. "All right then. Bet my bottom dollar Owen's bushed after such a long day."

"You're right, Daddy. He's plum tuckered from all that traveling." Glenda collected dishes and kicked off her shoes before bumping through the swinging doors to the kitchen. A series of explosions sounded from outside.

"Fireworks at the high school football stadium," explained Jack. "Was s'posed to go, but—"

Glenda was back to collect more dishes, and she finished his thought. "You can see'em from the front yard. That's what you always said." Glenda returned to the kitchen.

"Don't worry about cleanin' up, Punkin," Jack called out. "Got a Mexican lady comin' in the morning." Then in a lowered voice, he told Owen, "She's a real cutie." Jack winked at Owen. "Same one that brought out the whiskey."

Owen nodded and pushed his plate away. "I am kind of beat. If it's okay, I'll shower and call it a night."

Jack glanced at his watch. "Ten-thirty—boy, time flies. Tomorrow you got a writin' seminar in the library and lunch with the Shriners. I'll walk you up to your room."

As they ascended the stairs, Owen thought, *Soon, I'll be winging it back to the central San Joaquin. Crop-dusting helicopters,*

Monsanto, breadbasket of the world, water shortages. He'd return to a place where thirsty farmlands had greedily sucked water from the ground for decades. The land was sinking, and the remaining water was becoming too salty to use.

Jack showed Owen to his bedroom, spacious and well appointed. The queen-size four-poster bed was covered with a fluffy quilt and piled with lacy pillows.

"Night, night, don't let the coyote's bite," Jack said.

"Thanks, Jack, for everything."

"Pleasure. Breakfast around eight, that okay?"

"Perfect. Goodnight."

I'll shower in the morning, thought Owen. He was tired.

Downstairs in the kitchen, Glenda sat on a barstool. Her hand turned white around the neck of the cognac bottle, and she drained what was left. She stood and walked to a large trash bin with her copy of *The Journal of Desperate Living.* Using the foot-lift, she was about to drop it on top of a heap of leftovers, yet decided against it.

***

Owen slept naked, enjoying the cool freshness of the sheets and replaying the day's events in his drowsy mind—Glenda's enigmatic smile drifted in and out of his thoughts.

Colors are uniquely scented. Green smacks of fresh-cut alfalfa, yellow clings warmly to the nose, while black is spicy and erotic. Owen's room smelled brown, reminding him of dry cornstalks. Brown clings and survives a hundred spin-cycles. Even then, if the sun is warm and the wind swirls just so brown returns. You can wish for any other color, yet sometimes brown is what you're stuck with.

Owen was too tired to notice night sounds—chirping owls, yelping coyotes, the creak of footsteps on wooden stairs, the weathered moan of his bedroom door opening. He bolted upright as Glenda sat on the edge of the bed. She wore an oversized T-shirt, and her face looked beautifully surreal in the ambient light. The tilt of her smile and the smell of her breath hinted that she was well oiled.

Owen lay back and pulled the sheet up to his neck. Glenda inched it back down to kiss his chest. He closed his eyes and caressed her short, dark hair.

"Should've given Jenna another go," she whispered as her tongue followed the sheet further down.

"Mmm, think so?"

"This was my mother's room."

"Slept in her own bedroom?"

"Last few years, she did."

Owen wanted to ask why, but she was painting him with her tongue, and all other considerations left his mind. He arched his back as she took him into her mouth.

"Ohhh, my god."

Never had he experienced anything like Glenda. She performed an erotic ballet, dominant and graceful, full of breathy sighs and urgent exultations. She never allowed him on top, and he saw no reason to complain. After the final curtain, he lay semiconscious, stroking the smooth valley of her spine as they rested. Then she sat up and gazed out the window at the sliver of moon beyond. Owen wondered dreamily, *Am I the sparrow or the hawk?*

Facing on their sides, they whispered to each other.

"What does your father do for a living?" Owen asked.

"Nothing," she answered. "Mom won the Texas lottery ten years ago."

"That's amazing."

"Yeah, well, she didn't live long enough to enjoy it."

"What happened?"

"Money. It suffocated her. She wanted everybody to be happy."

"Sorry."

"Me too." Glenda got to her feet. "Night." She tucked her T-shirt between her legs.

"Do you have to go?"

She leaned over to kiss Owen. "You've a big day tomorrow."

"Goodnight, Glenda."

After the door closed, Owen reached down to feel himself, still moist. The memory made him stiff again.

***

In the morning, Owen showered, barely feeling the water. He cut himself shaving and put his socks on inside out, as he reveled in the afterglow of his night with Jack's mysterious daughter. *Don't push the envelope*, he warned himself. *Might drive her away if she thinks you're obsessed.*

Downstairs the pretty Mexican woman had breakfast prepared—hot biscuits with chicken gravy, bacon, coffee, and fresh-squeezed grapefruit juice.

"*Buenas días*," he greeted.

"*Buenas días, señor.*" She served him. "Miss eh-Stoakes— she ask me give you this."

The pretty Mexican maid lifted *The Journal of Desperate Living* from a large pocket in her apron.

"*Gracias*," he smiled.

"*De nada.*"

She really is a cutie, Owen reflected as she hustled back into the kitchen. His novel was bookmarked with a letter. He took a sip of coffee and read the words that were meticulously scrawled in pen.

Mister Zelenski (Owen),

After reading your book, I knew that Jenna deserved a better shake, so I took matters into my own hands. She was the only character I identified with. Everybody else was shallow, insubstantial, co-dependent, neurotic, or just plain dumb. At least Jenna had the guts to put in her two cents with that worthless bastard, Larry.

Know what I think? I think you identify with Larry. If that's true, then you're one sorry sonofabuck — means you've squandered your life without leaving your desk in search of the goddamn Cup of Life. Your book's pointless, which's why my father thought it was great. Bet he hasn't told you about the other great writers he's dragged into town. Ever hear of Martha Wood? She wrote a short story collection, My Travels with an Elderly Gentleman. *Surely you've read,* Flatulence: Shedding Light on an Embarrassing Subject. *Get my drift?*

Let you in on a little secret. Daddy selects honorees by the book cover. He hates to read. Ten-to-one he hasn't read your book through, and neither has anybody else in this godforsaken town. Most everybody voted for the Twitter-idiot president, so what can you expect? You may have noticed how folks pronounce the town name — Weevil. This town's chock-full of insects scurrying around in cupboards and hiding in cereal boxes. It'll eventually end up like your Russian hang glider, except it won't hit the ground — just spin around aimlessly until it disintegrates.

Came back thinking I'd find a clue as to how to turn my fucked-up life around. Married a gold digger after Mom died, and he burned through my share of the lottery money. Figured it was time for little bear to come home. But this isn't home. This is nowhere. By the time you read this, I'll be on an early-bird flight back to Sacramento.

You can't find truth in children's books, and it sure as hell doesn't live in the pages of that piece of shit you wrote. Maybe if you get off the treadmill and try living, you'll put out a decent read. Enjoy the biscuits.

Warmest Regards,
Glenda
PS: You have beautiful green eyes.

Owen returned the letter to the inside of the book, pushed his plate away, and leaned back. He folded his arms and focused on a cobweb in the corner of the coved ceiling, and felt the dull beginnings of a headache. His throat ached as if he'd swallowed a ruby slipper.

Who needs her? uttered a voice in his brain.

"Mornin'." Mayor Skag lumbered down the stairs to deposit himself across from Owen.

"Morning." Owen took up his napkin and wiped his eyes. Jack looked at him, questioningly. "Allergies?"

The pretty Mexican woman came in from the kitchen to serve the mayor. "*Todo bien?*"

"Yeah, Josefina, it's all good." Jack smiled and pushed his fork into the soft back of a biscuit smothered in chicken gravy.

CHAPTER 5
Owen Listens to the Voices

"Schizophrenia cannot be understood without understanding despair." —R.D. Laing—

After the Weeville debacle, Owen skulked back to Meadowland, unplugged the phone, slipped into bed with a bottle of Scotch, and cocooned. Various offers crowded his mailbox extolling the virtue of easy payment plans, free Netflix for a month, two-for-one pizza, and various other incredible one-time offers. Among them was a yellow Sorry We Missed You slip from United Parcel Service. Two thousand newly minted copies of *The Journal of Desperate Living* were waiting to be delivered. Vortex Publishing had shipped them to him instead of the distributor because he'd neglected to extend the agreement.

Yapping tirelessly, voices in Owen's head forced him to accept the cruel, unrelenting truth that was zipped in a body bag and jealously guarded by ego. Truth burst, spilling steaming, rotting reality over the floor of his apartment. Owen wondered how long it'd been in hibernation, this sharp fanged, rattlesnake truth.

Truth is, said voices, *no one gives a rat's ass. That bitch, Stoakes, was right on the money. Need to live a little.* Owen covered his ears with a pillow, but the voices were relentless. *Story of your miserable life would fit on a square of toilet paper.*

Truth jabbed Owen's ass with a scorpion barb, and the voices grew more self-assured. None had names, yet they used Owen's mind like a trampoline. He faced the medicine cabinet, read the label on the empty bottle, and considered his options. *Idiopathic*, he thought. *That's for goddamn sure.*

Let's jam, bone out, go on a walkabout — vamoose! They urged.

"Where?"

Doesn't matter. Half the fun's just getting there.

Owen quit his teaching job and announced his intention to leave Meadowland. No one pleaded for him to reconsider — not the ex-wife, his children, no one from the high school, not even the beautiful Ms. Payán.

See how easily you're forgotten? voices said.

Owen cashed out his retirement, had a big yard sale, and put his savings into an ATM account. He carried the card in his wallet, along with a picture of his children, taken when they were very young. The open road beckoned.

His first stop was a used motorcycle dealership. It was August the first, his birthday. Owen was fifty-one. Sitting on a proper Harley is like easing into your favorite leather chair to watch a Clint Eastwood spaghetti western. North America rolls by with the windows rolled down. Owen bought the only Harley he'd ever seen with a sidecar. No one said goodbye. In fact, he was sure he heard a scattering of applause as the Harley thundered past a city limits sign: You are leaving Meadowland, an All-American Town.

"Left a long time ago," he said as the wind whistled over the black half-helmet that resembled something from WW2. The voices were silent for a while, now that Owen had agreed to join them.

Within the hour, he picked up a pretty young hitchhiker just south of Fresno. She should've been in school studying how life was played, yet circumstances forced her to see for herself. Owen didn't know what those circumstances were and didn't ask. She said her name was Darcy — or Marcy. He couldn't recall. She rode in the sidecar without a helmet, and miraculously they weren't pulled over.

Owen checked them into a Sacramento hotel that'd seen better days. He'd found her just in time. Soon she'd have taken a lift from a porn addicted traveling salesman or an opportunistic truck driver with a sleeper cabin. Then she'd end up working for a pimp she met at the Greyhound station or would be found dead in a rubbish bin.

Owen guessed that Darcy, or Marcy, wasn't far removed from a small town like Meadowland, following dreams that were gradually drifting out of reach. She reminded him of Lesley with a Y. She focused on the soot stains around the air vent when he lifted her knees. Her sexual indifference, mixed with his guilty conscience, made him soften.

Don't be a pussy, voices teased. *Full steam ahead.*

Owen stiffened again. Her discomforted voice made Owen pause halfway in.

Follow the yellow brick road. She'll get the hang of it, they advised.

Marcy, or Darcy, clutched his shoulders, stiffened, and gasped as he pushed down and in. A short while later, he pulled out and spurted over her dark pubic hair. He went into the bathroom and wetted a washcloth in warm water. Then he cleaned his mess before making a new one.

***

The next morning the girl slipped out of bed and quickly dressed as Owen showered. Then she left the hotel. As Owen lathered, he began loathing himself, recalling that Tracy had been her age not so long ago.

Big deal, the voices insisted. *If they're old enough to bleed, they're old enough to breed.*

Darcy, or Marcy, was thumbing from the on-ramp to Freeway 99 North. Owen thundered past without looking back. After resting in Red Bluff for a night, he cut west toward Eureka. His love-handles began to melt away. The vibrations from the Harley were shaping his spongy English teacher body into something more useful.

We're starving, voices complained. Owen hadn't eaten since the previous morning.

She felt good, and you know it. Let's grab a burger.

He suddenly felt as if he could eat, if not a horse, then at least a good-sized cat.

After lunching at the Samoa Cookhouse, he thundered into the Trees of Mystery National Park, where all but a few voices in his head disembarked in search of some other poor sap to sponge off. Owen parked his Harley by two others. He needed a stretch-break, and the giant redwoods reminded him of how small he was. Spotting a public bathroom marked Lumberjack's and Lumberjill's, Owen went to wash his face and take a leak.

The entrance to Trees of Mystery was overseen by a fifty-foot likeness of Paul Bunyan. Someone sat in a control booth located inside the head and conversed through a speaker hidden in the cavernous mouth. A giant hand was waved from side-to-side by working a lever back and forth. As Owen exited the restroom, he saw a child approaching the fiberglass colossus with his parents. The boy tilted his head back to observe the swaying hand.

"Hi, little buddy," boomed a voice. The kid squealed and ran into the arms of his mother.

New voices were now bumping around in Owen's brain. Two grizzled looking men were admiring Owen's bike.

Feast your eyes on this mother, Owen heard one of them saying.

Cherry, remarked the other.

They took a step back to measure him. *Yours*? The shorter of the two asked. He was lean, with stubble-growth of brown beard.

"Yeah."

Fuckin' ay, this here's a work of art, said the taller one, sporting a large gut and a long, red beard.

"Thanks."

Where you headed, man? Longbeard wanted to know.

"Nowhere in particular."

This bike'll take you there in style, said Stubblebeard.

"So far, so good."

Trouble don't come factory with Harley's — ignorance is an add-on, said Longbeard.

Can say that again, Stubblebeard hawked and spit off to the side.

"From around here?"

Nah, ridin' up Oregon way. Longbeard placed a finger on each side of his nose to blow out the road dust.

"Mind if I tag along?" Owen asked.

The sun was on a lunch break, hiding behind a light drizzle. Stubble looked at Long. *No skin off my balls.* Longbeard held out a hand. *Name's Rowe...friends call me Skid.* He nodded to his friend. *This here's Madman.*

"Owen Zelenski, call me Oz," Owen said.

Like the wizard, eh? Well, Oz, Madman explained, *this's the thing — before you can ride with us, you gotta get initiated. Skid and me said if anyone was to join us, they'd have to prove themselves.*

We say that? Skid joked.

Other visitors stared at Owen as if he carried the plague. They returned to their climate controlled, air-bagged cages of steel and drove away from Trees of Mystery with doors locked and the windows up. A forest ranger had unraveled the mysteries of the trees for them, yet Owen provided fresh questions that couldn't be answered within the grove.

"What do you have in mind?"

A mischievous idea fermented in Skid's mind as he focused on Paul Bunyan. He motioned Madman off to the side for a private powwow.

When they explained the plan to Owen, he shook his head and laughed. "What kind of mushrooms were in your omelet this morning?"

***

They waited patiently for Paul Bunyan's rear hatch to open. When it did, a young man climbed down a ladder. *Bet he feels like a turd,* Madman chuckled.

Owen waited until he saw the operator headed to the Lumberjack's room. Then he snuck up the bung-hatch and closed it. It was dark. By feeling along the smooth walls of Paul's colon, he found a light switch and ascended spiral stairs to the main control room. A small stool sat in front of the console. A cell phone lay off to the side next to an open package of powdered mini-doughnuts. Owen stuffed one into his mouth.

A large red button activated the gooseneck microphone. From the eyeholes, he spied Skid and Madman standing by the bikes, waving. Paul Bunyan waggled his hand back at them like a parade princess.

An elderly couple stood below. The woman sneezed, and Paul Bunyan blessed her with, "Gesundheit!"

The husband laughed and yelled. "She got a whiff of those big feet of yours!" The wife punched his arm playfully.

"Do you have a cold, dear?" Bunyan inquired.

"Allergies!" she called.

Then, Paul Bunyan's voice boomed, "Grandma ain't sick. All she needs is Grandpa's dick!"

The couple stumbled back. "What the hell! Let's get a ranger," the husband raged.

"There's some lunatic up there!" his wife warned an arriving family in the parking lot.

Paul waved, as a gentle rain began to fall. "Bye-bye now," he called, "Don't forget to stop by the gift shop on your way out." He whistled at a teenage girl wearing braces. "Hey, doll, get a load of Niagara Falls." Owen pissed out of Paul Bunyan's mouth, singing, "Peein' in the rain, just peein' in the rain!"

The girl covered her mouth when she giggled. "Back to the car!" ordered her father.

The mythical lumberjack defecated Owen, and as he straddled the Harley, two rangers were jogging toward him. Madman and Skid were laughing so hard they could barely kick-start their bikes. Revving mightily, they spun gravel into the gray sky, passing the girl with braces on the way out. She was hiding her mouth, yet the eyes were still smiling.

That evening Owen found a raw potato in a dumpster. He doused his earlobe with Wild Turkey whiskey and used a straight pin to poke a hole. Then he fashioned a loop earring out of a paper clip.

Skid suggested they come up with a name for their affiliation. They settled on Desperados and used a permanent black marker to script it as best they could on the back of their faded denim jackets. Folks had more respect for affiliates.

It is a popular myth that hardcore bikers roll along, pillaging and plundering small towns. Rumor has it they spit on authority, blow noses on the shirtsleeves of society or, at the very least, scrape nails over chalkboards. Once a stereotype makes it to HBO, gets featured on Fox News, headlined in a tabloid, or trends on Yahoo, reality loses face. When watered by weak minds, ignorance acts as a fertilizer, encouraging stereotypes to grow into hearty misconceptions, weeds that never get yanked because they're mistaken for flowers. The result now sat in the Oval Office. Desperados minded their own business, and they expected others to do the same.

Once Owen had shared his academic past, Madman and Skid qualified him as the go-to intellectual. He was their philosopher, attorney-at-large, psychologist, confessor, and general medical practitioner. He paid room and board with his trusty ATM. They listened as he ragged on about global warming and how Earth had reached the tipping point. Best of all, he got them laid.

In the months that followed, a variety of women were drawn to the Desperados. Ladies are attracted to bad boys for a number of reasons. Some like rough sex and others are seeking punishment for past sins. Invariably they'd also reached a tipping point in their desperate lives. Owen was more than happy to offer services, and it was understood by his comrades that he always had first dibs.

Madman couldn't be serious even when he was fucking. *Takin' the tuna boat to China*, he announced as he buried his face between a pair of quivering thighs.

There were youngsters like Darcy, or Marcy, found at truck stops or hitching from onramps with cardboard signs: My sister's cuter next town over; U drive 70 x's faster than I can walk; and, I seek the Grail. Owen's friends sniffed out jailbait like abandoned chewing gum stuck to the bottom of a grammar school desk.

Somebody's gotta, may's well be us, they reasoned.

Owen contemplated life as they toured hamlets, brawny cities, and backcountry hole-in-the-walls. Vibrations from the road traveled through his balls and up into his brain, evoking strange sentiments. Every once in a while, Owen hit a pothole, and a new Desperado popped into his head. Initiates endured various humiliations to become members. Since Owen was the undisputed leader by proxy, he thought up the exams.

One task required the initiate to flirt with a brawny police officer, which went pretty well until the officer began to show interest. The candidate called the officer a poufy, and was immediately maced, slammed to the ground, hooked up, and charged with solicitation.

Desperados complained about helmet laws and debated about settling down in Illinois, Iowa, or New Hampshire, where it was still legal to ride without. As they hummed through Wyoming and Montana, prairie grass leaned, mountains shivered, and frozen lakes thawed.

Can't stomach California, Skid commented during a stretch break. He fired up a blunt and passed it to Owen.

Owen held the smoke in his lungs for as long as he could. "Remember when the Terminator was governor?

Dee Govinayduh, Madman mimicked.

Owen laughed. "Had a nice bike in the movie, though."

1990 Fat Boy, model FLSTF, Skid said.

Knocked up his maid, Madman added. *Believe that shit?*

The Harleys thundered forward. The wind dried out Owen's lips, and the sun turned his cheeks into leather, but he enjoyed the purr of his machine. Wildlife didn't mind the steady drumbeat of his engine. Red-tailed hawks circled, deer grazed, and coyotes maintained steady trots to nowhere. The Harley smoothed out at seventy, sounding like a sycophantic pat on the back. Together, man and machine formed a synthesis of steel and testosterone, an extension of the prick.

Who'd you vote for? Skid wanted to know.

"Didn't," Owen admitted.

Yeah, what's the point, right?

"Way I look at it."

In Yakima, Washington, Owen heard something rummaging around in a dumpster in back of a pizza joint. He figured it for a raccoon and was surprised to find something worse. It snarled in defense of a long, curved edge of pizza crust. He reached in, and the dog snapped at him.

"Motherfucker!"

The others howled with laughter. Owen lunged and trapped the dog around the neck. It growled and nipped, yet after a few tense moments, relaxed as he stroked it reassuringly.

"It's okay, boy, us guys're leftovers too."

Good for nothin' mangy mutt, said Tramp as the dog twisted around in Owen's arms to lick its balls.

"Oh yeah? Let's see you do that."

Nah, gotta admit, I ain't that flexible. Tramp was the newest Desperado and possessed a wicked sense of humor.

How long you gonna fuck around? complained Klein. Nicknamed Special K, he was always bitching. Straddling his bike, he ran hands through his dark, greasy, shoulder length hair and spat close to Owen's feet. Special K wasn't the least bit funny. *What's the matter?* he continued. *Mommy never let you keep a dog?*

K had challenged Owen's leadership from the get-go, and

Owen knew the time had come to deal with him. He set the dog
down and sauntered over. "Got somethin' to say, say it." He
hooked his thumbs into his front pockets as K busied himself,
making a ponytail with a rubber band.

Got a dick in your ear? Already did. Special K shot the
rubberband at Owen's face and folded his tattooed arms over
his chest. The rest of the gang tensed. Owen casually shuffled
sideways, smiled back at his followers, twisted suddenly, and
shattered K's nose with a right hook. K toppled like a scoop
of ice cream off a child's sugar-cone. Owen finished him off,
lifting K's head by the hair and crashing it to the pavement.
Blood poured, and K curled into a fetal position and begged
him to stop.

"Nothin' special about you," Owen deadpanned.

Skid burst with laugher, joined by the others. *You got served,
boy!*

Owen finished by pissing on K's bike. The smell of warm
pee on hot chrome was nauseating, but he made certain to
shake out every drop. Onlookers backed away respectfully as
he returned for the dog, whose eyes were too big for its head.
It sneezed and whipped around to chew on the hair around its
ass.

Skid put an affectionate arm over Owen's shoulder. They'd
traveled the longest together. Madman had shaved and stayed
behind in Oregon to work in construction.

That's one ugly fucker, Skid observed.

"Seen you lately?" Owen used the bottom of his T-shirt to
wipe sweat from his eyes. He clucked his tongue at the dog.
"Angel, that's what I'm gonna call you. There's a good boy."
He put the dog in the sidecar, and it made no move to escape.
Owen sat tall in the saddle, dressed in leather and denim.
Beautiful green-eyed Owen.

He'll slow us down, Skid said.

"Can't just leave him." Owen reached to pet his new friend.

All eyes 'n' asshole. Skid stopped after that, knowing better than to push the envelope at this stage of the game, especially after what had happened to Special K.

"Don't pay attention to Uncle Skiddy," Owen advised the dog. "He's one jealous sonofabitch."

They brought the Harleys to life and left Special K writhing next to his pissed-on chopper. The dog lay on the floor of the sidecar and curled into a ball. Near Grand Junction, Colorado, Owen picked up a hitcher named Dorothy. She'd got his attention with a cardboard sign that said, Fast Learner. She rode sidecar with Angel in her lap.

I'm a student sometimes, she'd explained.

Owen remembered her being way more — *feisty, thin, raven-haired Dorothy, with a few cards missing from the deck*. She liked underground parking lots and country back-roads, where she straddled him on the Harley. She was exclusively Owen's woman.

Gimme a shot, Skid often said.

"Ask her yourself."

Nope, huh-uh, you ain't gettin' near me with that thing, Dorothy said, alluding to the fact that Skid carried a weapon of mass destruction beneath his faded Levis.

Inevitably progress was slow, but it didn't matter. There was no place they had to be. There was something religious about cumming on a classic Harley, and Dorothy needed it three or four times a day.

Owen found a pair of Doggles and a leather jacket at a pet store in Park City. They were a distraction on the freeways and stuck to side-roads whenever possible. At rest stops, they patiently posed for strangers with cell phone cameras, and although he never knew, they were well liked on Facebook and went viral on YouTube.

It was late morning when they pulled to the front curb of a Mormon church in Provo that was having a parking lot yard sale. The scene resembled an archeological landfill. Everything you never needed was there. Dorothy decided to stick around. Owen gave her a long farewell kiss as disapproving eyes stabbed them in the back.

The rest of the Desperados had split for the holidays, but Skid had no place else to be. He clung to Owen like an old Band-Aid and spat on the sidewalk as Dorothy waved weakly to him over Owen's shoulder. It was chilly enough to see the breath fogging from her mouth.

Maybe I'll study here, she smiled, *marry a Mormon, and have a gazillion kids*. She stopped at Owen's bike to pat Angel, and then they watched as she strode away confidently, thumbing as she walked, and turned a corner down the street. Owen shook his head and told Angel to stay in the sidecar so he could check out the rummage sale. He joined other frowning patrons as they picked through the morass.

If you're browsing for a baby, you could do worse than shopping second-hand Provo. They're experts at procreation, and there's always a slew of cribs, blankets, kids' clothing, and whatnots for sale. Owen sifted through a stack of paperbacks sitting on top of five-gallon storage containers and half-buried beneath an avalanche of baby clothes. He thumbed through a coffee-table book about astronomy. He'd always enjoyed studying the heavens.

A puckered-face old lady scrutinized him suspiciously. His friendly greeting only caused her mouth to spill over further.

What's your problem, sour puss?

"Easy, Skid," Owen whispered.

The woman's eyes were slits as she kneaded prejudice into yeasty, narrow-minded dough. Owen breathed an impatient sigh and picked up the astronomy book. Then he saw it... sandwiched between a stack of cloth diapers and a copy of *Baby Names for Dummies*. He grew lightheaded, closed his eyes, and vigorously shook his head. Then he focused on the bold black title printed on the spine of a book:

"*The Journal of Desperate Living*," he whispered.

Best fuckin' book ever wrote, Skid praised.

"Trash," Owen confessed. "You have to admit it." Owen opened the book.

Chapter 13: Somewhere in England.
Larry hated the way fish 'n' chips soaked into newsprint, rendering it virtually unreadable.

"Christ," Owen moaned.

Me too...especially the sports page.

"You going to purchase that, sir?" Sourpuss woman's voice sounded like a squeaky wheel. "This isn't a library."

Owen gazed at the book, then into her sunken eyes. He stared until she turned away.

"Humph," she said as she left. He tossed the book back onto the pile and returned to the bike.

Where to, man? Skid wanted to know.

"Back."

Can you please be a little more specific?

"Meadowland."

Uh-uh, no way. We're through with that shithole.

Owen stomped the kick-start and revved. Mormons circled the old woman and smirked from a safe distance.

"I'm going alone," Owen bellowed. He shifted and pulled

away, raising a finger to the congregation that'd gathered in his name.

Wait up, dick-wad! Skid's bike, always temperamental, had decided to rest longer. His curses faded like the end of a soothing dentist office tune.

***

It's quite a ride from Provo to California, but once you cross into Nevada, time is no longer relative. Owen's '84 Harley was thunder and lightning. He doubted Skid would catch up. Yet before long, he pulled alongside.

Christ, man, what happened to your social skills? Fuck, don't know about you, but I'm horny!

They stopped at the Love Ranch in Nevada. It was buzzing about a famous basketball star that'd recently died there from a drug overdose. Owen chose a tiny Chinese girl, and if he hadn't known better, he could've sworn she enjoyed it. When he met up with Skid afterward, his alter ego bragged about having three girls at once.

Had me a black, Asian, and a Mexican.

"Which was your favorite?"

That Mexican was one hot tamale.

Hmm. Owen thought of Mariana Payán. She'd been hiding behind the black curtain of his past. Now the curtain had lifted, and memories floated in and out of his consciousness.

They crossed into California, downshifting from legal prostitution to vice-squads. In Nevada, you were free to try your luck. In California, good luck even trying.

Everywhere was Hollywood, small towns masquerading as movie sets. People living there were inseparable from the roles they played. Each town mimicked a popular soap opera or television series, and talk shows were found at every checkout stand. It was nearly Christmas, the emptiest time of the year for

Owen.

Skid watched Owen unlatch the dog riding in the sidecar. He was using a bungee cord for safety because Angel loved feeling the wind in his face. It was a small mutt, more like a rat on steroids, the color of dryer lint.

The closer they rode toward the past, the more Owen revealed to Skid. "I remember the day my old man left."

Not that shit again, Skid's tired voice shuffled into Owen's mind.

Owen's childhood memories rushed together like tectonic plates shoving up the Sierra Nevadas. He remembered taking a bubble bath with plastic boats. He wiggled his fingers under a boat, causing it to sway amid the fluff and crinkle of iridescent bubbles. His parents argued in the living room, and he put soapy fingers in his ears and hummed a tune.

"It's a beautiful day in the neighborhood...."

"Who is it this time?" Mother accused.

"...beautiful day for a neighbor...."

"Told you...I worked late!" his father answered.

"...won't you be mine, could you be mine...."

"I called, and you weren't there. Spotted your car at the Sundown!"

"Was at the bar with Frank and —"

"You weren't in the bar. I watched you come out with her."

"Jesus Christ, you're a bitch!"

"Your new little whore!"

There was a slap, followed by sobbing. The front door slammed, and tires screeched. Little Owen's boats took on water, and he watched them disappear, one by one, beneath the white foam. He finished the song in his head as a series of sobs escaped from his throat.

Forget about it, voices counseled. *C'mon, let's get you dried off.*

***

Lodi, Stockton, and Manteca rolled by on his journey to Meadowland. The closer he got, the clearer memories were. Thoughts drifted to a time before a Texas tornado crashed Glenda's house on top of his ego. Her letter'd been paper and ink. Why couldn't he shake loose of it?

Self-righteous bitch with an ax to grind, Skid put in.

Owen wondered if his children ever thought of him. As the wind scrubbed his face, he couldn't help believing they still did. "Meadowland," he mused, glancing at Angel in the sidecar, before adding, "Toto too."

Fuck me, Skid mumbled.

"Almost Christmas, Skid. What're you gonna ask Santa for?"

Twelve-pack, and a twenty-dollar whore.

"Ho, ho, ho," Owen chuckled. He was feeling sprightly as he neared his old stomping grounds.

Owen had always enjoyed watching the children open Christmas presents. It was the one time of the year he nearly felt happy. He knew it was superficial joy, fueled by the giggles of the children and the warmth of the fireplace. Something inside always prevented pure, unfettered joy. After the divorce, Christmas was a dirty bathtub ring. Owen never failed to send the children gift cards, but it was lousy insulation from the bitter chill of guilt.

After the split, Christmas rolled over and gave up the ghost. The chimney was non-negotiable for Santa, the roof too slippery for any business other than adjusting a satellite dish. Christmas was a sad and lonely time for washed-up fathers. Before the holidays, he remembered the mailbox, packed with glossy fliers, filled with flawless children sitting under perfectly coiffed Christmas pines, admiring impeccably wrapped gifts.

In the background, stockings were hung above the hearth.

Dad?

Owen heard a child's voice — or was it Skid up to his old tricks? "Tune it out," he commanded, twisting the throttle.

Daddy?

"Stop."

Will Santa bring us a pup? You think he might?

Owen glanced over to Angel, who wriggled and tucked his front paws beneath his chest. A lump formed in his throat as he thundered through Modesto on the 99.

Dad?

"For the love of Christ...." He spit and wished those painful memories could be expelled as easily. Skid pulled even, wiping his face.

Watch where you're spittin', jerk-bait!

Modesto is Anysmalltown, same as Merced, Reedley, Visalia, and Meadowland. Small towns are filled with people-watchers. Visitors garner tacit stares. Observers gather evidence against them before they go to trial, confident that God's on their side. Fear and ignorance have taken a toll on these folks. Parents vaccinate their children early to protect them from learning tolerance. Owen thundered into a Modesto filling station.

"Get a load'a this freak," piped an attendant to the mechanic on duty.

"Nice bike, though," the mechanic answered, clutching a socket wrench. "Check out the fuckin' dog."

Angel was barking excitedly from the sidecar. Owen filled the tank and slid his ATM card to pay. He walked Angel out to a grassy area, and it squatted to leave a gift. There was a small metal container attached to a light pole with a sign, Doggy Bags. Owen laughed, and they returned to the bike. The attendant reached down to pet the dog. Angel snapped, and the man jerked away. Owen strapped his shorty back on. The Hog started on the first stomp. They rambled through Merced and Madera, broke wind in Fresno, and were suddenly plunged into a thick San Joaquin Valley fog.

It began as wispy spider webs floating lazily above, evolving into dense, wet smoke. Then it closed in like sterile white gauze wrapped around an ugly wound. One moment Owen could see for miles, and seconds later, nothing. He downshifted and crept into the slow lane. It'd been a long while since he navigated the infamous clam chowder fog of the Central San Joaquin Valley. Cars, trucks, and Harleys were merely potatoes, celery stalks, and pearl onions in the deadly soup.

An explosion of glass and metal ahead made Owen quickly pull to the shoulder. "Stay here," he commanded Angel. The dog looked at him questioningly and then twisted to lick its ass.

"Keep an eye on the bikes, Skid." Owen took off his helmet.

Yes, Daddy, Skid answered in Patrick's voice.

Resisting the urge to smash Skid in the mouth with his helmet, Owen stayed close to the guardrail as he neared the source of chaos. Within the damp veil, he came upon a nightmare of twisted steel and flickering headlights. Two semi-trucks had an economy folded between them. A small pickup and an SUV were intimate, and it was difficult to see where one began, and the other ended. Other cars soon joined the heap. Glass sprayed, hubcaps rolled, and one sailed past Owen's ear. The chain reaction formed a crimped, sardonic umbilical cord. Fog absorbed each blow like a veteran boxer, jabbing, dancing, and then without warning, connecting with another jab.

"Jesus fucking Christ!" Owen gasped, stumbling into the wreckage. A totaled Honda Accord still was blasting techno, transforming everything around it into a macabre dance-club of flickering lights. Without sun, everything was a jumble of black and white—Tokyo in Godzilla's aftermath. He heard terrified voices, moans and screams, pleas for help. The smell of smoke and engine fluids permeated the air. He came to a Toyota Corolla, like the one he'd driven before he traded his life in. It was crumpled into an abstract origami shape. A muffled cry came from within. A cardboard Pizza Hut box had somehow been deposited on what was left of the hood.

A child, he thought to himself. Owen sensed the eerie, pulsing glow of CHP turnstile lights as he peered in through the shattered back window and saw movement. "Don't worry. I'll get you out of there, kid!"

The windows were inaccessible. He tugged on a chrome door handle. The door budged and opened a crack. He jammed in his fingers and pulled. The whimpering grew louder, and Owen smelled gas. He searched through the window but couldn't see anyone. Redoubling his effort, he braced a leg on the side of the car and tugged mightily.

Gonna fuck up your back. Skid was there.

The door squawked and squealed against the bent frame. Owen growled. The door gave way, and he flew backward, landing heavily on his back, his head snapping down against the pavement. Before blacking out, he saw a dog looking down at him from the rear car seat, a crust of leftover pizza in its mouth.

"Angel, you motherfucker."

***

Owen was awakened by the smell of piss and Lysol. His head throbbed, and his whole body ached. He was tethered to an intravenous bag.

"Mmm." His voice cracked, and there was an iron taste in his mouth.

A male nurse rushed over and lifted his hand by the wrist. "We're going to be just fine," he nodded, checking Owen's pulse.

"Bike...dog?"

"Fine, just fine. The CHP has them."

"Skid?"

"Pardon?"

Fine and fuckin' dandy. Skid mimicked the nurse's lisp from a chair in the corner of the room.

"When can we leave?"

"Two or three days is my guess," the nurse nodded. "You have a pretty nasty concussion, and your lower back's no picnic either." He shook his head. "Doctors will want to run some tests just to make sure everything's hunky dory."

"What's today?"

"Twenty-third."

"There's somewhere I have to be. Besides, I can't pay for any of this."

"Not to worry, the city of Fresno is footing the bill. After all, you're a hero," he smiled.

"Gimme a break."

"No kidding. That car burst into flames just after you saved that little dog. There's an article in the *Fresno Bee* about it. I'll bring it in tomorrow."

Skid folded his arms and shook his head. *Sounds marvy.*

"Anyway, here's the phone," the nurse pointed. "Press nine first. You can let friends and family know where you are."

"Thanks."

"Okey-dokey, then, if there's anything you need, give us a buzz." He lifted a cord with a red call button.

Shove off, faggot. Skid thought men shouldn't be nurses.

Skid was acting desperate. He hovered by Owen's side

and was frightfully courteous. The change in disposition made Owen queasy, and he quietly plotted his escape from the hospital and from Skid.

"First thing in the morning," he mumbled.

Huh? Skid jolted from a snooze.

"Sure as hell is boring," Owen amended. With a stitch of pain, he reached to click off the light.

Night, Ozzy. Skid's voice was sickly sweet.

"Night."

As he slept, a familiar tune entered his unconscious, a Christmas song rewritten and caroled by his children as he skimmed the *Meadowland Chronicle* from his recliner. They giggled and fell into fits of laughter before mastering themselves enough to sing.

Oh, Rudolph, the brown-nosed reindeer had a very snotty nose, and every time you saw him, he was blowing it on Santa's clothes!

Then he was faced with Patrick. *Why'd you leave, Dad? I hear Mommy crying at night. She doesn't play catch with me. Nobody does.*

"Son, I...."

Patrick was suddenly an adult, with a cigarette dangling from his mouth and dark circles around his eyes. *Kids need a dad — even if it's a fuckup like you.* Patrick smiled, and Owen noticed how bad his teeth looked.

Owen rolled to his side, and the children's voices faded, replaced with an image of Dorothy leaning against the door jam. She sauntered over to his bed, and with quickness possible only in dreams, stripped the tape from the IV on the back of his hand. Owen was powerless as she crimped the tube that carried saline into his body.

Time for a nice little detox, she announced. She lowered the sheet and lifted the green hospital gown. Then she moved his balls out of the way, pushed the tube up his ass, and squeezed the bag. *Hold it*, she wagged a finger and took his cock into her mouth. He tried to hold, yet finally gave up the ship, ejaculating and releasing a torrent of brown rapids at the same moment. In his dream, the sensational combination wasn't entirely disagreeable. *Merry Christmas!* Dorothy howled, pushing the call button and dashing out.

Owen woke up wondering where she'd studied that trick and checked the bedding to make sure no part of the dream was real.

Owen snuck out before daybreak, not waiting for the tile-grout oatmeal and hockey-puck toast to arrive. *Stay any longer, and I'll hang myself in the bathroom*, he thought. He painfully removed the IV, found his clothes, and dressed quietly, while Skid snored in the visitor's chair.

He learned the whereabouts of the CHP substation from a receptionist at the front desk in the lobby. It was an easy stroll from the hospital if you hadn't just been put through a ringer. The air was crisp and clear, but Owen felt as though he'd been trampled by a herd of bargain hunters. He shook aspirin from a green sample bottle and chewed. Each step sent sciatic pain down into his knees, every heartbeat punished his temples.

Pulling himself together as best he could, he communicated his request to the officers on duty. They didn't realize the dog was his and thought it was cool that the man who'd saved it wanted to give it a home. They were friendly, and the lone female cop went into the break room to retrieve Angel. The dog was so happy to see Owen that it peed all over the front of her uniform. Another officer, having just taken a sip of coffee, choked and sprayed on his shoes.

"Shit," she complained, handing the wiggling mass to Owen and glaring at her fellow officers. "Yeah, real funny, guys."

Owen stomped on the kick-start repeatedly, grimacing with each effort. The officers stood back, admiring the beauty of the machine and chuckling at Angel's seating arrangement. The lady officer, not one to hold a grudge, helped Angel into his jacket and Doggles.

An officer asked, "They make car-seats for dogs?" Everyone turned to stare at him. "Just wondering," he shrugged.

The dog's short stay had provided a much-needed diversion for the CHP. Fog season made their job doubly dangerous. As Owen wrestled to start his bike, they explained that they'd tried feeding Angel dry dog food but had much better luck with fast food and jelly donuts. He'd snarled at the lieutenant. They'd bathed the dog in flea shampoo and fitted a red nylon collar around his neck.

Throo, throo, throo, the Harley repeated, resulting in not so much as a smoky fart. Then, with a final out-of-breath lunge, the Harley blasted a bluish cloud into the cold air. Owen patted Angel and addressed the officers.

"Thanks for taking such good care of the dog," he said as the bike settled into a patented cadence.

"No problem."

"Our pleasure, heh, heh, heh."

"Some dog," put in the lady officer.

Owen smiled, lowered his head, and thought of the desperate journey that lay ahead. He scratched Angel's ears and then looked up at the officers. "Was wondering...any way you could look after him 'til after Christmas?" The officers glanced furtively at each other. "Where I'm headed, there's no place for a dog. I'll come back for him in a few days."

The lady officer nodded, and the others followed with shrugs. "Hell," she said, "Maybe we can teach him to whiz on fire hydrants instead of khaki."

"Lieutenant'll be thrilled," said another.

"Really appreciate it." Owen unhooked the bungee and lifted the dog to his face. "Have to do this alone," he explained to Angel with a reassuring hug.

"What'er you gonna name him?" Her badge directed the early morning sun into Owen's eyes.

"Angel." He handed her the squirming dog, and he promptly peed again.

"God*damn* it!" she yelled, "What's he got against lady cops?"

***

It was Christmas Eve as Owen thundered off. Fresno's an hour and a half northeast of Meadowland unless you own a Harley and drive a bit over the limit.

"Angel'll be fine," Owen reassured himself. "Found him in a dumpster. What's a little time with the fuzz?"

Where you think you're goin'? Skid pulled alongside, and his mood was worse than ever.

Owen twisted the throttle, but Skid hung with him.

Got an attitude problem, boy.

Owen rolled his neck and clenched his teeth.

Left me alone with that fag.

Owen's Hog sounded like an elephant farting in a mud puddle. Skid pulled even.

Ought'a know by now, you can't scratch me off like you did your wife and kids.

For a brief moment, Owen thought of kicking Skid off his bike as he'd seen in a movie once.

Where we goin'? LA? Mexico? Ain't been down ol' Mexico in a coon's age. Remember Cabo?

"Know damn well where I'm headed, and if you don't like

it, go fuck yourself!" Owen shouted.

Skid was speechless the rest of the way.

It was mid-morning when they made Meadowland. Owen stopped at a filling station to slop the Hog and to search for Nancy's married name in a pay-booth telephone book.

Johnson Albert, Johnson Atlee, Johnson Cleophus…. "Cleophus?" muttered Owen. Johnson Brandi, Johnson, Johnson, and Johnson. He couldn't remember the husband's first name. Dick, Peter, Jack, hell, they all fit.

Fuck it, let's go find some Mexican cooch, Skid suggested.

Owen tore out the Johnson page and bought a Meadowland map inside the filling station. Johnson, Albert, didn't ring a bell, but Al sounded like an accountant's name.

Meadowland had changed. A Walmart Superstore had usurped prime farmland. New residential subdivisions had erupted like psoriasis, and traffic was busier than he remembered. He wondered what Main Street looked like now if Big Ed's was still in business. He cruised by the old house, now repainted, with energy-efficient windows and an American flag jutting limply from a sconce at the front doorway. A wooden sign above the address proclaimed, The Payne Family.

At dusk, Owen parked across from the Ted Johnson house. The air was bitterly cold and crept into his joints. He chewed aspirin and felt his stomach burning. Skid blew heavily into his balled fists. A sign posted on the sidewalk just down the street said This is a Neighborhood Watch Area. Already several faces were staring out of windows.

The Johnson house was a cozy two-story, dripping with Christmas lights, a wreath snuggled against the front door and "Born is the King" chirping from somewhere. Owen knew better. Christ was born on April Fools. He suddenly craved pizza. Angel's eating habits were growing on him.

In the driveway was a silver Lexus with a *NANSLEX* license plate. Next to it was a 1982 Pontiac Firebird, purchased by Patrick from Sam, the garbage man. Hugging the curb was an aerodynamic Toyota mini-van, personalized with *KIDRIDE4*.

"Tracy's?" Owen asked aloud, "I'm a granddad?" A shiver coursed through him, and he rubbed his hands together. *What now?* he thought to himself.

Skid answered. *Knock the door and say, Merry Christmas, Daddy's home!*

Owen puffed into his hands as Skid continued.

They'd take one look and give you directions to the nearest homeless shelter.

Owen crossed his arms and rubbed his shoulders. He hung his head and bit his lip, hating the words yet powerless to stop them.

"Maybe not. Maybe they'd still love me," he whispered hoarsely.

March right up.

A police sedan cruised past and pulled to the curb in front of the bike.

Look Oz, hate to burst your bubble, but face it — smokin' ain't the Marlboro man, fightin' ain't Bruce Lee, and fuckin' ain't Sharon Stone. There's no goin' back to Kansas in a fuckin' balloon.

A stiff, plastic-looking officer stepped out of the cruiser and cautiously approached. Owen stared at the policeman's neck, straining the top button of his starched shirt.

"Sir, you having problems with your bike?"

"No." Owen saw small faces pressed against the front windows of the Johnson house, drawn by the flashing red, white, and blue turnstiles.

"Gonna have to ask you to move on, sir."

Owen squinted to see the children more clearly.

"Sir?" repeated the policeman sternly.

Little faces in the window were watching. Hot breath was fogging the glass with curiosity, and then a hand led them away.

"Sir, do you understand what I'm asking you to do?"

"I...." He looked down, seeing breath storming from his mouth and then fading.

"Sir?"

"Yeah, yeah, I get you."

The policeman returned to his car and waited. Monotone voices cackled on his CB.

"Move on where? No place to go," he whispered softly. He nodded toward the Johnson house. "My kids...."

The policeman climbed out again, stood by the cruiser, and hooked thumbs into his squeaking utility belt. Owen stomped, twisted, and clicked into first. He puttered down the street and hooked a U-turn, slowing to look once more at the Johnson house. A young boy had his face pressed to the glass, and he was waving. Owen pursed his lips and turned away.

Sorry, man. Why you think I brought you here? Had to see for yourself.

Owen rolled onto Main Street and let the thunder of the Harley drown out the clamor in his heart as it shattered into a million fragments. The officer escorted him all the way to the on-ramp.

***

Angel licked him with a garlic-flavored tongue. Owen thanked the officers, strapped the dog in, and took Freeway 99 North to find a cheap motel. Late that night at an Easy 8, ghosts leaped from his dreams like a vengeful jack-in-the-box. Nancy squawked like a crow, *Haw-haw-haw*, replaced by Patrick, who smiled and said, *Foo-foo*. Then Tracy taunted him in a singsong voice, *You'll never know your grandkids.* Finally, it was Glenda's turn, her lips moving wordlessly. *One sorry sonofabuck.*

Owen awakened before sunrise, weary and depressed. Angel was curled up asleep next to him. He turned on the television and surfed for five minutes before shutting it off. He took a long shower, and then, around eleven, they rode in search of a double Christmas cheeseburger. It was just the two of them. Skid had stayed in Meadowland.

Owen hoped he'd bump into Dorothy. Perhaps they'd settle down together. She could study up in Seattle, where steady rains kept the mind evergreen. "Yeah, maybe Seattle." It felt good on his tongue. *Maybe I'll renew my teaching credentials.*

There're lots of shacks claiming to serve the best cheeseburger. Just north of Fresno, there's a joint across the street from a neglected junior high school. While you eat, you can watch kids shoot hoops with scuffed, herniated basketballs on asphalt courts. Weather-blistered backboards are hung with iron rims and torn metal nets. Owen hated metal nets. Even when you shot the eye out of the basket, it clinked like loose change in a pair of sagging Dickies.

The burger joint didn't have a sign claiming to be the best of anything, just a piece of cardboard with *GOOD FOOD* scrawled in permanent black marker. As soon as he sank his teeth into it, he realized it was the best cheeseburger he'd ever tasted. The timid Mexican cook watched as he tore into it like a tiger shark. Owen pointed to what remained and gave thumbs up. The chef nodded and smiled, knowing he didn't need fancy logos to make a top-notch burger on Christmas Day—just quality ingredients and the secret sauce, love.

Owen bought Angel one too. The white plastic placa-scarred picnic table was filthy, so he sat Angel on the bike in front of him. The dog wolfed everything but the pickles and then glared up as if to say, *Where the hell're my curly fries?*

Across the street, a war raged. Latino teens battled under the boards, three to a team, jungle ball, no crybabies allowed. Owen fingered the last quarter-moon of his sandwich as he watched. Angel saw an opening and snatched it.

"Think that's funny?" he admonished. Angel cocked his head, waiting for a caramel sundae.

An argument broke out on the asphalt forum. Two opposing warriors squared off. One held a hand over his eye and cursed in Spanish. The other stood, fists on hips, nodding his head.

"Got checked, homes," the aggressor taunted.

"*Chinga tu madre!*" the damaged youth spat.

"*Qué? Dímelo cara a cara*, Angelito!"

The kid walked away, turning to give him the finger.

Angel's ears perked up when he heard his name called.

"Lop-eared muthufuckuh! You all *woof!*"

"*No le saques, cabrón!*"

The kid stopped at the edge of the street.

"Fuck you, bitch!" He raised a finger again and grabbed at his crotch. "Bite this!"

The other youth jogged toward him and then slowed to a menacing stalk as the other players watched with delight.

"Ven, fucker!" he challenged, "Let's see what you got, Angel!"

The dog was in the street before Owen could react. A blue lowered Honda Civic, sub-woofers buzzing with hip-hop, struck him. Angel rolled to a stop next to the two boys who were squared off.

"*Híjole!*" said one of the boys.

"*Ay, que la chingada,*" said the other.

The driver stopped, powered down a window, and spilled beer from a forty-ounce bottle onto the road, "One for the homies!" He laughed and cruised away.

Owen crouched next to Angel until the ragged breathing stopped. The boys backed away, shook their heads, and returned to the court. Jungle ball resumed, just as life always does in one form or other. He left the dog where it lay and returned to the Harley. The world's greatest burger chef shook his head sadly and turned away. Owen straddled the bike, tilted his face to the sky, and closed his eyes.

The burger chef always soaked his frying pans before he scrubbed them. The bubbles crinkled as he set one in a sink filled with soapy hot water. It floated a few seconds before sinking and leaving an oil slick.

As Owen took the on-ramp, a solitary tear blew to the side of his temple and was immediately swallowed by a cold wind.

CHAPTER 6
Owen Becomes the Voices

"Whatever is not commonly seen is condemned as alien." —
Iris Chang —

Fresno's Knob Hill, Visalia's Badger Hill, and the Pinnacle's development in Meadowland share one thing in common. They're oversized, hilltop homes with large picture windows that allow the upper crust to thumb noses on humanity below. Owen dodged around an unoccupied guard station and eased his bike up the steep, curvy private access road to the top of Knob Hill. If anything deserved the right to turn its exhaust pipes toward Fresno, it was the Harley.

He parked his iron horse beneath an experienced oak tree and sat there, watching the sun peek over the top of the Sierra Nevadas. He likened the scene to the cover of his defunct book, *The Journal of Desperate Living*.

Owen wondered if a yuppie teen would find the bike, the pink slip, and the simple note: Bike's yours, finder's keepers. Take care of it, and remember, the best, no less, or die like the rest.

He imagined the kid thundering off to become something more than a crooked lawyer, corporate whore or, God help us all, another Trump. He probed the saddlebags for his stash and carefully rolled a final doobie. He bathed in the gathering light, gazing down the hillside and slowly letting out a plume of smoke, which performed a ballet in the fresh morning air. Owen was bone-weary. The only voice left in his head was his, and it didn't carry much weight.

A swarm of mosquitos flew through the smoke, adding more buzz. Owen imagined his essence joining the swarm, entering the smoke, and bringing it to life. Lights flicked on in a few homes. Owen's mind cracked open like the front hatch of a '68 Beetle. Leaving the remainder of his stash in the saddlebag, he drifted down the hill along with his final smoky exhalation.

***

Owen was a speck at the bottom of the hill when a young lady, fresh as a new dandelion, cautiously approached the bike and stroked the soft leather saddlebags. The machine popped as it cooled, and the chrome sparkled in her eyes. She was enjoying her thirteenth winter, and the world was her oyster. Unlike most teens, she was an early riser. She felt that hopes and dreams had a better shot of lasting in the early morning before the sun dried them up.

The bike was beneath the oak where she'd shared her first real kiss with Bobby, who used to live just up the road but had moved to San Francisco. Cautiously she approached, half expecting a rough biker to jump out and manhandle her. She peeked into the sidecar. Lying at the bottom was a small leather jacket and a pair of Doggles.

Emboldened by the quietude of the morning, she unbuckled a saddlebag and discovered a sizable baggy of pot. She knew friends at school that'd tried. Hurriedly she stuffed the baggy into her jacket, frisked the other side, and found the title document. Below, the central San Joaquin Valley woke up to a fresh pot of Farmers Brothers coffee.

Later that afternoon, she smoked with her best friend. It took a few attempts to figure out how to roll a cigarette. Finally, they managed to make something that was smokeable. Taking turns on it, they giggled and discussed life's pressing issue: the cutest guy at school, the biggest sleaze, and who was a complete dweeb. They placed bets as to which of them would lose their cherry first. As they drew down on the doobie, they hungered for truth and were starving by lunchtime.

***

Owen picked up a discarded *Fresno Bee* and read as he slowly he drifted down the steep embankment and reached the bottom of the hill. Thoughts and voices filled his head. Scenarios covered the canvas of his mind with images that were both real and imaginary. A steady narrative kept him company. Often he heard his own voice within the steady chatter, especially when he was talking aloud to himself. It was a strong, surly voice. He was sure he'd heard the voice before, yet couldn't quite put his finger on where. It was a steady diatribe of fantastic ideas and philosophical meanderings, occasionally joined and rebutted by others.

"I'll cut to the chase. I'm an alien, and I'm going to kill myself. Checkout's long overdue. The prize inside this Cracker Jack world isn't worth the cost of the candy. It's my greatest hope that this telling will scratch your mind, infect it with some measure of understanding. Humans are more likely to listen to strangers because you're strangers to yourselves.

There's a flickering fly-fart moment just before a raindrop reaches pay-dirt, touching both earth and sky. As an accidental tourist on your planet, I exist in that moment. Looking for the big picture gets in the way of little snapshots. Here's an equation for you to chew on: 1 puddle +1 puddle = 1 big mess.

Science attempts to explain mystery. Religion tells you not to question it. More math: 1-1=emptiness. Scottish children understand the importance of mystery. If the Loch Ness Monster was captured and documented, tourism would dry up, childish innocence and curiosity would submerge deep into the brackish waters, and the Scots would forfeit something far more vital than tourist revenue. *Shine.*

SHINE. There's a word that deserves to be served hot with steaming bold letters!

In Spanish, it's written, *brillar*; Italian, *lucidare*; عمل in Arabic; and 亮 in Chinese. Shine is a spicy salsa that separates humans from gnats. It's so important that, herein, it will be fronted with a capital. Shine phosphoresces from curious children climbing trees or turning over rocks, lovers in a sunset meadow reaching for the stars. It emanates from those who are capable of harnessing positive energy to share with others. Shine makes you smile at toddlers taking their first chaotic steps. It brings tears to aged eyes as they flip through old photographs that prove they were once young. Shine is comforting. Forget nuclear subatomic particles. Shine's is the equivalent of Solar power. That's the ticket.

Shine inspires parents to lie about Santa Claus and how babies are made because you *want* your children to cling to innocence. When you become adults, you forget how to play. Through children, you bathe vicariously in the exuberance of youth.

Nearly everyone on your planet possesses a varying degree of Shine. Recently, however, Shine is suffering from a new ice age. Keep in mind that drop of water, earth and sky. Listen carefully to my tale, especially if you live in the Emerald City of Meadowland.

Shine has made my survival on Earth feasible. It's too complex to explain how, so I will dumb it down:

I went for a bike ride without telling my parents and got hopelessly lost. Here I am with two flat tires and no patch-kit in sight. You're probably dying to know what I look like in natural form. If you could see me, you'd complain, 'I've waited my entire life for ET, and this is what I get?' I can easily be mistaken for dust particles or mosquitos floating in a shaft of morning sunlight.

Getting here was fast and easy because my kind is composed mostly of energy. We use dark matter to fuel our travels, combined with other elements currently unavailable on your planet. It's an efficient, zero-emission way to bum around. But even if I could return home, Shine holds me prisoner. It's powerful and highly addictive.

Coming into contact with human Shine is akin to having a mindgasm. You won't find that in your Funk and Wagnall. Bathing my essence with positive neutrons literally makes my particles dance with joy. In other words, it ain't chopped liver. There's a bar just north of my universe that serves a costly concoction that packs a similar wallop. Barkeeps call it a Solar Flare, and I'm willing to bet that the main ingredient is an import from Earth. Cosmic corporations thrive in every corner of the universe, capitalists trafficking alien products, trinkets collected from billions of other life-supporting planets. Now you know what happened to Jimmy Hoffa. But I'm no better than those corporate thieves. Bartenders serve others. I serve only me.

I entered Earth's atmosphere without a green card and skidded to a stop on a hilltop just outside of Fresno, California.

Ever suffered from a flu that makes you want to crawl into a landfill to die? That's how I felt after I arrived on Earth. My tank was nearly empty. To save energy, I abandoned my bike on that hill in Fresno and started drifting.

Eventually, I floated my way into town, enjoying the primitive wonders of your world, despite growing weaker with each translucent step. Traffic noise, music, chatter, flesh, and technology rushed in all directions, replacing the primordial morning silence of Knob Hill. I rested in a place where apartments are the color of mud, the siding blemished with stylized letters and Roman numerals, sprayed blue or red. I've seen these markings almost everywhere — on overpasses and concrete walls surrounding subdivisions. It's the work of angry, disenfranchised youth with most of the Shine beaten out of them. In this Fresno barrio, I experienced my first contact with Shine. The boy's name was Hector Hernández.

Hector was crouched on a sidewalk, studying ants that were carrying crumbs, leaf bits, and conquered insects to their subterranean condos. Hector Hernández Shined. All humans have an aura surrounding the body, yet Shine is distinctive, thicker and brighter, a colorful kite flying higher than the rest.

There were other kids out playing, parents working in yards, fathers fixing cars in driveways, and sipping beer, yet none glowed like Hector. The brilliance he exuded made him larger-than-life. I was starving, and his energy was so inviting that I joined within him. We were dizzy for a moment, resting our head on the hot sidewalk until it passed.

"*Me lleva la chingada,*" were our first words together. We were flooded with so much information it took a while to adjust. My own thoughts crashed into Hector's. The sun's brightness was intense, yet the euphoria of sharing human Shine made it tolerable. Together we offered a Popsicle-stick to an ant, letting go before it clamped tiny jaws to our finger.

"*Pendejo*!" Was shouted from the front door. "Papa says to get your lazy ass inside." Hector's stepbrother made his finger into a pistol and pointed. "Pow." After delivering the message, he kicked a mangy cat lying on the doorstep and went back inside. Our throat tightened, and our pulse raced. We hoped the stepfather wasn't drunk. We got hurt when he'd been drinking. Our heart was ready to leap out of our dirty T-shirt.

The inside of the house was shadowy, and Hector's mother ironed clothes in the small living room. Our half-sister sat in a highchair, face streaked with mashed vegetables. Stepfather leaned against the kitchen counter, clicking the aluminum sides of a beer can. He was wearing a sleeveless T-shirt, arms tattooed with his sordid history, a snake eating an eagle, a naked woman licking a .45 automatic, Roman numerals on his neck, and three dots between the thumb and forefinger.

"God*damn*," he began. "What do we ask you to do around here? Jack shit! Not a fuckin' thing!"

"Don't cuss around the baby," the mother admonished.

"Fu-u-u-uck." He belched the word.

Hector's thoughts were habaneros. Anxiety quickly switched to anger. I shared his thoughts and feelings vicariously yet had no control over them. *If our real father was here...*, we were thinking, but we didn't remember much about him, so the image faded.

"Your room's a pigsty." The stepfather let out another prolonged belch.

"Ay, cochino," the mother waved her hand.

"Get your ass in there and clean up. Playtime's over." He crushed the can for emphasis. "Don't come out 'til I say."

The mother glanced up and returned glumly to her ironing. She'd forgotten how to protect us.

"Goal!" the television blared. Hector's stepbrother pumped his fist. A startled Chihuahua left his side and jogged to the sliding glass back door to be let out.

We went to our tiny room with its cracked window, the stained mattresses on the floor. A room we shared with the stepbrother, whose bed was unmade, his dirty clothes scattered all over the floor. Adorning the walls were the stepbrother's role models—50-Cent, Pacino's Scarface, and a blonde whose main assets were clearly visible beneath tiny strips of a leopard print. Hector wasn't allowed to post heroes even if he had any.

"When Papa comes back, he's gonna fuck you up," we growled through clenched teeth as our hands smoothed the top sheet on the stepbrother's mattress. Imagination transformed our father from the deserter he was into a savior, coming to the rescue and returning us to Mexico, where we'd live happily ever after.

I tried to communicate, but Hector was unable to decode the odd buzzing I produced in his head.

An argument ensued in the kitchen, the stepfather bellowing, "You only got a twelve-pack?"

The baby wailed. "*Por favor*, Manuel, you're upsetting her."

"Shit, let'er get used to it. That's what life is, a fuckin' scream."

In the middle of this, I was wondering why Hector Hernández Shined. Outside there were kids with loving parents and friends to play with, but none radiated like this Mexican immigrant boy.

We reached under his mattress to take out a sketchpad, sandwiched between issues of *Low-Rider* magazine. We flipped to a work in progress. The art reflected Hector's life—two twisted skeletons dancing a Mephisto Waltz, sharing the page with demons. There was an eye with tears dripping into a river of blood filled with angry sharks and an ear with a dick poking out of it. There were crosses, daggers, and filthy Spanish words, all wrestling together. At the bottom corner of the page was a crumpled beer can with a label proclaiming Only the Finest Ingredients.

The stepfather was coming. The door flew open, and he stood there with yellow stains rimming his T-shirt. Hector swallowed hard. The baby was still crying, and the mother cooed a Mexican lullaby.

"Don't maddog me, *cabroncito*!" he shouted.

"Fuck you, *pinche borracho*!" Hector's voice rose above it all—the metallic buzz of the refrigerator, the screaming baby, the senseless blare of television. Above the sound of a lawnmower and the incessant drone of hip-hop. Hector's voice was a mixture of pride, rage, and desperation. His knuckles were white against the sketchpad, nearly wringing the images to the floor. We trembled with loathing for this man who had replaced our dead-beat father.

Hector was frozen with rage, and I was swamped with emotions never experienced before, so much escaping all at once. Hector tucked his fear behind brown eyes and knotted cheeks.

"*Hijo de la, chingada*!" Stepfather raised his hand. We closed our eyes, and I left Hector before the hand descended.

Again, I wondered, *Why does Hector Hernández Shine?*

***

The next few months, I enjoyed excellent fuel economy with each pirated tank of Shine. I cruised your planet in the snap of a beer can. Reading from castoff newspapers, I found places of interest depending on the headlines. One excursion took me to a wedding party in Afghanistan. A seven-year-old boy was basking in the joy of having almost everyone he knew and loved beneath one roof.

"Son, I left the camera in the car. Would you please get it?" His father handed him the key.

He quickly obeyed, cautiously crossing the street, finding the camera, and turning to cross the street again. A massive explosion knocked him off his feet. Columns of flame, smoke, and dust filled the air. Deafened by the blast, the boy couldn't hear his own screams. Finally, he wobbled to his feet, only to find that his whole world was obliterated.

Later, he learned that a North American smart bomb had missed its intended target by three miles.

"I will avenge," said the Afghan son, whose hearing never fully recovered.

The following day I journeyed to the White House. It was as though the entire premises had been sprayed with a product designed to kill Shine at the root. It was an echoing oligarchy of divisive marble-tiled hallways, leading nowhere.

Along the Sudan-Chad border, Sudanese-backed Janjaweed soldiers rode into a small village on horseback. They murdered fifty villagers and raped able-bodied women. Twelve soldiers broke into a mud house where a mother and daughter lived. The mother pleaded with them to spare the girl, who hadn't yet completed her eleventh spring. They cackled, boiled a pot of tea, and forced the mother to watch as they took turns with the child, twenty-six times.

Notice how narrow and insensitive numbers can be? Humans thrive on statistics. Twenty-six divided by twelve. Someone got more than his share. That's how it works. Two of the attackers were child-soldiers, even younger than the girl. When she lost consciousness, the soldiers sodomized the mother, using leftover oil from a frying pan. Then they set fire to the house. The mother managed to crawl to her daughter and put an arm around her. For a moment, the combination of their remaining Shine blazed like the sun before fading like dusk.

Wherever I traveled, there was poverty and injustice. I truly wished for the existence of a just God, yet clearly, the rewards went to the spoilers. God, Santa Claus, Easter Bunny, Allah, the Tooth Fairy, Sasquatch, Jesus and his twelve…when will you ever learn? Yet, to be fair, I also discovered wonders in your world.

A Chinese grandfather was fishing Nanbei Lake with his eight-year-old granddaughter. He said she reminded him of her mother at that age. The little girl got a nibble, a bite, and hooked a small fish. As she joyfully pulled in the line hand-over-hand, I saw mist develop in the old man's eyes. The line went slack when the fish worked itself free, and he patiently helped her bait the hook again.

I found several heroes reminiscent of Mother Theresa, Gandhi, Mandela, Cesar Chavez, and Martin Luther King. There was Malala Yousafzai, who was shot in the head by Taliban gunmen for speaking out for the right of girls to be educated. Even when my thirst for Shine was at its peak, I never leeched off heroes. They're an endangered species.

I never witnessed a Boy Scout helping an old lady across the street, but I watched a Palestinian father standing his ground in front of an Israeli bulldozer. His thirteen-year-old son used all his strength to push him out of the way. As the blade crashed through their home, the boy shouted, "Someday, we will replace this house, but we can never replace you!"

For every human being that Shines to create a better world, there are thousands exploiting it. By my calculations, capitalism will soon dissolve the final vestiges of Shine. As always on your earth, it's boom or bust.

I've noticed how the word love is used. Sometimes it feels

like a cool breeze, yet most of the time, it's nothing but hot wind. Love is a main ingredient in Shine, yet there're countless efforts in your world to synthesize it. Money and power are manufactured to taste like love, yet it ends up as empty calories. John Lennon said it best—love is the answer. The cure for your ailing world is right under your beak.

Floating north on California Freeway 99, just north of Bakersfield, I spied a speeding blue '64 Mustang zigzagging in and out of traffic. I pulled in close to the rear bumper to observe the driver. She was an attractive, middle-aged woman. Her hands were white-knuckled around the wheel, and an unfiltered Camel was trapped between her lips. The convertible top was down, and her medium-length brown hair whipped around the headrest. She Shined as Hector had. My fuel light was on, so I hitched a ride within this mysterious blazing woman.

Strange sensations assailed me as I settled in—a strong feeling of nausea. Something was amiss. Her Shine satisfied my energy needs, but the queasiness remained and worsened. Our pain sharpened, and we reached into her purse to find pills. She shook some into her mouth.

"Jesus Christ." Her voice quivered with bitterness.

With the pedal to the metal, the wind lifted her test results from the back seat and deposited them on a weedy shoulder of the freeway next to a decaying sparrow. We thought of her sons. The older brother, Justin, was at a continuation high school, on probation for shoplifting. His thirteen-year-old brother, Chad, was proud of him. Their father was a stonewashed memory.

Hostility, fear, and guilt stirred our insides, yet she Shined. We were hungry, but eating always made the queasiness worse. Our eyes glanced to the rearview mirror.

"Goddammit!" we yelled into the wind. A CHP was chasing us, and his toys were winking, blinking, and whinnying. We let off on the gas and eased to the shoulder next to sloughed-off tire retreads, tears of glass, cigarette butts, a rusted tailpipe, a child's tennis shoe, a and fast-food bag with golden arches on the front.

Smokey barked license plate information to the dispatcher before stepping out of the patrol car. Our belly was filled with a red tide. The doctor promised that the pills would help…to take them on a full stomach. We wanted to cry, scream, laugh, and die all in the same moment. An SUV whizzed by with a faded bumper sticker in the shape of a yellow ribbon, Support Our Troops. He gave the officer an appreciative thumbs-up for catching the speeder.

A dispatcher responded to the officer's inquiry, and soon his boots were crunching toward us. Positioning himself at the passenger side of the car, he guardedly peered in.

"Ma'am," he said in a monotone. "Need to see your driver's license, registration, and proof of insurance."

We focused on the center of the wheel, our personal mandala.

"'Ma'am?" he repeated.

We almost heard his teeth grinding. An aluminum clipboard shielded his waist, and his thumb unsnapped the holster. He'd been trained — better safe than sorry. Tearing our eyes away from the wheel, we glared at him.

"Why?"

He shook his head, incredulously. "Ma'am, I have you clocked on radar at *twice* the speed limit."

Our eyes narrowed, admiring the leather pouches on his squeaking belt. "Gotta Batarang in there?"

"Please step out of the vehicle," he answered, dispensing with the formalities.

Dark clouds crashed together, and we thundered. His

Kevlar vest was useless, and his mirrored sunglasses didn't protect from the glare of her words.

"Listen up, Barney. I just spent three days at UCLA Medical Center, getting X-rayed, sonographed, echographed, Spirographed, you name it. I've been prodded, poked, sampled—"

"Ma'am," the officer interrupted. "Please step—"

"Lemme finish!" She lifted a hand. A sob escaped, and she swallowed it down. "I need to finish, please...I need to."

Something in the texture of her voice made the officer lift his hand away from his weapon. But he fingered his remote and prepared to request backup.

"You can throw me in the brig, the hoosegow, the joint, whatever the hell you call it these days, just let me finish." The officer listened as she swallowed and continued. "Dr. Dipstick informed me I'm dying of some cancer I can't even pronounce. They gave me these." We shook the pills in the officer's face, and another sob escaped.

"Ma'am, I still have to ask you—"

"So, as far as I'm concerned," we gulped for air, "You can take a flying fuck at a rollin' donut." We were trembling, nose running, our body ached, and we felt like puking.

She saw her reflection in his mirrored sunglasses.

He cleared his throat and stared at the ground. There was a penny there, and it was nearly worthless. After a moment, he looked up and shook his head. "Where you headed?"

"Delano," we managed.

"Think you can slow it down?"

We nodded weakly. "Yes, sir."

"Good. I'm really sorry about your troubles."

"Thanks," we whispered.

"Still need to see your papers—protocol and all that."

We handed him what he wanted, and he saw her name. "Victoria. My ex-wife's name." A corner of his mouth lifted for a brief moment. He handed the papers back, lifted his remote, and told dispatch he was clear. "Slow it down, Victoria," he said. "Think of the others on the road."

She nodded. "Okay."

The officer returned to his car. "Rollin' donut, have to remember that one." He turned off the toys and pulled slowly back onto the 99.

We got off at the next exit and parked at the entrance to the Kern County Waste Management Site. Bulldozers were working, covering refuse and belching plumes of diesel smoke into the air

Some garbage can't be covered, we were thinking. Desperately I tried injecting comforting thoughts, but wilted walls of cotton absorbed them. We marveled at the sloping man-made banks of dirt covering so much waste. There were candy wrappers from broken diets, unfinished letters of apology, dirty magazines, and somewhere, breaking the surface with a plastic arm or leg, deserted Barbies.

Victoria had played with Barbies when she was a child. Barbie kissed the boy sitting in front of her in first grade. He ratted her out, and Barbie was sentenced to solitary in the teacher's desk, joining slingshots, squirt guns, and a rubber tarantula.

Barbie was a cheerleader, senior class president, and drove a sports car without a license, registration, or proof of insurance. She didn't have to wear a seatbelt. Barbie was blonde, blue-eyed, and when she lost her head, it snapped back on. She only aged when a spiteful little brother threw her on the roof, where the sun bleached her tan and turned her perfectly coifed hair to dust.

Barbie never had cancer, couldn't get pregnant, and never had a slap-dick husband ditch her when things got rough, we were thinking. *Never a single mom with troubled boys, never lifted a lazy finger to help out.* She lived in a synthetic utopia with a permanent smile and ocean-blue eyes that never closed for sleep, sex, or death.

Our thoughts were clear and precious, and I wanted to hug her. Humans who Shine brightly are creative thinkers, and poetic ideas comfort them like an old family quilt. We imagined that in ten thousand years, archeologists would discover fossil Barbies. What would they make of it? No nipples or reproductive organs, just smooth plastic.

We lit a cigarette and gave voice to our final thoughts regarding Barbie. "Bitch, if you're out there, listen up! My punk brother used to take your clothes off, but he never learned a goddamned thing." Laughter dissolved into weeping, and we pounded fists on the steering wheel. "Sonofabitch!" We screamed at the sky. Then we fired up the Mustang and peeled out of there. Once on the freeway, we kept our speed at sixty-five for a while.

She determined, *When I get home, I'm gonna have a long talk with those boys. However long Dr. Slapdick gives me'll just have to do.* We accelerated to ninety. "Gonna give'em a big hug. Can't remember the last time." She let out a trail of smoke from a cigarette. The Mustang was at warp factor nine, and the steering was getting wobbly. Then she backed off out of respect for the compassionate CHP.

I got out before the Delano off-ramp, but not before returning her Shine to her. She'd need every drop for the coming weeks.

Human Shine's highly addictive. The urge to take a great big gulp and try for home was tempting. The monster under the bed, that was me. Comparably, Donald Trump is Prince Charles wishing he could be Camilla Parker Bowel's tampon.

***

I've spent lazy hours studying Hollywood war films—chaos and mayhem romanticized, romance bastardized into chaos and mayhem. In reality, modern warfare looks more like a video game, where lives are erased by joystick. Death is nothing more than a blip disappearing from a laptop. You can thank the Pentagon for cellphones, PCs, GPS, Xbox, laser pointers, and lots of other toys. World governments are well versed in the stratagem: Fear + Ignorance = Control. They have you divided and conquered, and you didn't feel a thing, did you?

On your planet, I've witnessed true horror, and it's right in front of your schnoz.

I drifted toward the dilapidated Evergreen Apartments in Meadowland, a ghetto owned by a slumlord posing as a developer. Evergreen used to be a decent place to grow a family. Along came a building boom. Legoland neighborhoods popped up everywhere, and before you knew it, Evergreen was where you were more likely to find a needle on the ground than a penny.

In the resident parking lot, I saw a beat up '82 Firebird, and something stirred within me. For a moment, I was consumed by darkness, the closest I've ever come to fainting on Earth. I attributed it to my need for a Shine fix. The feeling faded, and I refocused on a weedy flowerbed.

On the front door of apartment ninety-six, a wooden plaque proclaimed Home is Where You Hang Your Hat. In the living room, an elderly woman sat in a green rocker watching television. She hugged a family portrait in her arms as a game show host asked contestants to guess the price of a microwave. Her eyes lived deep within her skull, and they were dry except for a solitary drop of Shine gathered at the corner of a tear duct. Her mouth curved down, and a juice glass rested on an aluminum TV tray, half-filled with cheap red wine.

I explored the rest of the tiny one-room. The kitchen was Mother Hubbard bare—only an oatmeal tin, rubbery celery stalks, a dented can of Campbell's Chunky Minestrone, and an empty bottle of Two-Buck Chuck merlot. Photos of children dotted the walls. On her lap was a faded black-and-white portrait of her dead husband wearing a soldier's uniform.

The bed was unmade, and clothes littered the floor. As I checked out the filthy bathroom, she made a mewing lost-kitten sound that filled me with dread. I should've left immediately, but curiosity kept me tethered there. She mewed again. *What is that sound*? I wondered. It reminded me of something. Then I knew—it was the sound of a lonely soul trying to escape.

For a moment, the old woman revived. She ceased rocking and reached up slowly to wipe away the last drop of Shine with a palsied hand. It beaded on the tip of a finger, glowing, and then dripped silently to the picture glass in her lap. She touched the face in the portrait, leaned her head back, and closed her eyes. Slowly her fingers opened, and an empty prescription bottle fell to the carpet.

An unfocused blur of energy darted from her mouth, pin-balled through the living room, hovered on a cosmic thermal, and charged through the roof. I tried to follow, but it was too swift. The eggshell had broken. Perhaps her yolk spilled into another frying pan. Essence moves without leaving a forwarding address. She reminded me that nothing lasts forever, and with time, none of us are ever remembered.

As I left, an ambulance arrived, but it wasn't for her. A young man was brought down on a stretcher from an upstairs apartment.

"This kid gotta name?" A paramedic asked the onlookers.

A sobbing woman stepped forward.

"Patrick," she said. "Is he gonna be all right? He's gonna be okay, isn't he?"

"What was he using?" asked the paramedic.

"I don't know," she lied. She was a young lady with a face lined with premature wrinkles. I took a moment to read her thoughts...*Flush the meth before the police start snooping*.

The young man's eggshell had broken too, yet nothing lifted out from his body. I was overcome by an overwhelming urge to enter, to soothe him with kind words, to let him know someone cared, but I knew instinctively that entering the dead was a bad idea.

Something stabbed at my subconscious as I repeated his name. "Patrick, Patrick, Patrick." And then, a final thought emerged before I took leave. *He used to love dinosaurs....*

***

Withdrawal is unbearable. After that terrible experience, I tried going cold turkey but wimped out after a few days. Each time I tried, my essence began fleshing out and taking on a human form. The fear of being anchored to your world, ending up like the old lady, or like Patrick, terrified me.

Late one evening, I spied some Shine in an orange grove protected by dense thorny branches. A couple was in the back of an old mini-van with the back seats folded down into a serviceable bed. She was a petite, pretty Latina, and he was a lanky, middle-aged black man. Their kisses were so moist and inviting that I couldn't resist the prospect of an extraterrestrial ménage a trois.

Dopamine flooded me with pleasure when I entered her. Our burgundy slacks were down, and our top was unbuttoned. We wore a Rite Aid nametag that said, Miriam. We straddled him, and he filled us.

"Ayyy, ohhh ayyy!" Our voice was a textured celebration of human sexuality. Then I switched partners. Miriam moved her hips around us, and after a few minutes, the dam crumbled and flooded her valley. She continued moving until we were ticklish. I sipped enough Shine to carry me through another day and rested on the dashboard below the rear-view mirror. A crucifix dangled over me. Miriam reached to take him in her hand, fascinated by the glistening beauty of his attenuated cock.

"You're a messy girl." He raised an eyebrow and nodded at her lap.

"Maybe you should start wearing a—"

"Now, baby," he cut in. "Keep talkin' like that, and I'll have you dippin' ice cream for a month'a Sundays." Then he kissed her.

"You should at least pull out then."

"Let's think on that." His hand reached between her thighs.

I tried to escape Earth. My parents were, no doubt, hysterical by now. I'd be grounded for life. Yet with every attempt, I scarcely made it past your solar system before I was forced to coast back. Shine's a Toyota Prius on Earth and a Chevy Suburban outside the pull of gravity.

One Sunday, I traveled to Rome to attend the evening mass. Church architecture is more interesting than monotonous rituals and pronouncements. It'd been almost two days since my last meal, and I nearly wedged myself between a stone-carved saint and the cold marble he hung from. When I pulled free, a parishioner noticed and made the sign of the cross. Then he resumed his prayers. For him, I probably resembled a swarm of fireflies.

I was about to exit through a stained-glass window when I noticed a Shining woman sitting alone in a back pew staring straight at me. Her eyes were wide and beautiful, and I floated down to sit next to her.

"Are you an angel?" she whispered conspiratorially.

The texture of her voice was delightful. I doubt she'd yet seen forty years through those eyes. It was a shame no one else could appreciate how blazing she was.

"An angel?"

"I've been praying for one."

"Been called a lot of things, but—"

"Why're you here?"

"For you." I decided to play along. *If it's an angel she wants, then by god, it's an angel she'll get.*

"Let's go away from here," she suggested, taking my hand in hers.

It was my first experience with feeling a human touch, independent of my habit of sharing them. It was pleasant. "By all means, lead the way."

When she smiled, her eyes closed, and Shine created a crowning aura around her raven hair. The priest said something, and parishioners murmured like a flock of geese. I stroked her face to sponge some Shine, enough to make the journey. My hand trailed down to the top of a breast that was pushing up from her peasant dress. She shivered.

I'd experienced a variety of vicarious human emotions, yet the sensation of touch was a whole new ballgame. I theorized that she noticed me because believing in what you can't see is vital to faith. As we took to the cobbled streets, I shadowed her like a newly hatched sparrow that has imprinted on the first living thing it sees.

My species is asexual, yet I have reasons for preferring women. For the sake of simplicity, let me use a shoe allegory. Women are emotionally well armed. They aren't timid about pointing out a pair of shoes in a storefront window and saying,

"Aren't those adorable?" Ladies' shoes describe the type of men they're destined to attract — loafers, clogs, flats, and mules. Smelly memories are soaked into each pair. The lady I walked with was wearing a simple pair of black sandals.

Standing at the altar of her closet, a typical North American woman's narrative regarding shoes might sound something like this: "I met Jonathan in pumps. These stacked heels were on sale the day Johnny popped the question. This pair of black stilettos helped when Joe was having equipment failure. I used them again in divorce court, where my bulldog lawyer chewed away half of John's assets. Oh, haven't seen these in ages, the sandals I bought in Mazatlán after the settlement. Mazatlán. Ramon, ay yi-yi. Ramon's equipment never failed."

"Where're you taking me?" I asked my mysterious guide.

She smiled. "Nearly there."

She was short and stout. You'd never find her gracing the cover of a checkout stand magazine. Her curves left no doubt as to where the lower spine ended, and the rise of her buttocks began. New feelings stirred as I followed. We walked streets worn with the passage of a thousand years, arriving at a crumbling apartment house and climbing four flights. Her studio was meager yet immaculate.

"Don't even know your name," I said.

"*Mi chiamo*, Maria. Easy to remember — there're millions of us."

She never asked my name, though I'd recently settled on one. Oz. At this juncture, I'd overstayed my welcome in your Emerald City and desperately wanted to catch the first balloon home. There's no place like home.

It was a pleasant surprise that I was able to close the entry door behind me. The furniture arrangement was simple — four wooden chairs and a table topped with fresh flowers. The kitchen was tiny, just a few iron pots and a red-clay jar bristling with wooden spatulas and spoons. Next to the open French window was a twin bed festooned with fluffy multicolored pillows. Beside it was a floor length mirror. I gawked at my reflection, a dazzling array of energy particles taking shape.

"As you can see, I'm a simple woman." She tilted her head, and a thick lock of raven hair swung over one eye, nearly covering her mouth.

"Not simple," I said. My voice was watery yet steadily improving. It felt wonderful to have a voice. Maria glowed like a woman with a secret, waiting for the right time to share. "How do I look?" I asked.

She moved close, her breasts contacting my lower back. "Like an angel with sparkling green eyes."

"You're an angel, not me."

She smiled, walked to the double windows, and opened them wider. "Listen," she whispered as a gentle breeze filled the room with the smell of sun.

I heard the unstructured poetry of children laughing in the street. Clothes were strung from one side of the street to the other and were snapping in the breeze. A vendor rang his bell, announcing, "*Fresco, ristóro, gelato!*" A screech of brakes was followed by unpleasant words, and dogs harmonized with a distant siren.

"Maria?" I stared into the mirror, and green eyes blazed back. "Am I really an angel?"

"You're *my* angel."

"Look." I gestured to my shoulders. "No wings."

"But you will fly," she answered. Maria touched my back with her fingers. Her Shine weakened for a moment, and I became more defined. I asked no more questions. Humans infatuated with solving mysteries should be more concerned with preserving them. Opportunity sneaks away while you text, surf the Internet, and zap through TV channels. At this crucial moment, knowing facts would have poisoned the seed before it had an opportunity to grow into a flower.

For all wants and purposes, I *was* an angel, wings flapping, horn blowing, and halo spinning like Saturn's rings, an angel with a throbbing erection. Maria pressed her lips to my back and flicked the tip of her tongue there. Reaching around, she filled her hand with my attenuated cock. In the mirror, I watched as she bit her lower lip and smiled. She led me to her bed, bathed in late morning light.

I lapped Maria's flower, and she smelled like a stormy tropical sea. Her natural essence was as nutritious as Shine because it originated from desire rather than need. Ocean breezes, fruits, and flowers emanated from the center of Maria's galaxy. Her head was thrown back, and she filled the room with instinctive sounds as I lapped her.

"Mmm," I moaned.

"Ay, my angel." Her impassioned voice harmonized with my mantra. Then I sat up and scooted between her thighs. I found her and was slowly sheathed, a pleasure so profound that all else was lost. I wasn't dead, wasn't alive, but somewhere in between…Nirvana!

Exhausted, we lay on our sides, still connected, breathing as if we'd sprinted the length of the heavens. Her hair smelled like sun-dried tomatoes, and her silken legs trapped me inside.

"Angel," she sighed.

"I love you," I said, and she smiled before drifting off to sleep.

I slept for the first time. Where I'm from, we rest without dreaming. That night I dreamed of a naked little boy, just out of the bubble bath. I woke with a start as the child jumped from the balcony window and smashed into the cobblestoned street. Maria wasn't there. Throwing off the blanket, I rushed to the window. It was dawn, and the street was empty. It's good to sleep, but dreams make fools of us. There was a paper napkin on the dining table held in place by a deep red rose. My hands trembled as I read the writing on it.

My Angel,
I desperately wanted to wake up in your arms. Perhaps one day, we will meet again. Meanwhile, I pray you find the will to keep from fading. You belong with substance. Arrivederci,
Maria
PS: There's beer in the refrigerator.

I stared at the note. My throat hurt, and surges of pain throbbed in my chest. Before I could stop them, tears spilled from my eyes. Leaning against the windowsill, I sobbed until my nose ran a river.

A bread vendor looked up from below. *"Volete dello pane?"*

I put a finger to one side of my nose and blew. He scampered back, hissing obscenities and slapping the underside of his chin with the back of a hand.

***

Ancient Earth civilizations studied poetry as seriously as economics. Music and the theater were considered as important as commerce. Today, fine arts and humanities are deemed unprofitable, an annoying requirement for the world's freshmen classes who are taught to live for the bottom line. You're cutting out the heart and replacing it with a stone.

My greatest frustration with your world is that you're becoming like me, energy without form. I'd give my ethereal left nut to possess sustainable Shine. Why is your race determined to trade in humanity for a pot of gold?

Trying not to fade was like begging a Christmas tree not to shed. I wandered Rome searching for Maria. As I faded, a few Italians squinted at me curiously. Mostly I went unnoticed, although one sighting was chronicled in a sleazy Italian tabloid.

Debilitated by grief and frustration, I tried my hand at being a Good Samaritan. By then, I appeared ghostly, shaved ice with artificial syrup. Summoning as much substance as possible, I helped carry groceries for an elderly man from the trunk of his car to his doorstep. When he saw bags floating next to him, he crossed himself, dropped his load, and scrambled into his house, clicking a series of locks in place. I rebagged the groceries and set them on his doorstep.

I helped an elderly widow plant begonias in her back yard. She watched delightedly as flowers freed themselves from plastic containers to enter holes she'd troweled in the earth. She believed me to be her dead husband.

"*Enrico, amore mio*, you still have a green thumb."

She Shined, yet I didn't have the heart to satisfy my self-indulgent thirst with her. Later I walked to a park, pushed a child in a swing, fed ducks, and managed to trip up a purse-snatcher pursued by police.

There was substance still growing inside me, residuals from my experience with Maria. It gained strength when I helped others. Mahatma Gandhi said, "Earth provides enough to satisfy every man's need, but not every man's greed."

***

I feel a diatribe coming on — can't be helped, here goes.

Capitalism begins with a weekly childhood allowance for taking out the trash, doing dishes, or mowing the lawn and evolves into more costly paybacks as the child ages. Where's it written that you should be paid to do the right thing? Materialism erodes early childhood development. Kids grow into adults and follow the money trail over a fiscal cliff. North American adults receive a FICO credit score…anywhere from 300-850. This is considered your *standing* — yet you realize too late that you're standing on a financial landmine. And so the struggle begins.

When you're unwilling to write your own horoscope and can't separate the wheat from chaff, life gets ugly. The land of the free and the home of the brave makes up six percent of the world population yet consumes over half the world's products. In the culture of make believe life's a video game, and if you don't have the latest version, you're behind the eightball.

I've been to military school. Shine is well camouflaged there. Presidents, chancellors, prime ministers, and other so-called world leaders are patsies for the special interests of the two-percent. For them, a beautiful tree represents lumber, clear blue lakes are development opportunities, and peaceful valleys have fracking potential. North Americans are no longer ignorant; they're downright stupid. Ignorance implies the lack of knowledge — stupidity is having knowledge and ignoring it. The president is a result of the latter. Throughout history, egomaniacs have snipped away at the fabric of Shine.

I've enjoyed reading North American history books, although much of what is published is lies and half-truths. The worst are lies of omission, stuff that's left out to ensure the purity of the image you wish to create.

Historically speaking, men are responsible for the brunt of atrocities on your planet, invoking the Almighty in times of war. Take a clear look at *The Pledge of Allegiance*, published in 1892 by a (heh-heh) minister. "Indivisible" was added in 1923, and "under God" in 1954. This thirty-one-word document is the best example of hypocrisy I've found in your world.

I pledge allegiance to the flag of the United States of America and to the republic, for which it stands, one nation under God, indivisible, with liberty and justice for all.

What a load of crap! Yet in many public schools, children are ordered to stand, put hands over hearts, and mouth this drivel. The results speak for themselves. Mob mentality = the lowest IQ in the herd (minus) twenty percent.

***

No trace of Maria. Couldn't last three days without a fix, and Shine was getting harder to score. A deep depression tethered concrete to my ankle and tossed me into the cold Pacific. Hundreds of feet beneath the sea, I squatted on the ruins of Atlantis. Don't expect me to furnish coordinates. If that information fell into the wrong hands, pieces of the lost city would end up on knick-knack shelves inside Trump Tower. I was strung out and rationalized that time beneath the sea might do me good—perhaps there was alchemy amid the mythical rubble.

An immense shape glided into view. "Christ!" I burbled. It was the largest living thing I'd ever seen. She pushed forward with powerful unhurried strokes of her tail. Blue whales can grow to 120 feet in length, and she was every inch of that. She used baleen to filter congregated swarms of two-inch, luminescent krill. She was an impressive reminder that mankind isn't the Snob Hill of the food chain. When humans are extinct, life will flourish. If krill disappears, the chain is broken. The smallest life forms are the most essential. You've forgotten this tidbit, my friends.

Seeing Her Majesty sent sparks up and down my essence.

I joined a mass of the krill and was sucked in, following the shrimp into her great stomach. Considering the human atrocities that've been inflicted upon these gentle creatures, it's a wonder that any survive. Aristotle Onassis swilled ouzo on his yacht perched atop a whale-penis barstool. What a prick. In the Guinness Stout of the whale's belly, I wondered, *Are whales' foreskins used in the manufacture of luxury wallets that, when stroked, turn into a briefcase?*

A mysterious voice interrupted my musings. "Knock-knock."

Without thinking, I answered, "Who's there?"

"Avenue."

"Avenue, who?"

"Avenue gotten your head out of your ass yet?" His laughter was deep and raspy.

I tried to be more specific. "Who are you?"

"Here to help your stupid ass."

"I don't understand."

"You're tweakin', got the shakes, need a score, right?"

Whoever he was, he knew me well enough. Indeed, if I didn't find some Shine soon, I'd begin to flesh out again.

"How long you been in this shit-hole, man?" he asked.

"Too long."

"Hear you've got a thing for the ladies."

My energy blushed. "Just one."

"What'll happen if you stay clean?"

"Burn out, I guess."

"Haven't you heard? It's better to burn out than to rust." There was a metallic click, followed by a brief flame as he fired up a blunt with a Zippo lighter.

I caught a glimpse before he snapped it shut—he was a dead-ringer for the Zig-Zag man caricatured on the roll-your-own cigarette papers.

"Smoke bad for the whale?" I was concerned.

"How the fuck should I know?"

"Who are you?"

He inhaled deeply and held it. "Gotta lot of names." His voice was squeaky now.

"Anyone will do."

He exhaled slowly, and his voice returned to normal. "Call me whatever you want, but you were thinking Zigzag. Let's get down to business." Even stoned, his voice was commanding. "Know how rare Shine is? Shit, man, it's been on the intergalactic endangered list for over two thousand years. Shine's harder to score than this grade A White Widow I'm smokin'."

"Tried to kick it, but—"

"Know what your problem is, pecker-head? Afraid to live your best and die like the rest."

The whale swallowed another mouthful of bioluminescent shrimp, and I was able to see my companion clearly. His long, greasy, limp hair hung over to a threadbare T-shirt that said Taoism: Shit Happens, Hinduism: This Shit Has Happened Before, Zen: What is the Sound of Shit Happening? Rastafarianism: Let's Smoke This Shit!

He exhaled, and I felt the smoke move through me, causing a rush of euphoria. "What do you mean?" I asked.

"Can't cheat death." He shook his head and took another puff. "Ain't no comin back." Another cloud of smoke closed in, and it felt like a swarm of bees buzzing within my essence. "Death's the least of your worries, Oz. That's what you call yourself these days, ain't it?"

"What'll happen to me?"

"Chill out, man. Gotta find your own answers." He took one last toke on the glowing nub. "Yuh see, man, life is different strokes. Safe to say it's the last real mystery. That, and those who still support Trump." He gave a self-indulgent laugh.

"Cold turkey?"

"Up to you, man—free choice and all that rot."

The shrimp had stopped glowing. In the darkness of the whale's paunch, a cell-phone played *Sucker for Pain*. He fished it from the pocket of his holey, acid washed blue jeans and checked the caller ID.

"What the hell's He want?"

"Anyone ever told you you're a dead ringer for the Zigzag man?"

"One million six hundred and forty-three, make that forty-four, times. Gotta jam, man."

"Hang on, you didn't answer my—"

"Stop whinin', dumbass. You can put the pieces together."

"One question."

"Shoot."

"You wouldn't happen to know an Italian woman named—"

"Maria, shit." He cut me off and dug into a pocket. "Almost forgot to give you this."

He handed me a wadded piece of paper and lit the Zippo so I could read it. I immediately recognized Maria's handwriting. "You know her?"

"Been around the block together a few times." He snapped the lighter shut. "Hang loose, Oz. Follow the Yellow Brick Road." His voice faded, and he was gone.

The blue whale contracted her bowels and shit me near the surface. I rose into the sky to scan for Zigzag. The whale regarded me with a bloodshot, dinner-plate eye that looked like a cetacean roadmap. Maria's note floated inside me. I smoothed it out and read:

"I want to be with you, but it's not possible yet. I love you."

"Ye-e-e-s!" I soared, circled Mars, kissed Venus, and returned to Earth exhausted and famished. Maria was out there, loving me, and I loved her back. She was watching over me. Moisture from the sea floated within my essence. I climbed toward the sun and, for a brief moment, became a rainbow.

***

I checked rehabs, attended AA meetings, and studied withdrawal sufferers. Heroin and meth are the worst. The user's body becomes a menstrual cramp when denied, and it's nearly impossible to keep sanity from boiling over like milk in a saucepan.

Crystal meth is your favorite means of self-destruction. It's cheap, easy to find, and you can eat it, snort it, smoke it, or shoot it. First use provides a rush of confidence and hyperactive energy for six to eight hours. Then your body demands more, and more, until one day you stare into a mirror and pick at yourself because you think worms are living under your skin. Cranksters look like extras from *The Walking Dead*—like someone I once knew…can't put a finger on.

I've watched you sniff, shoot, huff, and swallow products manufactured for taming hair, removing paint, cleaning kitchens, and powering cars. You're self-destructive, self-indulgent, and you're fucking up the cosmic balance. You seek to dominate rather than coexist. Believe me, Mother Nature's going to spank you and send you to bed without supper. Shit, I feel it, another diatribe, it's coming….

The human need to dominate was necessary for survival thousands of years ago, yet now it's governed by ego. You share an overpopulated Mario Brother's world, seeking higher levels before mastering the ones you're on. Kurt Vonnegut warned about this, intimating that Earth is a living organism, has detected parasites, and is taking steps to get rid of them. Guess who the parasites are?

Your quest for the Holy Grail leads you further from the truth. TV, smartphones, social media, drugs, dead-end jobs, religion, money, and power each lead you further from yourselves. You're afraid to live your best and die like the rest.

I'm fond of this planet, its rivers, oceans, forests, and mountains. I've been forced to watch the on-going war you're waging against yourselves. You're brokering disaster. My remaining shreds of sanity were held together by periodic messages from Maria.

I was sharing Chinese take-out in England within a Shining old man. He cracked his fortune cookie. YOU ARE LOVED BY YOUR ADORING MARIA

"Bloody hell...?" He handed it to his wife of fifty years.

"Two-timer." She shook a finger in his face, and their laughter was warmer than Oolong tea.

I resided within a marvelous Nuba woman in Sudan. She was carrying sacks of sorghum balanced on her head. Along the way, men tried one-liners, and she ignored them. As she slept that night, I found a message from Maria embroidered on her tob.

Angel, I've a confession — the man you met in the whale's belly is an ex-boyfriend. Don't be jealous — we split up over two thousand years ago. I'm glad you met. I love you more than Belgian chocolate! — M —

I left Africa and raced to Belgium — no sign. New and powerful emotions were draining Shine nearly as fast as I could refuel. The thought of Maria sharing herself with Zigzag man torched me with the jealous flames she'd warned me about.

A few months ago, in the jungles of Paraguay, I thought the absence of light might entice Zigzag man as it had in Atlantis. I descended deep into a cave until I was totally immersed in blackness. The odor of guano was heavy. Bats clung from the ceiling, and water dripped from stalactites into shallow pools.

Ex-boyfriend or not, Ziggy knew where Maria was. I discovered a blind salamander, but no Zigzag man. When the bats yawned, stretched wings, and flew off to harvest their bug quota, I followed into the evening sky. With Shine becoming more difficult to procure, I fed like a mosquito as people slept. Sleepers dream and dreams share ghostly partnerships with reality.

Binghamton, New York, was bitterly cold. A few mummified souls tramped the streets, snow squeaking beneath their boots. Tree branches didn't sway for fear of snapping. I floated toward a little girl who was warm and safe within the walls of a Brownstone apartment. She was dreaming about a black stallion. As she rode along a shoreline, I joined. Happily, we galloped along, with the sun in our long, brown hair. Then, the dream developed into a nightmare:

The girl faded, and now the stallion galloped down a frozen city street in Binghamton, nearly losing its footing several times. He veered into a dead-end alley that was strewn with garbage, crawling with rats that wore bright red wool sweaters. The great horse bucked me off and pranced away, snorting vapor through his nose. An orange-striped cat peeked from a dented garbage can.

I stood and brushed myself off. Detecting movement close by, I searched the rubbish, spotting a pair of worn sneakers wriggling beneath a discarded shower curtain. Anxiety burned at the edges of my remaining fuel supply, and I began materializing. My reflection in a dimly lit puddle of runoff water was tall, gaunt, balding, wrinkled, and disheveled, with eyes the color of emeralds.

A man sat up, pulled the shower curtain aside, rubbed his eyes, and stared at me. Illuminated by a dim fingernail-clipping moon that peeked through snow clouds, he resembled other destitute I'd seen. His face was covered with gray stubble. He wore a grimy sweater and a battered army surplus jacket. His head was topped with a gray beanie. Green blazed from his sunken eyes like a blowtorch.

I shivered and continued to flesh-out, feeling the bristly itch of a beard. I wanted to wake up, yet self-will wallowed in quicksand, and my heart pattered like an idling Harley. With Maria, having substance had been pleasurable. Now I ached with arthritis and felt a gnawing hunger.

The apparition rose to his feet with the help of a long bamboo staff. He stood tall and thin, a spitting image of me. There was a mouth beneath the alfalfa sprouts of beard, and it moved to speak.

"You've met my son," his voice bellowed, resounding off the mossy walls of the alley.

"Shut the fuck up!" a voice shouted from an apartment window. "Some of us gotta work tomorrow!"

The old man raised a reproachful eyebrow to the window. The sliver of moon hid behind gathering clouds, and a light snow drifted. I'd seen his like wandering the streets, gibbering as if they had a mouthful of mashed potatoes. He twisted his lips and blasted a thunderous fart that made a gathering of rats scurry for safety.

"I will sing and make music, Psalm 57:7."

"Shut the fuck up!" was repeated from the window.

In this dream, I morphed into a naked synthesis of human

imperfections, skin covered with scars, tumors, lesions, warts, and moles. I trembled from the bitter cold and knew that I'd need to score some Shine quickly or become a one-man geek show.

"What's the matter, son?" the stranger asked. "Stressed out?"

"Gotta feeling, you know."

Suddenly a quilt appeared in his hands, and he put it over my shoulders. "Here, liable to catch your death," he said stonily.

"That's what I'm hoping."

The old man stiffened. His eyes burned like glowing green jellybeans, and his whiskers quivered. He took a deep breath and blew on me. I was instantly encased within a thin sheet of ice. He stepped forward with his staff gripped in both hands and slowly raised it over his head.

"He lies in wait near the villages, and from ambush, he murders the innocent!"

"I never murdered —"

"They fall under his strength!" he continued.

"I never hurt a fly."

He chopped down, and the layer of ice above my head cracked into a spider web, spreading until I shattered into a pile of glassy fragments. Rats in red sweaters poured forth from every hidden crevice to feed on me.

Then, as dreams are apt to do, I was within the child again, and we were sleeping peacefully. She moaned and threw off her covers. I had enough substance remaining to tuck her in and stooped to kiss her forehead. The smell of a sleeping child awakened something buried deep inside.

"Tracy." Familiar, yet elusive. *Patrick* was on the tip of my tongue, and I swallowed quickly. *Newspaper…Evergreen.* I couldn't shake the image. I gritted my teeth and growled. My head filled with a rhythmic shushing noise. Finally, it subsided.

It was then that I searched earnestly for a way to blow out my flickering candle.

*****

My story's come full circle. I'm an alien, and I'm going to kill myself.

I breakfasted on a woman who was out birthday shopping for a sister. Our feet were tired, and we couldn't decide on anything. We sat in a coffee shop and wondered if the sister would enjoy a gift card to Macy's. She Shined enough to get me out of Binghamton, the birthplace of Rod Serling. Indeed, my experience there had *Twilight Zone* written all over it.

I slowly orbited Earth in search of an ashtray to stub out my substance. There's so much high-tech garbage circling the planet that it has formed an orbiting ring. Satellites buzzing, bleeping, flashing, and beaming signals so you can choose from two-thousand channels, eavesdrop, or find a shortcut to Walmart. There're orbiters you don't have an inkling about, designed to cook humans like a sow bug beneath a magnifying glass, guide missiles, and direct drones from laptops.

I'm an alien, and I'm going to kill myself. The question is, how? Stuff a handful of blood-diamonds in my mouth and chase it with a shot of Iraqi crude? Enter Paris Hilton's brain and wander the emptiness forever? Discuss foreign policy with Donald Trump? Then an idea clamped onto my ear like Mike Tyson.

She wasn't difficult to locate. Desperation has wings, and hope slogs it out in army boots. She sat alone on a barstool in the kitchen, having just baked two dozen of her famous chocolate-chip swirl squares. No one was there to share with. Absently she cannibalized the corner of one as it closed its pores on a cooling rack. Light streamed in through a window and made the porcelain sink glow white.

There wasn't a hint of Shine emanating from her. It was as if, while vacuuming, the Hoover had sucked it into the dirt-bag along with the hairpin, a nickel, and a Lego piece. Dark puddles filled with desperation had accumulated below her eyes. Tentatively I inputted myself, having never shared someone without Shine.

It felt like being zipped into a garment bag filled with dry ice and tossed from an Alaskan Princess cruise-ship into Glacier Bay. She nearly lost consciousness when I arrived. After the dizziness passed, we felt like weeping, yet willed the tears from our eyes before they could escape. We lifted a note that lay next to the cookies.

Ginny, sorry it happened like this. Wish you could understand how she makes me feel. I'm not getting any younger, the kids are grown, and the time's ripe for a change. I'll stop by for my things this afternoon. — Richard —

Thirty years and four sentences. See what I mean about numbers? The phone rang, and I wanted her to pick up. We pursed our mouth as an old-fashioned answering machine kicked in with Richard's generic voice. *Hi, you've reached 732-4523...*

"Pick up," I coached.

We're not able to come to the phone right now....

"Please," I begged.

But if you leave your name and number....

"Goddammit, pick up!"

We'll get back to you.

An irritating beep followed. "Hi, Mom. Kristy needs some new school shoes, and we wondered if you'd like to join us...

just a second, Kristy wants to say something."

"Hi, Grandma," said a sweet loving voice. "I got a new pup—"

Ginny turned the machine off. "Thirty years," she murmured. *Thought Richard would come to his senses. Would've forgiven him.* A faded memory drifted lazily into our head. "Jim." We shook our head. *Can't imagine him hurting anyone, let alone his own wife.* She recalled Jim's image splashed on the front page of the *Meadowland Chronicle* and featured on *Fox News.* In her mind, we pictured a young man with a crucifix dangling from his neck, the pizza night. "Meadowland." She shook her head. *No meadows in sight.*

Ginny shuffled into the bedroom closet and tiptoed to reach a shoebox on the top shelf. So far as we knew, Richard had never fired the thing. It felt heavy as we lifted it from the box. We saw the tips of deadly larvae snuggled in their chambers. "Just in case," he'd explained when she questioned the purchase. "Because you never know."

"Thirty years." The phone rang again. *Four sentences.* The phone stopped ringing before the machine clicked on. "Yeah, you never know."

We narrowed our eyes and squinted into the barrel. A killer bee was waiting there.

"Yes, Richard, stop by for your things." A distant memory arrived. *When a bee stings, it's the worst of all stunts. Take pleasure in knowing he'll sting only once.* Her favorite English student, Robert, had written it for her a lifetime ago. "Lord, how that child loved to write."

Should I write something? We wondered? *What's left to say?*

Our hands were earthquakes, thumb pressuring the trigger, the hive buzzing.

"For the love of God!" I pleaded.

The phone rang again. A voice said, "Sorry, we missed you. Did you know that you could save up to twenty percent on your next phone bill just by switching to Sprint?"

"Thirty," she sighed, placing the barrel inside her mouth.

As I passed through the roof, there was a single shot.

***

I'm a greedy, good for nothing, yellow through and through…as useless as the toy in your Happy Meal. I'm the void inside a billionaire's power suit. *Why isn't suicide as simple as ordering fast food?* I wondered. *Sharing someone else's suicide is out. Has to be another way. Where's Kryptonite when you need it?*

On my world, death is meaningless. One day you notice someone's not around anymore. They drifted away without fanfare. Some believe they travel to a parallel universe, yet most of us don't waste time on afterlife philosophy. Solitude has forced me into self-reflection. I've taken without giving, bitched, moaned, and dished out unsolicited advice. Miss Maria…haven't heard from her for so long.

As I sat atop the iconic Hollywood sign overlooking Los Angeles, an idea occurred…a long shot. My story ends in California.

And a rock feels no pain. So said Paul Simon. If you wanted to find the edge of the world, where do you look? Antarctica, the Middle East, Africa, Timbuktu, Meadowland? None qualify, although Meadowland comes pretty damned close. I stood at the rim of the world, the funky LaBrea Tar Pits in Los Angeles. Replicas of giant mammoths, fierce saber-toothed cats, and voracious vultures dot the area in and around the gooey pits. The scientific name for the saber-cat is Smilodon. Bet they weren't smiling when they became ingredients in black-bean soup. The surface of the fossil-fuel lake was calm and peaceful; easy to imagine why creatures were tempted to skinny-dip.

A little boy stood at the fence, Shining to beat the band. He had a stone in his hand. He wasn't experimenting with weapons of mass destruction or promoting preservatives that could mummify white bread for twenty-five years. He just wanted to see what would happen when the stone met the tar. So did I. A chain-link fence separated him from the pit. He was debating if he should.

"Of course, you should," I answered. I entered the rock. Inanimate objects don't Shine. I've nothing against abandoned tires, gum wrappers, or Persian rugs, but it's true. The rock gave neither pleasure nor pain. It was amoral. They don't listen to gossip and could give a shit about the ozone. It was dark and silent inside the rock. I felt the rocking motion of the boy's arm and was suddenly propelled upward.

"Jesus!"

The rush caught me off guard, and a second later, I landed in the antediluvian goop. Immediately the temperature inside the rock changed as we slowly sank. A wave of survival instinct nausea swept through me—every particle of my being begged out. Somewhere deep inside me, the patient voice of my developing conscience counseled, *When you think you're dead, the rock will exist, and you'll be part of it. No matter what, you'll always be a part of something.*

"There's no such thing as nothing!"

A penlight shone through my dusty blinds. The light broadened into a substantial beam of awareness. It grew colder inside the rock as we were incrementally ingested.

"I'll always be something, always something!"

A sudden burst of light flared from deep inside me. Borrowed fragments of souls liberated themselves and scattered in all directions to find home. There's no place like home.

I narrowly escaped, launching myself into the brown Los

Angeles sky as thick tar pulled its black cloak over the stone. A warm wind gusted through my essence. I took to the sky, spinning, performing barrel rolls, and laughing. The boy shaded his eyes to watch his experiment, which was more successful than he could've imagined.

A turkey buzzard with a red featherless neck snatched me out of the air.

"What the hell?" I giggled, sliding down its throat and landing on a dead mouse fragment. What a stink! The prospect of becoming bird shit wasn't particularly appealing, but nothing could diminish my joy.

A stick broke as it was struck against a cardboard matchbox. "Fuck."

"Zigzag man, I presume?"

"Shut the fuck up." He tried another match, and it snapped as well.

"Is that what you're here to say?"

"It's a start." Another match sparked and died. "Fuck me! They can put a man on the moon…."

I laughed so hard I had trouble catching my breath.

"Yeah, yeah, real funny. Finally got your head out'a your ass. Tar pits, rocks—you're a real piece of work." He finally managed to fire up a blunt, taking a long drag and exhaling through me. "Just dropped by to say that your parents've been worried."

"You found them?"

"My job."

"Thanks."

"De nada."

"When are they coming to get me?"

"Told'em you were okay."

"So, when are they —?"

His hand reached out to grab me by a scruff of energy. "Listen up, amigo…what you've learned on Earth will define who you are forever. No pain, no gain, comprende?"

"Yeah," I squeaked.

He let me go and smoothed out my wrinkled ego. "Sorry, get carried away sometimes. I'll tell'em where you are." He licked a thumb and forefinger to snuff out the cigarette.

"Hold up."

"Can't see a fucking thing." The faceplate on his cell phone glowed eerily. "They'll shit a brick. I'm callin' collect."

"Wait," I said as a kernel of thought microwaved and popped into two words. "Hang up!'

"Bite me. Got a job to —"

I focused my remaining energy to knock the phone from his grasp and trap his wrist. "Your job's finished," I said.

Ziggy put a gentle hand on my shoulder and squeezed. I heard my father's voice on the answering machine. "We're not able to come to the phone right now, but leave —"

We both laughed hysterically. The bird shit us out, and before I had a chance to ask about Maria, Ziggy took to the air, singing a skyward version of Elton John's "Goodbye Yellow Brick Road." I landed on the monkey bars at a grammar school and knew exactly where I was — the tiny labor-camp community of Woodland, less than an hour's drive from Meadowland.

In the distant skies, I heard Zigzag singing, "…where the dogs of society howl," as the sun dipped beneath the Sierra Nevada Mountains, in a scene reminiscent of a book cover I'd seen. I climbed down from the bars and found an old newspaper to use as a blanket. Totally exhausted, I fell asleep beneath a nearby mulberry tree.

***

A poem rushed into Owen's head without punctuation or

spaces between words.

Lifeisjustanendlessflighttomakeitthroughtheyellowlight.

"Sir?" A voice fought to get a toe in the door.

Maria.

"Sir."

There it is again. What's he selling?

"Sir, you'll have to leave before the kids start arriving to school." His voice was gentle and made Owen smile and open his eyes. The name Floyd was embroidered on the front of his shirt. Owen sat up and carefully folded the newspaper to read later. Floyd offered him five dollars. "Go get yourself some breakfast."

Owen shook his head. "Thanks, I've got money." He patted a pocket and felt the wallet, still there.

"I've got a sack full of aluminum cans in the bus shed. You're welcome to'em." Floyd had seen this man around town, collecting cans and rummaging around in dumpsters.

"Thanks. I'd be happy to take those off your hands."

Floyd went into the shed and returned with the sack. Owen hefted it and figured it to be enough for a few bottles of Thunderbird wine.

"Thanks again."

"Welcome."

A pack of dogs argued over a female on the railroad tracks next to the school. The janitor whistled "Strangers in the Night" as he walked back to the bus shed. The morning bus driver arrived and started up a yellow school bus. Floyd greeted the older man with a pat on the back. Owen was sure, even though he could no longer see auras, that Floyd was Shining.

Owen walked to a nearby Shell gas station to use the public bathroom. The S on its sign had recently been shattered by a rock.

Owen's green eyes reflected in the cracked mirror. "Owen Zelenski," he said as if greeting an old friend. "Long time, no see." A thought surfaced — *Play your song, and if you're fortunate, someone else'll hear.* He splashed his face with cold water from the sink. Every drop was a bursting flower, part Earth, part sky.

Schizophrenic, bipolar, manic depression, idiopathic, he reflected. "Freeway leading in, a tiny back road out, and lots of voices shouting directions."

Owen found a small market with an ATM. He bought cigarettes and stood outside to smoke. A sanitation truck positioned itself next to a dumpster. The hydraulic hiss sounded like a giant snake. He returned his attention to the yellowed, month-old *Meadowland Chronicle* he'd slept with. On the front page was the president, his face distorted with rage.

Last election provided a conduit for everything wrong in the US, thought Owen. *Prejudice, racism, bigotry, and hatred are gum stuck beneath a table. You never know it's there until you run your fingers underneath.* Now the table was flipped over for everyone to see, and still, they were blind. On the next page was a list of local crimes, mostly robberies and simple assaults.

Owen wandered to a small public park next to the Memorial Building and sat on a green steel bench. He lit another cigarette and reopened the newspaper randomly to the obituaries. At the top was an advertisement for a funeral home, a two for one sale. Then, as he skimmed down, he saw a small photo with a summary below it. It was a high school graduation picture.

Blood drained from Owen's face. His chest felt as though he'd been shot clean through the heart with a compound bow:

Patrick Kenneth Zelenski, twenty-eight, died from an apparent drug overdose...he is survived by...services will be held....

Owen's mouth opened, yet nothing escaped. He sunk to

his knees and took in as much air as his lungs would hold. Then he let out a long, blood-curdling howl, filled with loneliness, sorrow, and self-loathing. He crumpled the newspaper and clutched at his head, beating it on the sidewalk.

"No, no, no, no, no!" His chest heaved. Tears and blood soaked into the grey cement.

Crows were resting in the uppermost branches of a nearby oak tree. They stopped arguing to listen. An elderly Mexican couple was out walking. They paused a moment to watch Owen and turned to walk the other way. His body shook with the force of his sobs. The crows lifted almost soundlessly into the sky with a faint whirring of wings.

"Oh no, ohhh god...I'm so sorry! I'm sorry, my son! My boy, my little boy...oh God! Forgive...."

CHAPTER 7
Eleventh Summer

"Life is short, but it is wide."
—Unknown—

We were eleven, going on twelve. Twelve was the golden ticket, the age when dreams and fantasies high-fived with hope. How could I have guessed that sequestered within the magic of twelve was a dark reality, waiting to pounce like a feral river cat?

My best friends were Rodney Rooster Martin, Arnulfo Goofus Rodriguez, and Joey Reece. My nickname was Stick... Andrew Stick Johnson. Our epithets were cruelly accurate. Together, we attended Woodland Elementary School.

Rodney and I lived on small family farms. Arnulfo's father labored for a large corporate farm, and they lived in low-rent housing on one of the properties. Joey lived in Woodland and didn't have to ride the bus to school with the rest. He didn't have a nickname, and I can't recall why. His ears stuck out from his head like dollar pancakes. We could've come up with something. We gave ourselves nicknames before enemies had the chance to tag us. Kids like Stinky Sandoval, Pork Edwards, and Fishface Turman had waited too long.

We gambled with pennies on the ancient rickety school bus dubbed the Crackerbox. Wherever it squealed to a stop, dogs gathered to race us to the end of their territory. We bet which one would keep his lead the longest. The ancient bus shuddered as it ground through the gears. In between shifts, it popped a smoky fart. Sometimes the dogs were lazy, especially if they were trying to impress a female, which was nothing we could lay odds on.

The big kids, eighth-graders, sat in the back seats firing lentils through straws or flicking pennies, which we collected for gambling. The morning bus driver was Mr. Hernandez, a timid old man. Stern warnings were generally ignored, and his knuckles whitened around the steering wheel. Big kids lowered windows to spit on stop signs and talked nasty to the girls. Mr. Hernandez crinkled his forehead, turned up the radio, and tapped the steering wheel in time with Mexican tunes he listened to.

Floyd drove the afternoon bus to take us home. He was an entertainer. The Crackerbox was equipped with a long-armed microphone that swung in front of him. Floyd sang into it while he drove. He crooned songs about bowlegged women, impersonated Frank Sinatra, and took a stab at rock'n'roll once in a while. Sometimes he let us talk on the microphone before we stepped off the bus.

Once, when I was in bed with the flu, Floyd's rich voice drifted lazily over the farm as he cruised by. "'It never rains in California, but girl don't they warn yuh…'" As I remember, it was pouring cats and dogs.

Every Friday, I asked Floyd about his weekend plans, and

the standard reply was, "I'm gonna go out and chase wild women."

I imagined what a wild woman would look like. When he wasn't driving the bus, something always needed fixing at Woodland Elementary. Floyd could repair just about anything. He kept classrooms clean, umpired baseball, and refereed during flag-football and basketball season. Keeping gophers from taking over the soccer field was next to impossible.

Floyd made up his own job descriptions. "I'm an environmental engineer. Studied at the Harvard Institute for Custodial Arts." He always found time to teach jump-shots, scooping grounders, and how to throw a spiral with the football...important stuff.

Most Woodland teachers used our tiny school as a stepping stone to get into the Meadowland district, where they were paid more. Instructors came and went every year. We were all pleased when Ms. Payán arrived. Lupe Payán was my sixth-grade teacher. After lunch, she read us poetry in her soft, lilting voice, filling boys' heads with cobwebs. She had long, shiny black hair and sleepy brown eyes. Her curves were barely concealed beneath brightly colored Mexican skirts and blouses she preferred wearing. When she walked by our desks, the breeze created by her skirt floated the scent of her perfume.

Ms. Payán had a twin sister, Mariana, who taught at Meadowland High School, adding further fuel to our fantasies. Boys all agreed that we'd take her classes if we made it to high school.

There was a pencil sharpener bolted to the front corner of Ms. Payán's desk, and we took turns going up there. We'd let a pencil slip from our fingers. Stooping to retrieve it, the rest of the guys would count off seconds while the perpetrator examined her smooth, dark legs. I held the record—seven seconds. I gawked at her satiny calves, the contour of her thighs beneath the thin fabric of her skirt, while seconds were counted, and the rest of the class bubbled in answers on a grammar worksheet.

One morning, as we were taking a quiz on the Civil War, Rodney Rooster Martin passed me a note that said, *Going for the record*. I signaled the others that the game was about to begin. They looked up from their papers, grateful for a temporary reprieve. Rooster gripped his pencil and walked to Ms. Payán's desk. He stuck his pencil into the sharpener and began cranking the handle. He practically ground it to a nub before he got up the nerve to drop it.

Rooster had a rooster-tail lock of hair sticking straight out from the back of his head, hence the nickname. Patty Rodriguez sat behind him, and sometimes I saw her stare angrily at it, as though any second she'd spit in her hand to slap it down. With hair like that, Rodney was doomed to failure. Sure enough, as he bent to retrieve the pencil, Patty got Ms. Payán's attention with hand signals and ratted him out. Rod was sent to Principal Muller's office, and my record stood.

Recess and lunchtime gossip usually focused on Ms. Payán. She filled us with desire, curiosity, and butterflies. I still remember comments she wrote on my final report card that year. *Andrew's a bright young man, and he will do well in seventh grade if he keeps his mind on his work.*

Nelda Morales shared top billing with Ms. Payán because she had the biggest tits in class. But Payán was the star attraction. Some days she wore button-up blouses that gapped open when she leaned over, giving us a brief glimpse of the tops of her breasts. Age and inexperience defeated serious attempts to put our desires into words, yet we often walked around with boners at school.

The following year Lupe didn't return — she nailed a job

in Meadowland. She'd join her twin sister, and in a few years, we'd double our pleasure. In many ways, her replacement was noteworthy — Ms. Crooninghill.

Ms. Crooninghill was a petite woman in her early sixties, ramrod straight with sunken cheeks that ceaselessly flexed. Her hair was a mass of fine gray wire ordered into in a tight bun. She had a prominent wart on her cheek, and her voice was shrill and grating, like the screech of fingernails on a chalkboard. Yet her eyes were mysteriously beautiful, deep blue searchlights on a moonless night.

She kept a yardstick at her desk, which she slapped down hard when classroom decibels reached unacceptable levels, anything above a whisper. She routed boys to Principal Muller's office daily for passing notes, making animal noises, or sleeping during class. I was shipped out for passing a drawing I'd made of Crooninghill riding her yardstick beneath a full moon. Principal Mueller ordered lunchtime detention and demanded I offer a formal apology. I was sent back to class during recess.

"Sorry about the drawing," I stammered. "Didn't mean to hurt your feelings."

"Thank you, Mr. Johnson," she scowled. "But the main issue is respect."

"Yes, ma'am," I droned.

She used a long pause to study my eyes as if she were reading my thoughts. "I have an assignment for you to complete this weekend." Her face was stone. I winced, knowing it was payback time. "You'll write a three-page report about witches."

No sweat, I thought, *I'm lookin' at one.*

"You must include a title and a reference page, and do not plagiarize. Do you remember what that means?"

"Yes, ma'am." I didn't really but figured I'd look it up in a dictionary.

"You'll turn it in to me on Monday morning before class. If I deem it satisfactory, there'll be no need to contact your parents. Do you understand?"

"Yes, ma'am." Her eyes penetrated me, and I felt my armpits getting wet.

That weekend I worked sluggishly on my report with the aid of *Funk and Wagnalls* encyclopedia's, which still cracked with newness even though they were going on ten years old. My mother had purchased them one-by-one during a grocery store promotion, one free for every twenty-five bucks you blew. My parents used them as filler in a bookshelf previously dominated by *Readers' Digest* magazines and a collection of ceramic Victorian ladies. I watched some Sabrina reruns on *Nickelodeon* to supplement the brief paragraph I found in the encyclopedia regarding witches of Salem. I wrote big and concluded my impressive tome by saying how much it would suck to be burned at the stake.

During Monday morning recess, Ms. Crooninghill asked me to stay in. She silently reread my thesis as I stood before her desk. I'd managed to fit about five words per line. She'd corrected it with a red pen, and the pages looked as though a pig had been slaughtered on them. Occasionally a slight twitch gathered on Ms. Crooninghill's face and died.

I was twirling my pencil, nervously. It slipped from my fingers and rolled beneath her desk. Her head snapped up.

"Interesting, Mr. Johnson," she droned and pointed a boney finger at the paper. "You say here that the accused were burned in Salem for practicing witchcraft."

"Yes, ma'am."

"Hmm." She puckered her wrinkled lips. "Do you still think I'm a witch, Mr. Johnson?"

There was no doubt in my mind—if I'd had on the ruby

slippers, she would've demanded them. "No, ma'am," I meekly replied.

She reached into her desk, took out the drawing, and handed it to me. "Would you do the honors? Please tear it up and throw it in the garbage." She nodded to the canister sitting by her desk. I did as she asked. "Thank you, Mr. Johnson. You're free to go."

I rabbited for the door, but Ms. Crooninghill's voice stopped me before I made a clean getaway.

"Andrew?"

"Ma'am?" I turned, with one foot bathing in the sunshine.

"You didn't mention the laugh."

"Ma'am?"

"Come now...surely you've heard how witches laugh." Her sparkling blue eyes widened.

"Like on *The Wizard of Oz*?" I took a stab.

"Precisely. Run along now."

I exited, gulping for air like a fish out of water. The door closed behind me, and suddenly an eruption of hideous cackling laughter came from within. The gang hurried over, hungry for the low-down. But I was speechless.

Ms. Crooninghill served her purpose and stayed at Woodland until her retirement. She was the bottom slice of bread, and Ms. Payán was the top. Sandwiched between was a cathartic summer. Lessons were learned that summer that weren't found in books or on worksheets. Ms. Crooninghill cast a spell to help us forget what happened. So did Nelda Morales, whose tits grew bigger over vacation.

Each summer, the gang whiled away weekends at the river. Arnulfo worked in the raisin vineyards with his father and brothers and could only come on Sundays. Joey played summer baseball, but games were on Tuesdays and Thursdays.

Rodney and I were more fortunate. As long as we stayed out of our parents' hair, we could roam around freely.

Mexicans provided most of the sweat-labor on our farms. Sometimes, my father had me work alongside them because he believed it was important to know hard work. It was strange working the fields with Mexicans. I didn't understand their language, but they always seemed happy. They laughed and sang as they labored under a thankless sun and were kind to me. They called me little *güero*, and even though I didn't know what it meant, it sounded better than Stick.

My work experience with the Mexicans helped me to engender a deep affection for the culture. Sometimes they offered me a quesadilla filled with cheese, meat, or potato and hot peppers. More than once, I made a beeline for the water canister to douse the flames.

The river was actually a wide, man-made canal that carried irrigation water to thirsty Central Valley's farmlands. The name river provided the canal with a more adventurous image. Dry weeds and thorny brush dripped down the inner banks into the bamboo. Segmented bamboo shoots were sheathed like corn stocks, and when stirred by a rare summer breeze, the leaves rubbed together, sounding like the swish of Ms. Payán's skirt.

During summers, the river was a lengthy white streak of dry sand, dotted with bottles, cans, abandoned tires, and other cast-offs. We exhumed shopping carts, animal remains, spent shotgun casings, and other junk — everything a boy needed. The wrinkled trunks of mighty oak trees rose from the riverbanks, red-tailed hawks perched like giant teardrops among the top branches, and woodpeckers hammered out Morse code.

On the river that summer, we fantasized about skinny-dipping with Ms. Payán or finding an unopened six-pack of Lucky Lager. Instead, we discovered marijuana sprouting from

Folgers coffee tins deep within a tangle of bamboo. Joey Reece found them while clearing a trail into a thick strand of bamboo. Joey had sharp, bony elbows and curly clumps of black hair that camouflaged his pancake ears. He was thin, wiry, and easily the best athlete at Woodland. He stumbled upon the coffee cans, fifteen in all, and yelled for us.

They were neatly arranged in three rows of five. In the middle of each earth-filled can grew a small plant. The soil was still moist. Close by was a paperback book, half-buried in bamboo leaves. Arnulfo snatched at it, but I was quicker.

"*Puta madre*," he snapped.

Everyone gathered. The cover was faded and torn and looked like a man facing down a burnt tortilla — *The Journal of Desperate Living*, by Owen Zelenski. I opened to a weathered, dog-eared page and read aloud.

Larry remembered that summer morning as if it were yesterday. He was just a kid, eleven or twelve, forced into surviving two weeks at Camp Rising Sun so that his parents could enjoy some private time away from him. Spying through a cover of pines, he watched as his cabin counselor, Mike, kissed Veronica.

Rodney grabbed at the front of his pants. "Skip to the good part." Rod was the only one of us that carried a cellphone. It belonged to his mother, and it started playing "Strangers in the Night." "Hold up." He answered the call. "Yeah…yeah, okay… all right…uh huh…okay…bye." Then he hung up. "Gotta go in an hour."

I continued reading.

Veronica was my age, nervous and unsure. The counselor whispered something in her ear as his hand moved beneath her Camp

Rising Sun T-shirt.

"Ay!" Arnulfo grabbed Joey's butt.
"*Pinche Joto!*" Joey pushed him away.
"Shut up, this's the good part," I admonished.

The pounding in my head was joined by the insistent throbbing of my....

"Shit, the pages're stuck together—"
"Load'a crap anyway." Joey interrupted. He wanted us to focus on the plants.

Arnulfo always carried matches. Once in a while, we found a half-smoked cigarette, and he'd fire it up and do a perfect impression of Principal Muller. We cut Arnulfo's name down to Nulfo. He was squat, chubby, and easily the worst athlete at school. His lack of athletic prowess was easily overshadowed by a sharp sense of humor. He could distort his cherub face into the oddest shapes imaginable. No matter how hard the rest of us tried, when Nulfo pulled a face in class, we all busted up. He got us into a lot of trouble that way.

What Arnulfo lacked in physical ability was replaced by his dauntless farting skills. He was able to control tone and volume and would occasionally blast one during class as the teacher turned to scratch something on the blackboard.

During baseball season, Nulfo was the equipment manager. He parked himself at the end of the bench, and when he let one go, those of us who felt the vibrations raised a hand. This unit of measurement was dubbed the Rectum Scale.

As we circled around the Folgers cans, he let one go.

As the rest of us backed away from the smell, Nulfo gingerly removed several leaves, snatched the paperback from my hand,

and tore out a page.

"Fucker."

"Chill out, Stickman."

Carefully he rolled the young leaves into the paper, twisted the ends, and lit it. After a brief puff, the paper caught fire, and he dropped it. Dry bamboo leaves immediately caught, and we stomped around to put it out.

"Dumb ass, tryin' to burn us all up?" Rod screamed.

Nulfo suddenly transformed into a stoned Mr. Muller, staggering and knocking over coffee cans.

"Ms. Payán, I called you into my office to see if there's *anything* I can do to change your mind about leaving Woodland."

Then, he changed his voice into a falsetto.

"I'm sure you'll find somebody else who's qualified, Mr. Muller."

"Not with an ass like yours, Ms. Payán." Nulfo held his palms out. "It's like a ripe apricot."

We were hysterical. Then he picked up one of the Folgers cans to read the label. "Good to the last drop. Rooster says that after he finishes sucking my —"

"You wish!" Rodney smoothed a hand over his hair. He'd painstakingly tamed the rooster-tail with an experimental mixture of his sister's mousse and his father's Brylcream. Yet it was rebelling again.

"What should we do with this stuff?" I asked.

"Plant one in my backyard. Hell, it's so full of weeds, nobody'll notice," said Rodney.

"Just leave it," cautioned Joey.

"If we get Nelda high, maybe she'll put out," Nulfo suggested.

"Heard she did it with Ramon," Joey shared.

"No shit?" Rod was all ears.

"You know who this shit belongs to," I said, changing the subject back to the pot plants.

"The Fuckabees!" We cried in unison.

The Huckabee's encompassed identical twins, James and John, and their older brother, David. They'd all been kicked out of Meadowland High and were at the continuation school.

Huckabee spelled trouble. Teachers at Woodland still gossiped about them. They lived on a ramshackle farm four-and-a-half miles east of mine. Their father was a farmer of sorts and was usually soused. Every so often, I saw him at Ali's Market buying booze. There was no Mrs. Huckabee that we knew of. The boys grew up wild, scruffy, and good-looking in a coarse way. The twins' long red hair complemented their fair complexions. David was taller and kept his brown hair short. He had a long scar on his forehead from a knife fight, or so it was rumored.

Moments later, our afternoon became a chaotic whirlwind of happenstance and synchronicity. In the distance, we heard the hum of a motorcycle. The Huckabees each owned Choppers in various stages of disrepair.

"*Vamos!*" urged Joey. The graveness of his voice lent wings to our feet. We fought our way out of the bamboo and onto the sand, which swallowed our feet with each stride. Even so, Joey easily opened up a spacious lead.

"Wait up, *hijos de la chingada!*" Arnulfo begged as he puffed along. He soon wore out and found a clump of tall weeds to hide inside. I glanced back and saw him.

"Goin' back for Nulfo," I panted. My self-esteem would benefit from macho points. Back then, imagination was the only thing I had going.

Only eleven years old, I towered at five-foot-ten, providing an easy target for every skinny joke or nickname known to man. Beanpole, Gumby, Stringbean, Twiggy, and Curly Fry were favorites. One joke went, he's so skinny, when he wears yellow, he gets mistaken for a number two pencil.

Stick Johnson. At least I had more talent than Arnulfo, who farted and made goofy faces. When I reached him, he motioned for quiet.

"David Fuckabee came down the bank with a girl," he whispered. "They're on the other side of that dune." He pointed to a dense stand of weeds crowning a sandy ridge.

"Yeah?" My heart was pounding.

"Bet you ten bucks, they're humping."

"Let's find out."

"*Híjole, gringo loco.*" He put a hand on my elbow, but I jerked away.

"Gotta know," I said. A familiar ache swept into my loins, imagining what David was doing with the girl. My bravado surprised me, yet it was the growing pressure in my pants that imparted courage.

"You're on your own," Arnulfo said, sneaking away, glancing back to see if I chickened out.

Sonofabitch, I thought. *Risking my life to come back for him, and he deserts me.*

I crept forward, and belly crawled toward the dune, topped by skinny reeds and milkweed. I heard voices. One was deep and gravelly, and the other melodious, shrilling like an exotic bird. I peeked over the dune through the crowning weeds.

Having sneaked a few of my father's *Penthouse* magazines out to the hay barn, I thought my education was complete. I'd even learned some from the big kids at school. Yet I was a fool to think any of that would prepare me for what I saw. David Huckabee and a Mexican girl were locked together, and her long black hair was splayed on a blanket they shared. The sounds they made clouded up my mind.

She urged him, "*Ay si, huh, ayyy!*"

My whole body jittered, and my head felt as if it were filled with helium from a county fair balloon. As their movements grew frenzied, I suffered a huge cramp in my left thigh. Thankfully my suppressed squeal blended with the noise they were making. I backed down the dune to straighten my leg and massage the knot. As soon as the pain eased, I stood and began to limp away.

"*Ay, me vengo,*" the girl cried.

I had witnessed magic and was feeling transcendent when I rejoined the gang. I articulated every detail, and they didn't believe a goddamned word. Even Nulfo shook his head at me.

Joey and Rooster had stumbled upon another mysterious denizen of the river. They put fingers to their lips as we entered a tangle of bamboo, one of our abandoned fortresses. It'd once been a labyrinth of trails leading into various rooms—the treasure room, bathroom, and jailhouse. The bastion had stood empty for quite some time, yet a few trails were still negotiable. Rodney led the way until we saw a man. He lay tucked in a fetal position, snoring loudly.

"Seen him around town collecting cans." Joey pointed to a burlap sack.

"Yeah, me too," I whispered. "Digging in the dumpster at Ali's."

"Smells like shit," murmured Rodney.

The transient rolled to his back and smacked his lips. Then he sat up on his elbows to regard us, blinking and wiping his nose on a tattered shirtsleeve.

"What you want in here, boys?" His words were textured with phlegm, and he cleared his throat.

"Fucked up," Arnulfo whispered, pointing to a collection

of Thunderbird bottles littered around him.

His first effort to stand met with defeat. Then, with cracking knees, he finally did, brushing leaves off his soiled pants.

"If I'd known company was coming, would've tidied up." His voice was deep and croaky. The man's weathered face was obscured in white stubble, and his long, greasy hair was littered with flecks of dirt and leaves. He mostly squinted, but occasionally his eyes flew open to reveal green eyes as intense as a lime-flavored jawbreaker. He stooped for a baseball cap with an R stitched to the front. A faded red T-shirt hung below the waist of his baggy gray trousers. A pair of beat-up tennis shoes completed the dress, and he wore them without socks.

"You live here?" Arnulfo asked.

"Home sweet home," he replied, gesturing grandly with his arms.

"Don't you got family?" I wanted to know.

"Had."

"What happened to'em?"

"Better to ask, what happened to *me*?"

"Gotta get home," said Rod, lifting his cell phone.

The others turned to leave, but I hesitated.

"What did happen?"

"What's your name, son?"

"Andrew."

"Well, Andrew, I sort of just drifted here."

"Okay. Take care."

"Will do," he nodded.

As I turned, something came into my head. "Need somethin' to read?" I handed him the book and left to join the others. Turning once, I saw a surprised look on the transient's face as he held the book up to his green eyes. His hands were trembling.

"Well, I'll be goddamned," he said.

We rehashed the day's events, etching details into our memories to be retold later with liberal dollops of bullshit. Trying to convince them about David and the Mexican girl proved fruitless, but they believed Joey when he claimed to have seen a red-tailed hawk swoop down on a cat and lift it skyward. Go figure.

We talked about the future, an oral form of magic realism. None of us wanted to be farmers, teachers, or janitors, although Floyd was pretty cool. We dreamed of being DJ's, winning the lottery, or racing stock cars. Joey was going to play baseball in the big leagues.

"I'm gonna be a pimp," Arnulfo announced.

Now that Ms. Payán had traded Woodland for Meadowland, we focused on Nelda Morales. She sometimes wore dresses to school. Thanks to Rooster, pencils wouldn't work. I came up with the idea of using mirrors taped to my tennis shoes, and Joey mentioned the micro-telescope advertised in all the comic books.

"Let's just ask her to show it to us," offered Rodney. We all looked at him for a moment and shook our heads at the same time. "Send Goofus," he amended, "Maybe she'll feel sorry for the poor bastard."

"Ah, Nelda," Nulfo rehearsed. "Let's blow this hick-town and set up house in Meadowland. Whatcha say, dollface?"

In a girl's voice, Rooster replied, "Why that sounds delightful." Then he pulled up his T-shirt and pinched his chest to look like a woman's boobs.

"Yeah, baby." Arnulfo reached for one, and Rooster ran away.

Joey laughed and shook his head. "She'd take one look at your Tootsie-Roll and…."

Only I knew the truth. Even Joey Reece, with his love for baseball, was stranded at third base. Nulfo and Rooster begged him to tell about the red-tailed hawk again.

Christ, I thought, yet I joined the fray. "Wish it'd swoop on my sister." My sister, Brenda, was a high school sophomore.

"Shit, I'll swoop on her," Arnulfo volunteered.

We climbed up the banks of the river, and Joey began his long trek to Woodland. Woodland was a funny name for a town nearly devoid of trees, a farm labor community where most residents were illegal immigrants and worked the fields. Joey's dad worked for the irrigation district.

Rod's farm was a few miles south of mine. His bike was hidden in the riverbank brush. Looking back, I wonder why our parents ever let us out of their sight. Guess it's because farm communities are tight-knit and seem impervious to the nasty deeds man is capable of. Parents clung to romantic visions that nothing bad could happen in such a small farm community. Rodney rode off, his rooster tail sticking up like an antenna. We heard his cell phone go off in the distance. "Strangers in the Night...."

Arnulfo's father had dumped him at my house earlier, and we'd walked together to the river. My bike had a flat because of my bad karma with bullhead stickers. Nulfo didn't own a bike. My ranch was about a mile away. When we arrived, my mother finally surrendered to my petition for Arnulfo to spend the night. It was rare for my parents to allow a Mexican friend to sleep over. Like gum stuck beneath a student desk, you don't know racism's there until you feel it.

Nulfo called his dad to make sure it was all right to miss a day working in the vineyards. By then, his father had probably finished a six-pack of Corona, and he gave a quick stamp of approval. Goofus never complained about being poor, packed like a sardine in a room he shared with three younger brothers. When we were together, he wanted to ride my bike, look through my comics, or sneak off to the barn to study my collection of purloined girly magazines.

My mother politely inquired about our day at the river. We left out the part about motorcycles, pot growers, sex, and hobos. As far as our parents were concerned, the river was a day at the park.

That night I let Arnulfo have my bed, and I built a nest on the floor next to him with some old quilts. In the darkness, we whispered.

"Think Nelda did it with Ramon?" I asked.

"Saw'em kissin' behind the cafeteria a couple of weeks ago. Should'a seen it. He had her pinned up against a wall."

Ramon was an eighth grader and already wore sideburns. He put tacks under the heels of his shoes so that they clicked with attitude when he walked on hard surfaces.

"Bet they did."

"Let's make crank calls," Nulfo suggested.

"Nah, my sister's got ears like a bat."

On hot summer days, my fifteen-year-old sister, Brenda, wore next to nothing. Nulfo drooled over her like a street dog. She was a light sleeper and regularly caught me raiding chocolate chips from our mother's baking supplies or liquor from the forbidden kitchen cabinet.

"Think she'd wake up if I started balling her?"

"With you, she wouldn't even notice."

"Kiss my ass."

Thanks to the intoxicating newness of summer, an idea distilled in my mind — one that would change our lives forever.

"Let's sneak to the river," I whispered.

"Yeah," Arnulfo answered.

We waited until we were sure the rest of the household was asleep. My father was a light sleeper, too, as well as an early riser. Silently we slipped out into the warm night, and I slowly pulled the door shut and left it unlocked.

Our house was built at the end of a long lane, edged with tall palm trees. My great grandfather had planted them when he emigrated from Germany. In the darkness, they looked like giant Q-tips. As we reached the end of the lane, we were startled by a noise coming from a clump of weeds. On farms, an opossum, a badger, a coyote, or the rare mountain lion that sometimes wandered down from the Sierra Nevada's could've made such sounds. I turned my pocket flashlight on the source. A dark shape leaped out at us. It was Ike, the family dog.

"*Chingada!*" Arnulfo's favorite word sprung from his mouth. I bent to scratch Ike's belly, and the old Australian shepherd wagged the stub of his tail like a hairy thumb. Arnulfo took a lock-blade out of his pocket. "I'll cut his nuts off," he threatened and slapped at a mosquito on his arm.

Ike sniffed at a clump of weeds and marked it. He spent most waking hours pissing. Ike had an uncanny ability to hit any object he chose with a lift of the leg. My sister once spent hours creating an early California mission out of sugar cubes for a third-grade social studies project. I helped her with it because she promised to give me the mission after it was graded so I could change it into a fort for green plastic army men. When it was finished, she set it on the picnic table in the back yard to dry.

Ike used the back lawn as a toilet, and I earned fifty cents a week by going on poop patrol with a flat shovel and a plastic bucket. That's what I was doing when Brenda went into the kitchen for a glass of tea. I watched Ike slink into the yard. He made a beeline for the table.

Ike loved challenges. He sniffed around the table, figuring out the calculus. As my poor sister returned, he unleashed an arching yellow fountain on the mission. The tea glass slipped from Brenda's grasp and shattered.

"I'm gonna kill you!" She picked up a yellow plastic Wiffleball bat and gave chase, weeping and shouting. Ike escaped.

Later, I heard my father whisper to Mom, "Ike's an atheist."

Ike tagged along with Arnulfo and me. There was a twisted comfort in having him there. Perhaps he'd piss on any enemies we encountered.

Arnulfo began telling one of his fragmented urban legends. The way Arnulfo told stories, you had to fit the pieces after he was done.

"Hear what happened last year?" He never waited for an answer. "Car was parked at the river, right around here somewhere, it was in all the papers, think it was a '69 Buick Electra, windows were down." He paused long enough for me to patch it together. "Dude picked up some chick at the 5-Hi Club, and they were fucking in the back seat, mean-ass Rottweiler jumped in through the window and...." Arnulfo finished predictably by making a grab for my crotch. "Bit his nuts off!"

"Fag," I said, twisting away.

"*Maricón*," he countered.

That signaled the start of a never-ending insult game, and I didn't feel like playing, so I kept quiet. Arnulfo fished a Snickers bar out of his pocket and offered me half. The hand that was holding his half dropped to his side for just a moment, and Ike snatched it.

"*Pinche perro!*" Nulfo tried to kick Ike and slipped on a patch of Johnson grass that Ike had pissed on. "*Chingada!*" He sprang up and sniffed his shirt.

"Now you're Ike's bitch!" I laughed and backpedaled as Arnulfo tore off his shirt to chase me with it. "Your tits are bigger than Nelda's!" I pointed.

He soon ran out of gas, put the shirt back on, and we continued journeying toward the banks of the river. Weak batteries made my flashlight nearly useless, so I turned it off. Under a toenail-clipping moon, the river's steep sides looked like a sleeping snake. Muscle-bound oak trees loomed hauntingly, filled with unseen life. Chirps, croaks, and screeches reminded us that life was all around. Skunks, weasels, bats, frogs, and owls were some of the critters working nightshift. There were feral cats that had been born on the river. We'd learned the hard way to leave them alone. Mysterious coyotes were seldom seen. Their nightly keening fed our imaginations with primitive grist. We suspected that feral cats were a primary food source for them.

As we arrived at the river, Ike disappeared. Secretly we missed him, not that he'd offer any real protection. Ike was a chicken-shit dog. Ranch cats regularly beat the hell out of him, and I personally witnessed him fleeing from gophers, toads, and field mice. Still, the sound of his license tag jingling against the metal chain of his collar was comforting.

A warm breeze swept over us, rustling the bamboo leaves. Soon, melted snow from the Sierra Nevada would swell the river. Every year we built a raft and braved the easy-going currents we referred to as the rapids. But for now, the river was the Sahara. Whispers of the night were more intrusive than the whine of a diesel tractor. Even crickets were unnerving. Every creaking branch, hidden screech, or distant bark of dogs brought us closer to full retreat.

"Pact," I suggested. "No scary stories."

"Deal," Arnulfo answered quickly.

Sudden rustling from a stand of bamboo caused Nulfo to cross himself. "*Ay, Dios mío!*" Ike sauntered out, wagging his stub and flipping over for a belly rub.

"Christ," I scolded, reaching for his collar. "Wish I had a leash or a piece of rope." The rare summer breeze drifted lazily over the bamboo and lifted the soft sound of harmonica music. Ike rolled to his feet, ears straining, head cocked to the side.

"Hear that?" I whispered.

"Betcha it's that ol' tramp."

"Maybe," I said, gripping Ike's collar even tighter.

Arnulfo's face lit up. "Floyd with a wild woman."

I laughed into my hand. Arnulfo's comic timing was impeccable. We sneaked toward the source of the music until we spied firelight. Creeping forward until we were about thirty yards away, we hid behind a large mound of catch-weed, so named because of the painful quarter-size burrs they carried. Peeking over, we saw the transient's face glowing eerily in the flames as he pressed the harmonica into sad service. I changed my grip on Ike's collar so his license wouldn't jingle.

Fingers of flame seemed to dance with the music. I didn't recognize the tune as the hobo's mouth moved from one end to the other. He played awful, but it provided a pleasant ambiance, and the darkness swallowed his mistakes.

After a while, he stopped, tapped out saliva on his knee, and slid the harp into his shirt pocket. He picked up the book I'd given him and strained to read by firelight. I kept Ike steady as he licked his balls. The hobo stopped and stared into the flames for a time. Then he resumed thumbing through the pages. A short time later, he began weeping softly.

"What the fuck?" Arnulfo whispered.

We were both uncomfortable with hearing an adult crying.

After pulling himself together, he fed the book into the fire, lay down on the sand, and broke into sobs, which grew louder as the book flared and the pages curled. Wood settled beneath the flames, and the resulting updraft lifted the front cover away from the spine of the book. It spun around, rising from the fire, edges glowing. It gained height and drifted toward us, landing a few feet away. I picked it up. What survived was the smoking image of a man walking toward an all-encompassing, creosote darkness.

Moments later, we heard motorcycles. Our knees quivered, and we sat with our backs to the protective clump. Arnulfo motioned wildly that we should go, but I put my hand up and signaled for silence, thinking they'd pass us by.

"Maybe there's girls," I whispered, tightening my grip on Ike.

Nulfo calmed down a bit. He licked his lips and smiled. "Tell me again, how did she sound?"

"*Ay, me vengo,*" I mouthed the Spanish words chiseled into my memory.

"*Órale.*"

The tramp sat up as the bikes parked on the bank parallel to him. Arnulfo clenched his fists as boots tromped down the bank through dry weeds. Ike nervously licked his chops, tugged against my hand, and whined softly.

"Shhh," I admonished, soothing him with my free hand. I swallowed hard and peered through the brambles.

The three brothers wore T-shirts and jeans. The twins' hair had been sculpted wildly by the wind. James and John walked arrogantly over to the bum. David brought up the rear, shuffling, stumbling, and sending sand in all directions.

Ike's rear leg lifted for a scratch. His license slipped from my grip and jingled against the chain. Quickly I recaptured it. I thought to slip it off, but then he'd be free to give us away. His muscles were jittery with pent-up energy. Arnulfo's eyes were wide, and my head pounded with each thump of my heart. I was glad Ike wasn't much of a barker.

"What the hell we got here?" spat James or John. We couldn't tell them apart.

"Hey boys," the hobo murmured and stared down at the sand.

One of the twins patted his pants pocket, "Got a cigarette, old man?"

"Nope."

"What's that, then?" He gestured at a square in his shirt pocket.

"Nothin'."

The twin snatched the harmonica out of his shirt pocket before the transient could stop him. He stepped back and began playing and slapping his knee in time. The other twin clapped and sang, "Grab your partner by the tits, swing'er 'round until she shits, throw'er up against the wall, and shove your dick in balls'n'all!"

"Yee haw!" shouted the player.

Arnulfo covered his mouth, and I could tell he was storing the lyrics for later. David was swaying and smoking a cigarette ten yards away. John, or James, disappeared into a bamboo stand.

"Check it out," chortled the other twin, humping a phantom woman, accompanied by the harmonica.

"Idiot." David shook his head.

Again, Arnulfo fought the urge to laugh.

"What the fuck?" A shout came from the bamboo. "Cocksucker's been into our shit!" The twin returned with an empty coffee can and squatted next to the tramp. "This your work, old-timer?"

David mumbled something and then fell on his ass. "Fuck, what was in that shit?"

The twin with the harmonica cupped his hands around it and blew high notes into the transient's ear. Reflexively the old man's boney elbow came up and smashed into the twin's nose. The harmonica flew from his hand, and he staggered back. With the bottom of his T-shirt, he wiped a trickle of blood from his nose.

"Motherfucker!"

His twin brother laughed. "Caught you a good one."

David was passed out with his mouth ajar. Occasionally he flung up a defensive hand against an enemy in his nightmare. The injured twin made sure David was out, and then he closed in on the transient.

"Sonofabitch!" He toppled the old man with a roundhouse to the face. He lay motionless for a moment and then tried to crawl away.

Ike gave a short woof, and I clamped a hand around his mouth. Mff, mff.

Smelling blood in the water, the other twin circled and kicked the tramp in the stomach.

"Oof! Lemme alone," he gasped, tucking into a fetal position. His plea was ignored. The brothers stomped and kicked. "Mama!" he cried, trying to cover his head.

A short time later, sweating and puffing, the twins stopped.

"Stupid ol' fuck," chimed James, or John, dabbing his nose with the back of his hand. The other twin wiped his forehead with the bottom of his T-shirt.

"Man, that's a helluva workout."

Ike was struggling, Nulfo's mouth hung open, and his eyes were closed. The vagrant lay twitching, one leg kicking spastically. Gradually the motion slowed to a stop. A wet spot formed at the front of his pants as a piece of firewood settled, sending fireflies into the summer sky.

"Dead?" asked the bleeding twin.

"Playin' 'possum most likely." The other twin poked the body with his

foot. "Nope," he said, shaking him by the shoulder. "Deader'n a doornail."

A twin tossed some sand on David's head. "Get up, man."

"Wha...? What the fuck?" David fought to sit up.

"Ol' man screwed the pooch."

David's forehead crinkled. His chin tucked in as his mouth tightened and curved downward.

"Was just havin' some fun," the other twin explained.

"Cocksuckers," David scolded, rubbing hands over his face. "Hide'im in the brush, and grab the plants."

Ike was still struggling, so I released his mouth and fell to petting him as he panted. The twins argued as they kicked sand on the fire, but David wasn't listening. They were background noise, a dull humming in his head, annoying and unrelenting.

"Ain't nobody gonna miss the fucker," grunted one of the twins as they dragged the body into the bamboo.

A jackrabbit suddenly burst from its hiding place in the bamboo. Ike tore from my grasp to give chase. The twins watched as Ike sprinted past them in hot pursuit, jingling all the way. David groveled to his feet and turned toward our hiding place, narrowing his eyes. I prayed he wouldn't hear the beating of our hearts. He took a few lurching steps forward, squinted into the darkness and moving his head from side-to-side.

The twins emerged from the bamboo carrying the bare-root plants. David glanced back and turned again toward us. He reached into his pocket for a cigarette, fired it up, took a long drag, and exhaled slowly.

Christ, I thought, *what if Chickenshit comes back?*

"Hey man, better get these home," advised a twin.

"Yeah." David whirled and followed his brothers up the bank.

Nulfo and I stayed frozen until the choppers were a distant thunder.

My jaws hurt from gritting my teeth. I wanted to check on the old man, but my quivering legs refused to take me there. Arnulfo tugged aggressively on my arm, and we crept silently away. Reaching the upper bank, we jogged until we reached the boundaries of the farm. Arnulfo dropped to his knees, gasping and holding his side. I hugged my arms to my chest and felt my childhood slipping away.

"Christ," was my first word.

"*Chingada*," Arnulfo added.

That rest of the night, imagination was our worst enemy. We sat atop a haystack in the white barn. Heavy crossbeams above our heads creaked and groaned. The metal roofing popped. Cooing pigeons flapped and scurried, showering nesting material to the barn floor.

We weren't sure David Huckabee hadn't seen us. They certainly knew Ike. Funny thing about farm communities — you knew your neighbors' dogs as well as you knew the neighbors. The sky was a gathering mass of unseasonable clouds, blotting out stars and the crescent moon.

"Gotta tell," said Arnulfo.

"Know what'll happen to us if we rat 'em out?" I cautioned. A cow mooed laconically in the distance.

"Rod and Joey?"

"Especially not those fuckers," I said emphatically.

Arnulfo nodded. He was terrible with secrets, and I fully understood the torment he'd face when we returned to school, and others bragged about their summer adventures.

In the ensuing hours before dawn, we nearly convinced ourselves that the drifter wasn't dead, or if he was, he was somehow better off. Didn't work. Only grown-ups can justify themselves that way.

Toward daybreak, we watched a coyote loping across a field toward the river. Before sneaking back into the house, we emptied sand from our shoes and picked cockleburs and foxtails from our socks and pants. The tang of nervous sweat, dirt, and weeds clung to our bodies and pervaded the air as we lay, lost in our own thoughts.

Later, as Arnulfo snored, I heard the patter of rain on the wooden shingles of the roof. It helped me relax. Somehow, rain would make everything clean again. Maybe the tramp would come to after the first few drops and crawl beneath a strong oak to recover.

He'd cried for his mother, and the memory of it made me sick to my stomach.

At sunrise, my father went into the kitchen, and soon the coffee machine was dripping like the rain.

"Ike, where've you been?" I heard him ask. I got off the floor to look out the bedroom window. Chickenshit was trotting up the lane toward the safety of his doghouse. "You look like hell," my father added.

By then, my mother had joined, and bacon was soon sizzling, as a radio voice droned on about the effect unexpected rain might have on the raisin grapes. Arnulfo snored softly, mouth twitching, practicing goofy faces even as he slept. I listened to my parents' warm voices, the sound of rain, and the clink of silverware as it was laid out. I knew when my father was putting on his jacket to go out to the workshop, as he always did on rainy days. It was all very familiar, and I liked it that way.

Looking down the lonely lane, where Mr. Hernandez would pick me up when school resumed, I half-expected to see three motorcycles, the soggy riders hatching plans to shut us up. But there was only the emptiness and the rain.

Hours later, Nulfo's father drove up in his battered grey Chevy pickup. Alone I was more vulnerable. We didn't say much to each other, just gave the complicated handshake that was popular at the time.

I wrote a last will and testament and left everything to Ms. Payán—my bee-bee gun, stamp collection, comic books, but not the magazines in the haystack. Perhaps she'd make such a fuss at my funeral that I'd achieve a post-mortem erection. The rest of the gang would double their fun if her twin sister showed too.

It rained hard the rest of the day and part of the next. My father said the river was rising and asked if my friends and me had begun building a raft yet. I thought of the river, the lazy current, and imagined us floating while I wrote fantasies in a spiral-bound notebook. *Life on the River*, by Andrew "Stick" Johnson.

Ms. Payán was nervous. "Andrew," she said. "If this gets out, I'll lose my job."

I took her into my arms. "Don't worry, doll-face, this's between you and me."

But I knew there'd be no rafting this year. Perhaps never again. The rain stopped. I scanned the *Meadowland Chronicle* and watched the local television news for information that would shed light on the transient's fate. My folks translated this sudden interest in the news as a good thing, a sign I was growing up.

My conscience held me hostage. Often I saw the Huckabees humming down cracked country roads, hair blowing and faces scowling. Finally, I realized they didn't have it out for me. Arnulfo was itching to spill the beans, and I threatened him with castration.

"We'd look like idiots if we say something now," I argued.

Nearly two months passed before an Irrigation District employee discovered the remains. Joey Reece's father returned with the man, and then they reported it.

The county coroner's office assigned natural causes to the death. The obituary was perhaps the smallest ever written in the *Chronicle*. Joey's father had told him that an expired ATM card revealed the name of the diseased: Owen Zelenski.

Owen Zelenski was unceremoniously tendered in a pauper's grave at the Woodland cemetery. No one came to say farewell, and a gopher made his home in the fresh dirt. The Huckabees had gotten away with murder.

Resentment and guilt filled me. We should've said something…would've been heroes. Celebrity may have induced Nelda Morales to show us her tits, and there's little doubt Floyd would have sponsored our show on the bus ride home.

Would've, could've, should've—empty words. All evidence had been rinsed and carried downstream by brown river water as we entered eighth grade. I was Andrew Stick Johnson, cowering in the back row of a new classroom ruled by Ms. Crooninghill.

Time has a way of letting dust collect on dreadful memories. Eighth grade gave us Ms. Crooninghill, who allowed us to return to the Emerald City of our youth, where the great and powerful Oz fielded requests amid the dissipating smoke of our remaining childhood. Floyd serenaded with songs and talked of wild women. On the bus ride home, I gazed north toward the river and the swishing bamboo that shrouded dark mysteries.

One late afternoon, just after eighth grade graduation, I walked to the river. Arnulfo and his family had moved to Texas, where much of his family lived. He was the only one I would've wanted with me. The river was smaller than I recalled. I breathed in the straw of bamboo, the spicy aroma of earth and brush. Unrelenting irrigation waters had reshaped the river bottom. I found a rusty Folgers can half-buried in the sand, dug it out with my foot, and kicked it.

Zelenski had a history, I reflected. I'd heard stories about homeless people who were once lawyers, doctors, teachers, and fathers. How had he become so lost? What caused a life to shift like sand on a river bottom?

Two weeks before my freshman year at Meadowland High, Arnulfo and his family returned to Woodland for a short visit. He got a kick when I told him Lupe Payán was my English teacher.

Patting his shirt pocket, he said, "Sorry, man, I didn't bring a pencil."

I asked if he'd kept our vow of silence.

He giggled into his hand. "Think by now, everybody in Texas knows."

At first, I felt betrayed, but then it was okay. After all, Arnulfo never could keep a secret.

***

The following school year was shortened. Covid-19 delivered a new reality to the world of man. It made me realize that life is ethereal. Depends on us to make the most of our time. Life is short, but it's wide.

The End

Ty Spencer Vossler lives in Pacific Grove, California, with his BMW (beautiful Mexican wife) and their daughter. A prolific author, he has published over seventy works in the past four years, including five novels and a collection of short stories. Refusing to be typecast, he writes science fiction, magic/realism, romance, as well as literary fiction.

Ty's work has published on four continents, including, *The Eye of Espinoza* (magic/realism) and *Seedlings* (apocalyptic science fiction), World Castle Publishing.

Vossler holds a Masters in creative writing and has created award-winning creative writing programs in the United States and Mexico. He attributes his originality to trashing his television over two decades ago.

www.ingramcontent.com/pod-product-compliance
Lightning Source LLC
Chambersburg PA
CBHW071854220626
47052CB00002B/117